Praise for *Hidden*

"I have not only enjoyed reading Corinne Joy Brown's new novel *Hidden Star*, but have learned so much about the lives, traditions, and history of the "hidden" Jews of New Mexico, that I intend to tell everyone I know, as well as my students at UTEP, to add this important book to their personal libraries. The author truly engages the reader with vivid descriptions of the personalities, ideas and journeys of each of the book's characters. I am deeply impressed with the story, the way the author tells the story, and the inspiration it gives the reader to deal with the some of the challenges that life presents us every day."

—Rabbi Stephen A. Leon
Founder and Director of the Anusim Center of El Paso, Texas

"*Hidden Star* is an engaging, fast-moving book, set in a well-realized Southwestern landscape. The book raises important questions about how history and identity intertwine, even as the novel itself weaves together the oft-knotted threads of family, religion, and romance. An enjoyable read!"

—Dr. Gretchen Starr-LeBeau
Associate Professor Principia College
Author of *In the Shadow of the Virgin: Inquisitors, Friars, and Conversos in Guadalupe, Spain*. Princeton University Press

"*Hidden Star* is an ambitious, complex novel, spanning from the seventeenth century to modern day, yet easy to read and difficult to put down. Corinne Joy Brown's thoughtful look at the crypto-Jews of New Mexico, then and now, is enlightening and inspiring."

—Johnny D. Boggs
Six-time Spur Award winner and distinguished New Mexico author

"*Hidden Star* intricately weaves the gray and faded threads of our ancestral memories into a rich and colorful tapestry that comes alive before your eyes. A nostalgic and poignant must-read!"

—Genie Medina Milgrom
Author of My Fifteen Grandmothers and How I Found My 15 Grandmothers *(Como Encontre A Mis 15 Abuelas:* A Step-by-Step Guide: *Una Guia Paso a Paso)*"

"As you read these pages, begin a journey that takes you into a past most do not fully understand. As I celebrate my faith and culture, I acknowledge a history hidden and not fully comprehended, but embraced with wonder, sorrow, happiness and inquiry. How can what occurred in 1492 resonate in 2015? Reverberations ring true through the passage of time and space. Enjoy this story, as the past is the present and strives to become the future."

—Lorenzo A. Trujillo, Ed.D., J.D.
Attorney/professor/author and fourteenth generation descendant of the original settlers of New Mexico

FriesenPress

Suite 300 - 990 Fort St
Victoria, BC, Canada, V8V 3K2
www.friesenpress.com

Second Edition — 2016

Author photo by Stephen Collector

ISBN
978-1-4602-7577-1 (Hardcover)
978-1-4602-7578-8 (Paperback)
978-1-4602-7579-5 (eBook)

1. *Fiction / Hispanic & Latino*
2. *Religion, Judaism, History*
3. *History, Latin America*

Distributed to the trade by The Ingram Book Company

Hidden Star

A novel by

Corinne Joy Brown

Corinne J. Brown

The town of Estrella in northern New Mexico and all names and characters in this story are fictional with the exception of select, well known figures from history and Rabbi Stephen Leon and the Anusim Center for Return in El Paso, Texas.

I am the catch
in your throat;
the wordless cry, the unexplainable

I am the cloud
that follows you
raining
at the slightest provocation

I am the scar
that has become a flower;
I am the pilgrim
you brought home:
the Jew you hid from the fire.

I am your dark sleep.

I am your dream
of finding someone
whose arms will hold you
when daylight comes.

—Lisa Alvaredo

ACKNOWLEDGMENTS

TO THE MANY FRIENDS and readers who gave me feedback along the way and expressed empathy, enthusiasm and encouragement for the writing of this story—I hope I haven't missed a one. Sincere thanks are owed to:

Becky Benes of Denver, published writer and respected *compadre* who has believed in me since the very beginning and listened while I read this story out loud on our various trips to Santa Fe. To Sonya Loya of Ruidoso, New Mexico, whose early confirmation of the *converso* experience, as I have drawn it, was so important, and whose own journey back to the faith of her ancestors has been an inspiration to many. To Genie Milgrom of Florida, born in Cuba, who traced her family's history to its sixteenth century roots in medieval Spain and who joins me in the search for facts within the Society for Crypto-Judaic Studies; and to the remarkable, talented and insightful Dr. Lorenzo Trujillo of northern New Mexico and Denver, noted musician, legal expert and humanist, who has shared his traditions, his music, and his own family's history with me. Your unwavering support over a decade has helped me tell the best story I could.

To all the content, plot, and line editors like Tom Howe, literary friend and child at heart, who drove the actual trail of the runaway boys all across New Mexico and photographed the journey; to friends Jacqueline Hirsch and Debbie Wohl Isard, who both read for clarity, grammar and meaning; to Sandi Gelles Coles, former Dell editor and professional plot doctor, for seeing all the holes; to Mary Metcalfe from Friesen Press, and Sephardic genealogist /editor Schelly Talalay Dardashti, for the excellent final cleanup.

Thanks also to the crucial academic professionals who helped me stay true to history and tradition: Seth Ward, Professor of Comparative Religion (University of Wyoming), the late Dr. Jack T. Sanders, Professor Emeritus of Religious Studies (University of Oregon), and to Professor Gretchen Star Le Beau, Professor of Religion at Principia College,(Saint Louis, Missouri), expert on the plight of women during the Middle Ages. To Leonard Stein, Professor of Literature at Ben Gurion University of the Negev (Beersheva, Israel). To my friend Cheri Karo Schwartz, poet and storyteller, for feeling the spiritual heartbeat within the lines, and a very special thanks to Frank Morgan, Navajo, from Corrales, New Mexico, who provided translations and confirmed the Native American characters so important to the tale.

To my all important Spanish language editors such as SCJS member Arnold Trujillo, Seventh-Day Adventist Church of California, (a native son of southern Colorado and its rich Spanish heritage), and to Aida Souviron, book club colleague and Spanish-speaking linguist from Bolivia. Also to Regis College professor and Spanish instructor, Obdulia Castro, for the important final language critique. To law enforcement professional Sheriff Pete Palmer, Chaffee County Sheriff in Salida, Colorado; to David Kice, FBI Special Agent in Santa Fe, and to long-time mountain rescue volunteer Bill Barwick, Alpine Rescue Team, Evergreen, Colorado.

To Rabbi Stephen Leon of El Paso, Texas and his Congregation B'nai Zion, who open the doors to any and all seeking a Jewish experience, whether historical, traditional, educational or other. Thank you for allowing me to attend your summer anusim conference, meet your congregants and speak at the inauguration of the International Anusim Center for Return. And thanks to the many attendees I had the privilege to meet there, interview and learn about their journey (you may remain anonymous). To film maker Joe Lovett of New York for his creative work telling the story of the anusim in his documentary *Children of the Inquisition*; I support and applaud you.

To the women whose talents connected with this story so deeply, I had to include your work: Lisa Alvaredo, poet, whose poem sets the stage, and Sushe Felix, painter extraordinaire, whose love affair with New Mexico begins with her heart and ends with her brush. The exemplary painting on the cover captures the landscape perfectly.

And most of all, to my beloved sister Vivian (Viesha), whose start in life was marred by the most evil event known to man, the modern-day Inquisition known as the Holocaust. Although your mother perished in the Warsaw Ghetto, she had the foresight to secure you, a child of five, with Christian friends, protected by your blue eyes and a Catholic religious medallion placed around your neck.

Hidden for months by those who cared and protected you until the siege on Warsaw, your tumultuous survival, rescue, and eventual return to our family in America after the war (to our father, who was really your uncle) was nothing short of a miracle—something I do believe in. Once I understood your story, learning its truth only as a teen, the ensuing years made me realize that anyone can be unjustly persecuted for who they are. Hiding behind a false identity becomes a method of survival shared by many, whatever the reason, whatever the risk. People do what they must.

Your experience worked its way to the surface until I felt myself compelled to forge a tale in which I could personally explore how yet another woman, part of a hidden community, unknown even to herself, sought to understand her true identity, but only when circumstances dictated that she must.

Finally, to the memory of all the Jews persecuted in Spain and Portugal who died simply because of what they believed in, I write this book for you. You are not forgotten.

PROLOGUE

May 24, 1790

Village of Estrella, Northern Territory of *Nueva España*

Rebeca

THE SOUND OF MORNING bells pealed into the pale southwestern sky as the sisters of *Las Hermanas del Sagrado Corazón* sent hosannas to their Father in heaven. Gratitude filled their prayers, for each and every one of them believed that He alone helped provide for His beloved daughter, Rebeca Elena Morales, soon to be leaving the convent to wed the local *alcalde mayor*, Don Ricardo de Córdova.

Churchgoers in the village of Estrella and around the valley for miles awaited the deliverance of their virgin bride to her infamous groom. The much talked about match would surely end the loneliness of their love struck leader once and for all. Hopes rose that the *alcalde's* irritable temper might also finally improve. Though vigilant in protecting his people's needs, making sure that food, fuel, and water were accessible at all times, the Don ruled with impatience. The smallest error in grain tax or a poorly loaded mule could trigger his fiercest lash.

De Córdova had long been plagued by bad luck with women. Rumor followed him from one post to the next—wild and scandalous tales laced with jealous lovers, tempestuous affairs and a trail of vengeful concubines in *Ciudad de México.* Prior to his assignment in the north of *Nueva España,* he'd been left humiliated at the altar in San Antonio when a promised bride failed to appear. His reputation clearly preceded him.

The Don knew he had little time left to take a wife. At forty-seven years of age, with his pride and lineage at stake, the thought of plucking the young novitiate Rebeca from the convent renewed his courage and his faith. God had surely blessed him. He felt more than young again. He embraced the girl's father, Enrique Morales, owner of the nearby *Rancho de Las Palomas,* with lusty bravado, daring to joke about his talents in the nuptial bed.

"She will swoon with delight," he assured his future in-law with a wink. "And bring me many *niños*."

* * *

Rebeca fidgeted as Sister Alicia tidied her head cloth and tucked away strands of her long, dark, silky hair. "*Ay, preciosa.* Stand still. You must look your very best today."

The girl gazed in the mirror and frowned. "*¿Yo? ¿Por qué?* Me?" she repeated. "A wedding? But why?" She wished this day had never come. How could she marry a stranger? The orphaned child of Morales' first wife, long deceased, Rebeca's fate had become the cause of much concern. Raised in the convent for a proper Catholic education after her mother died, she'd grown into a comely young woman whose sensuality fueled speculation. Locals gambled on who might one day win her heart. Therefore, the Sisters watched her every move, lest she be abducted or led astray.

* * *

De Córdova first found her while assessing the village holdings. One morning, unannounced, he entered the convent doors. The Sisters were at matins at the time. He slipped into the chapel, sat upon a pew, and watched the proceedings unnoticed, unable to take his eyes off the young girl, deep in pious veneration.

Such lips, he sighed, so ripe and sweet. He peered further, studying her hands; so fine and unblemished. He savored every part of her.

When at last Rebeca looked up and found the unfamiliar man staring at her like a ravenous fox, she reverted to her prayer book, a chill raising bumps along her arm. *¿Quién es el? Who is he?* she wondered. *And what does he want with me?*

De Córdova continued to pin her with his gaze. His admiration turned to lust as he felt himself grow aroused. "This one I must have," he vowed. "This one must be mine."

* * *

Dressed as convention required in a gray woolen habit, Rebeca appeared as seductive as she was innocent. The more the Sisters attempted to hide her beauty, the more it seemed to show. At fifteen her skin glowed as if illuminated from within, and her chocolate brown eyes, fringed by thick lashes and delicately arched brows, demanded undivided attention. In truth, few men in Estrella did not yearn for her, openly or in secret. Therefore, the nuns breathed a collective sigh of relief when they learned she was to be taken off their hands—married and possessed—by such an esteemed, wealthy, and desperately single man.

"But marriage?" asked Rebeca, when informed of the plan. "*Por favor, no gracias.* I am not ready. I wish instead to take my vows."

At peace with her lot and her love of God, the girl had little concept of life outside the convent, and certainly not of marriage—the last thing on her mind. But the decision to betroth her to the Don was agreed upon by both her father and the Reverend Mother, "as a match made in heaven," one to benefit them all.

Even Señor Morales himself saw no harm; only the honor that had come to them. No matter that the Don was old enough to be her grandfather. Surely, she was of age to be wed, more than of age, in fact. Not even her tears could soften his determined heart.

* * *

Rebeca entered the chapel, bathed in the light of many *luminarias*—oil lamps, large and small. On each side of the altar, hand-fashioned rosettes of ribbon intertwined like colorful, flowering vines. Rays of morning sunlight beamed through a small stained glass window bearing the design of a crimson rose, each segment illuminated as if in holy bloom.

In the center of the apse, an upright harmonium accompanied the familiar hymns, while the pure voices of the Sisters sang in unison. Church members took their places, smiling, as though each mother might be giving away her own daughter in gratitude, or each father, standing by Rebeca's side.

High above them on the whitewashed wall, a wooden carving of Our Lord Jesus on his cross lent solemnity to the occasion, but not even the anguished eyes of the Son of God could diminish the festivities. An event as great as this rarely came to Estrella, the quiet center of a remote agricultural valley along the upper Rio Grande, just one of several land grants made by the Viceroyalty more than a century before. But as the locals gathered, they sensed a kind of foreboding, like an ill wind rising beneath the air of joy and happiness. How could one so young and pure be given to another with such a dark and tarnished past?

* * *

Altar boys proceeded down the flower-strewn aisle swinging urns of fragrant incense; the guests took communion and, at last, the Don and Señor Morales stood before the priest. Rebeca, swathed in ivory lace, and pale as an apparition, approached. She stared at the assembly gathered before her, straining to better see her betrothed, then shrank at the sight of him—a heavy-set man in riding boots and a black military coat, his beefy hands and wrists covered with leather gauntlets. Sweat stained his collar. His pointed gray beard reminded her of the whiskered goats she often tended on the hill.

"*¡Ay! ¡Pobre de mí!* What will happen to me?"

Rebeca's eyes met the Don's, focused upon her as she approached. Her heart struggled within her chest. Was there no way out? She escaped from his lascivious stare, seeking refuge in the wooden cross above. Earlier that morning she'd begged her father to refuse his offer, but neither Morales nor the Abbess would hear of it.

"A cause for celebration," Sister Atencia insisted, wagging a finger at Rebeca. "Be of gratitude."

Rebeca approached the altar, tight-lipped and unsteady, ushered by a flank of nuns behind her. She trembled at what was about to unfold. The good Sisters, by contrast, radiated happiness, their usual stern expressions softened by subtle grins. The unprecedented wedding would enrich their holdings substantially. If they could not offer their *niña querida* as a bride to Christ, they would happily escort her to her waiting groom, and add a much-needed schoolroom to the convent because of it.

* * *

Blessing the couple, the priest recited in Latin the vows of the marriage ritual, repeating them in Spanish for the congregation. The Don, beads of sweat glistening across his brow, stood erect, smiling at his easy conquest. He licked his lips. Indeed, he would take her that very afternoon.

Morales fidgeted, celebrating his good fortune, dabbing away the occasional tear.

At last, the cleric addressed the congregation and asked, according to tradition, "If there be any who object to this holy union, may they say so now, or forever hold their peace."

Silence settled over the room. Heads turned this way and that. Not a single reply. One and all waited for the service to continue. Then, from the back of the church came a shuffling as a woman in a tattered black mantilla arose. Aged and bent, she leaned heavily against a polished hardwood cane, a spindly, vein-crossed hand on its worn knob.

"*!Déjalo!* Stop this! Hear me, *padre,*" she said in Spanish. "You must stop this proceeding—now."

"What?" Rebeca startled, turning to see who had spoken. "What did the woman say? Who was she?"

Only one other in the packed sanctuary knew the answer. Enrique Morales, Rebeca's father, could see the crone had aged much these forty years. Yet, he caught his breath when he heard her husky, distinctive voice. It had to be her. How dare she speak out thus? Or come forward now? What did she want from him, after all this time?

The old one stepped to the end of the pew and straightened, standing as tall as she was able. "I object," she said, clearing her throat, her bony fingers clasped before her. "This woman cannot wed this man, now or ever. It is forbidden."

Rebeca's lashes fluttered as she stared. "*¿Qué? ¿Qué pasó?*" She turned to her father, tugging at his sleeve. Then she gripped his arm like a vise, almost unable to breathe.

Morales stared at the once familiar figure; his face drained, his pallor ashen. A muscle in his left cheek pulsed. *Incredible*, he thought, imploring the plaintiff with pleading eyes. *Someone stop her, now!*

Rebeca's heart thudded again in her chest. *Could this stranger be my salvation? This vieja?* If only she had heard correctly. *Please God.* All heads craned toward the speaker.

"Come forward, grandmother," ordered the priest, his usual impassive expression turning into a dark scowl. He closed the prayer book and clasped his hands. "*Por favor,* speak."

"I say to you, *padre*, this girl cannot wed Don Ricardo de Córdova," the old one repeated. "Not now, or ever."

"*¿Qué es esto?* Who are you?" he demanded. "And pray tell, old one, why not?"

The woman threaded her way into the aisle, her black, heavily lidded eyes glittering, a fringed *rebozo* around her shoulders. Undaunted, she pressed forward.

Morales began to tremble. Fear turned into rage. How dare she come into his life now? Memories flooded back of the unresolved love between him and this crone, more than a decade older than himself, and once, so very beautiful. Irresistible, in fact. Their brief affair was a passionate one, but impossible, nonetheless. She was married, but had taken him as her lover in secret. How many nights had he enjoyed her, at such great risk? She never forgave him for choosing another and leaving Albuquerque to start a new life in the north. Decades passed. He had not thought of her in years.

But she never forgot. She discovered where and how he lived, and that he had a daughter raised by the Church. She knew his first wife had died, exactly how and when. Could it be she was here to expose him?

Rebeca gripped her father's arm. She searched his eyes as they waited for the old woman's reply.

De Córdova turned toward the aged figure, his heavy brows knitted into a dubious frown. What gall—this hag, an unexpected barrier between him and his immediate future? His face flushed to scarlet, his eyes narrowed to slits as he focused upon her. "Who stands in my way?" he demanded, his lips curled in a snarl. "*¡Bastante!* You lie! Remove yourself, *abuelita.* Get out of my sight!"

Undaunted, the woman stepped closer, raising an accusing hand. Pointing at Rebeca, she rasped, "Hear me well, Don de Córdova. *¡Verdad! ¡No está bautizada*! This girl has never been baptized!"

Enrique Morales stepped in front of his daughter, shielding her from the words he hoped he would never hear. "*¡Silencio!* he shouted. "Enough! She is one of us, a Christian. I swear!"

"I will not be silenced," the crone replied. "I know who you are and who her mother was before her. Rebeca Elena Morales cannot wed Don de Córdova, for she is the daughter of a Jew!"

A collective gasp escaped from the parishioners. Heads shook in disbelief.

"Impossible!" said the priest, shaking his head.

"Impossible," echoed the parishioners from their seats, the meaning of the words rising like some abomination in their midst. Some sat too shocked to move, others crossed themselves and bowed their heads, afraid to witness what might ensue. De Córdova swore an unspeakable insult under his breath and then slapped the face of Morales with his stiff, black leather glove. The force of the blow stunned the rancher, causing him to close his open mouth with a clack.

"¡Puta!" de Córdova hissed, turning to the priest and spitting in disgust. "Not baptized? *¿Esta judía?* You dare attempt to pass this daughter of the devil to me? A curse upon you!"

With that, the outraged servant of the most northerly outpost of New Spain stormed from the church and into the waiting carriage that was to escort him and his young bride to the *alcalde's* abode. As the hooves of his white Andalusian horses clattered away, not a soul in the sanctuary dared utter a single word. The faithful sat as if stone, not even daring to breathe.

Rebeca sank to her knees, her world imploded, unwound, undone. The church seemed to list and pitch, like a ship foundering at sea. But what did it all mean? Should she rejoice or lament? Weep, or shout for joy? The words the old woman uttered had robbed her of her senses, her identity, and in fact, her very self. Not baptized? How could it be?

Silently, she begged Jesus to forgive her. Clutching the silver cross hanging from her neck, she released her father's arm and fainted, a tumble of lace upon the floor.

CHAPTER ONE

October 2015

Township of Estrella, Río Arriba County, State of New Mexico

Ángel

THE SCREEN DOOR SLAMMED with the clatter of metal hitting warped wood. Ángel Ortega, fourteen years old—less one month and two days—stepped into the diner dragging his canvas backpack, half-zipped and falling open. A faded pair of red sweatpants hung out like a dog's tongue, the cords of a cell phone headset trailing alongside.

"*Hola, mi hijo!* You're early," said his mother, looking at her son over the yellowed Formica counter. Ángel usually showed up at the *Taco Stop*, Rachel Ortega's fast-food luncheonette, just after school let out at three p.m. The grease-obscured face of the clock mounted above the stove read 2:40 p.m.

"*¿Qué pasó?*" Rachel asked, pushing her hair back from her forehead and squinting into the light of the open door. "What's up?"

The boy avoided her gaze and studied the toes of his worn, high-topped sneakers instead as if seeing them for the first time. Straight black hair, cut blunt at the shoulders, fell around his face and eyes, half-covering them. Looking up at last, he reached for a pack of cigarettes in his shirt pocket but stopped, catching his mother's steely gaze. It said clearly, "Don't you dare."

"Nothin'. Nothin's up." He lowered his hand, flipped his bangs out of his eyes, then pushed his fists into his jeans, waiting.

Ángel straddled one of the round stools in front of the counter and peered into a cake platter covered by a glass dome, preserving what was left of the morning's pastries. Two glazed sweet rolls, a cinnamon-covered *sopapilla,* and a stale donut wilted in the afternoon heat. A fly circled inside, a blissful prisoner.

"Umm ... can I have a soda?" he asked. "With some ice?"

Rachel stood with a damp rag in her right hand and her head cocked to one side, more than sure that the answer to her earlier question lay somewhere behind her son's customary pout and an afternoon snack.

"Maybe," she answered. "That depends. First tell me what you're doing here so early."

Ángel fidgeted and wrinkled his nose, his sealed lips a hard line.

"Okay, *bandido,* one more time. *¿Habla conmigo?* What's going on?"

Rachel often spoke to her son in Spanish, switching to her favorite nickname as well whenever she meant business. Her little bandit hadn't been getting along at school lately and she hoped the answer wasn't the one she feared. His presence in the new junior high in nearby Española seemed to be no more welcome than it had been at the boarding school in Roswell. The fall semester started off OK, then things fell apart—expelled after just four weeks. Ángel just never seemed to get along.

Rachel hated to admit it, but remembered feeling much the same when she was his age, out of place, unable to fit in. Back then, she always had the feeling that somehow she was different; she never knew why. Her family was part of a close community, yet often kept to themselves, except for attending church. By contrast, Rachel tried to help both her children—Ángel and his younger brother, Juan—feel connected, especially to local events and festivals. But in spite of her efforts, her older boy was often withdrawn, in trouble with his teachers, and hard to reach. She wished she could take him in her arms and comfort him with all her mother's love, but hugging him just made it worse.

"Don't," he'd say, turning away. "That's mushy stuff."

If the kid could just stick it out a few more weeks until the semester break, maybe there'd be some peace. A few days off at least. Why wouldn't those kids at school just let him alone?

"You get into a fight?" Rachel asked gently, bribing him with a can of ice-cold Orangeade.

"Sorta. Not really."

"You want to talk about it?" she probed further, filling a glass with crushed ice.

"Nope." He poured the can over the ice and drank, emptying the glass in one gulp.

She knew she'd never get an answer by pressing him. She'd wait until the drive home when he'd feel more relaxed, or until his grandfather would ask how his day had gone. Papa Héctor had a special talent. He could get his grandkids talking about anything.

"Okay," she said. "Never mind, then. Here."

She lifted the glass dome and the chocolate donut found its way into the boy's hand. Rachel turned back to scouring the grill. Another hour and the shop would close. She'd leave him alone until then.

* * *

Rachel Ortega loved her boys, but lately, felt overwhelmed by work and family. She hated the arguing and the spats, especially when she fought with her husband, even simple conversations spinning out of control. She and Gerry couldn't agree on how to make the *niños* mind, especially Ángel. Or, they scrapped about money, since they often ran short, stretched to cover the bills and expenses, mostly due to Gerry's gambling—cockfights, races, card games—anything he could place a bet on. Lately, things had gotten worse. He avoided her, often sleeping in the tool shed behind the house where he kept his motorcycle and an old army cot. He said he liked working on his equipment late at night, but she knew better.

Okay, so what? she consoled herself. *It's his choice. What the hell? Let him sleep where he wants. Besides, I have to get up at five to get those boys out the door and open the diner by six. I sleep better without him.*

It wasn't any easier with Gerry's father, Héctor Ortega, either. He lived in the spare room. How many years had it been? Nearly five since Gerry's mother had died in her sleep, leaving her devoted husband of forty-two years heartbroken and helpless. After the funeral, they all agreed it would be better to just lock up the trailer in Antonito and bring Grandpa Héctor home to live with them.

Rachel didn't mind having him under their roof. He always tried to help, but with his vision almost gone, most of the time he just listened to the television or the radio, or napped. When the boys were home from school though, that was another story. He'd greet them at the door and ask for every detail: like what they learned that day, joking and teasing about teachers, and the names of pretty girls.

Ángel didn't care much for the banter, but Rachel's younger son, Juan, loved to climb right onto his grandfather's lap. "Tell me a story, *abuelo*," he'd ask, pulling on Héctor's white beard.

"You first," said Héctor, wrapping his arms around Juan's slight body and bouncing him on one bent knee.

"Faster!" Juan giggled, pretending he was riding a runaway horse.

Even with Ángel's grumbling, Héctor's grandchildren were the sunshine in his perpetually dark world, two bright orbs of wonder and love. And when brotherly fights erupted, or an argument between Rachel and Gerry arose, the old man simply listened and never took sides. Hard as it was, he knew better than that.

"Just once, couldn't you tell him he's wrong?" Rachel begged the last time things got out of control. Maybe it was unfair to ask a parent to judge his own son, but Rachel wished Héctor would get involved, just once in a while and tell Gerry how to behave. Or maybe, take her side. She resented feeling overpowered all the time.

Lately, she'd learned to dismiss Gerry's insults and turn the other cheek, or ignore him altogether. What did he know, after all? He couldn't stop her from being herself and expressing how she felt. She wasn't a kid anymore. And since Ángel returned home from Roswell, she needed to protect him from his dad. Sometimes, things got ugly. It wasn't fair. Once in a while, Ángel dared fight back. He'd call his father names, swing a fist, or kick and run. Then, all hell would break loose: Gerry threatening to use a belt, doors slamming, tears flowing.

"This has *got* to stop!" Rachel insisted after the last eruption. "I'm telling you, Gerry, for your own sake. Enough! You've got to control yourself. He's just a boy. I can't live this way."

"You don't say? Well, I don't see you doing anything to stop him, straighten him out. He's spoiled rotten, a little mama's boy. Somebody's got to teach him how to behave."

* * *

Through it all, Rachel held on to her home. The house gave her strength. It belonged to her parents after all, and to her mother's mother before that, and maybe even more ancestors before her—she didn't know exactly, a place where generations had been born and raised. It was left to Rachel and her older sister Carmen after the Martinez's died in a road accident one fog-blanketed night on their way to visit relatives in Chama. Rachel was barely fifteen at the time.

Carmen, almost twenty, stepped in to help. She pulled out of a junior college in El Rito and, along with a state-appointed guardian, Sister Conchita, an administrator from the high school, finished raising her sister until the persuasive Gerry Ortega came along three years later. Rachel had just started her senior year. By June, Gerry had managed to talk her into marriage and put a ring on her finger. Nothing fancy, just a gold band from Wal-Mart, but enough to make her his. After the wedding, he moved into the family house like he owned it, and nine months later, helped baptize their first son. New life filled the old adobe with joy. The child was christened Ángel Martinez Ortega, a lusty, healthy dark-eyed boy.

"My happiness is my *niños,*" said Rachel to anyone who asked, especially after little Juan came into the world, seven years later. Motherhood came easy, as long as she was at home, spending time with her sons, baking, cooking, playing with the boys. But things shifted once she went to work and the children started to mature. Everyone's needs seemed to change.

CHAPTER TWO

Coming Undone

"I'M SORRY, BUT I can't take this," Rachel implored one night after another argument. "Why am I always putting out fires? We're not a family anymore, Gerry, we're an inferno! And now, because of a stupid letter that came by mail this week, things are going to get even worse—an order from the state of New Mexico that says we have to move."

"What? When? Nah, that can't be," said Gerry, not even looking up.

"I know. But it is. I don't know when exactly. I was afraid to show it to you but here it is. Maybe we'll get a retraction, or another letter saying it was a mistake. How can I be sure? If it isn't, how will I tell Héctor and the boys?"

"Dunno. You'll figure it out. You always do."

"I don't know about this time. Hey, look at me. Listen. I can't imagine your father adjusting to a move and a new home, especially with his handicap. And it's going to be hard on the kids, too."

"One thing at a time, OK? We're not goin' anywhere so relax. It's just a threat. Like I said, you deal with it."

Rachel hoped it was a mistake, but when no retraction came, she broke the news to the rest of the family a week later as simply as she could.

"Whatever God wills," said Héctor. "*No problema.* I go where you go."

As for the boys, she explained, "There's no reason to be too concerned, *mijos.* At least, not yet. We have time."

In her heart, she had not fully processed the fact that the New Mexico Department of Transportation had given them three short months to pack up the house and find another place to live.

* * *

At first read of the second letter's details, Gerry exploded. It came in the mail ten days after the first one, a special delivery on a hot, clammy August afternoon.

"Christ! Who are they kidding? Pushin' us around! Don't they got nothing better to do? Let 'em go build a road somewhere else. Hell, nobody comes through Estrella anyway. We're not going anywhere." He crumpled the letter in his palm.

Rachel shook her head. She wasn't sure he understood. It didn't sound like they were being given a choice. The message was clear, spelled out in black and white. That's how progress came to small towns like theirs, by decree, and without warning. And because some engineer in Santa Fe had drawn a plan that would plot a new access road to the main highway right through their front yard, they had been given two options—move the house back three hundred feet, or leave.

Since an irrigation ditch ran behind the back fence, they couldn't reposition the building anywhere else on the lot. Relocation was out of the question. But if they moved, they could accept a check for the appraised value of the house and its one-acre site, in full. Then, the treasured home would be razed to the ground.

Gerry asked Rachel to go get him a beer while he unfolded the crumpled letter for a second look. By the time she returned, he'd discovered the second page with the assessment and the full offer, the paper shaking in his hands. He couldn't stop laughing.

"Holy Jesus, girl, it's like winning the lottery. Did you see these numbers? Come on! We're finally gonna get out of here! It's payday!"

"Wait, Gerry, please," Rachel interrupted. "I don't want to go. I mean, we can't let them do this. I think we should protest. This house has always been home to me. And I still have a lease on the diner, too. There must be some law in our favor that protects people from situations like this one. Someone we can call."

"Are you crazy? Keep this house? No way. We can't lose. Besides, once they finish the bypass, this town is gonna' die a slow death. You know that. No one will drive through here anymore unless they have a good reason to, and I can't think of even one. We might as well get out while we can. And the offer is decent—two hundred thousand dollars, clean! What's keeping us? Your two-bit restaurant and this ancient ruin? Hardly. We can finally move to a real town and get a life."

"No. Please wait," protested Rachel. "I'm not giving in just like that. Maybe we can get an appeal or something. Hire a lawyer." Rachel knew little about legal procedures but couldn't imagine they could be forced off family land practically overnight.

"Pay a lawyer? With what? Are you kidding me? This is bigger than us," Gerry laughed again, swigging a can of Bud. "They can have it, babe. And I mean all of it, right now. Tell 'em we're in. It's theirs!"

CHAPTER THREE

An Inheritance

GERRY HAD NEVER PUT down roots in Estrella. He had no attachments. He'd always hoped the town would be a stepping stone to somewhere else all along. At least, that's how it seemed when he'd met Rachel fifteen years earlier, and not much had changed since then. He'd been in Estrella but a few weeks when he first learned that the beautiful eighteen year-old was not only single, but owned some serious real estate as well. That was all he needed to know.

After the wedding, attended by a few of Rachel's friends, plus Gerry's parents who'd come down from southern Colorado, Gerry went to work for a mechanic in the town's only repair shop. "This is just for now," he told Rachel. "You'll see."

But that was then, and life went on, and nothing ever changed. Only now, who'd have guessed, it actually looked like it might.

* * *

"Come on, work with me," Gerry said, waving the letter in her face. He spun around, giddy with elation. "I mean, what's holding us? We're finally able to get out of here, just like I told you we would someday. It's a done deal. Let's get moving. I've got things to do."

In some ways, Rachel knew he was right, and resented it. They had no control or leverage. Unable to postpone the inevitable, she called her sister Carmen who needed to know about the offer too. The house was partly hers, after all. She had to be involved.

Carmen, always the big sister, always one step ahead. When Rachel married, Carmen moved out, glad to see Rachel stay in the house and start a new life. A year later, after Ángel came, she moved back in to help her sister with the baby, but didn't get along with Gerry at all. She did what she could for a few months and finally moved in with Pedro Gonzales, the guy she'd been dating. They stayed together for close to a year in the two-bedroom adobe she'd rented across town on Twin Pine Lane. After the relationship ended, Carmen bought the rental for herself, comfortable where she was.

"What do you want me to say?" asked Carmen, eyeing her sister after hearing the news. "I don't think you have a choice. Sure seems a shame somehow. I loved that old house. Hate to see it go. Just remember, I get some of that money when the check comes, like fifty percent, right? I'm still a co-owner."

"Hmm." Rachel stopped her. "I'm not so sure about that. I've been taking care of it all these years, paying taxes, upkeep. I haven't seen you contributing to its cost. I paid for the new kitchen and bathroom, after all. So let's say maybe 40/60 at best. I mean what's yours is yours, but to be fair, I get more. That's the way I see it."

Carmen shot her a look somewhere between contempt and disbelief. "Is that right? Are you kidding me? Well, I'm not so sure. I'll have to think it over."

Rachel stood her ground but didn't like her sister's reaction and hated it when they didn't agree. *Too bad, that's the way it goes. Now, what else? What's next? So many decisions.* Her head hurt trying to sort them out. Cutting ties and undoing a life seemed much harder than building one. *Where to begin?* All she knew was, that without a miracle, by Thanksgiving an army of bulldozers would turn their narrow winding road and one-acre lot into a four-lane byway and everything they owned and loved would have to be gone.

* * *

Ugh, she deliberated. *I know I should go along with Gerry, wherever he wants to move. Isn't that what wives do? But maybe it's time to think about myself for once, what I want. Or don't. Maybe this is the turning point, the one I've been waiting for—the time to say no to what feels wrong—no matter the consequences.* In her head, it sounded doable, telling him it was over and time for them to go their separate ways, but Rachel hated to imagine the confrontation if she did. Besides being impatient, Gerry had a nasty temper she unfortunately knew too well.

* * *

"First thing I gotta do is find a storefront with a warehouse," Gerry said, pacing the kitchen. "So I can work on a couple of new cars." He was as excited as a kid making a Christmas wish list. "Then buy a bigger bike. Maybe two bikes. Maybe I'll upgrade the four-wheeler. Damn! We could get a boat and tow over to Navajo Lake for a change. What do you think about that?"

Rachel listened to him as if to a mad man, full of talk and wild plans. Yet she never heard him ask once what she wanted, or what he could do for her, or what might be good for the boys.

Back when he used to suggest moving to Farmington or Albuquerque she'd let him ramble. Fat chance. It could never happen. Now, it had become a bizarre reality and she felt like she was just going along for the ride.

"Forget it," she fumed, the aggravation following her to work where she mixed up orders and misplaced deliveries. She just couldn't imagine leaving the town that had always been her home. Estrella, a familiar story with a happy ending. She loved its warmth and familiar faces, its wooded hills and clear, bracing climate all year round. She loved its people and how they cared for one another and its green fields filled with cattle and horses and long-haired, gentle *churro* sheep. This story just had to have another chapter. It just *had* to.

She didn't want to abandon the small restaurant where she'd developed an adoring clientele either. The diner might be old and worn, but was always busy. Clients often waited half an hour for a seat, swearing that she made the best enchiladas in the county. Besides, the lease had one year left. She couldn't imagine losing both the diner and her family home at the same time. Above all, the house had been a place of refuge for many since it was built more than two hundred years earlier. The old weathered adobe with sturdy *piñon* trees in the courtyard and thick sculpted walls seemed as permanent as the earth itself. Rachel always assumed she would live out her days there, as did her mother, grandmother, and who knows how many ancestors before them.

CHAPTER FOUR

The Painful Truth

"HEY, CAN WE TALK?" Rachel ventured, hoping Gerry was clear-headed and sober for a change. "How do you think this move is going to work out anyway? Time-wise, I mean."

Gerry put down the wrench he was holding and looked up at her. "What are you talking about?"

"Logistics. You know, cutting loose. Just maybe, you could leave first and I could stay on, at least until the school year ends and my lease is out. Then we could talk about what's next."

Gerry nodded. "That might work. Yeah, why not? Sure, you can stay," he answered. "I'll find us a place to live meantime. Not too big, right? And I need to find a place for Dad to live too, once and for all—a senior home or something. He can't keep hanging around with us the rest of his life. And maybe we can find a military school for Ángel, some place that will straighten him out real good. That would be a goal. Give us some peace for a change."

"Excuse me?" said Rachel. "Military school? I don't think so. Besides, we've been there and done that. Maybe I don't want Ángel to live away from us anymore. Maybe that's the whole problem. You keep pushing him away. Did you ever think about that? And I don't mind Papa living with us either. The boys love him. What's wrong with you, Gerry? Don't you care about anything? We're a family. We have a life here. I don't want to leave or change any of it."

"Well, it's too late for that, sorry. Change is in the works. We'll make new friends, move to a real town and not wallow in a dead end place like this. You can make tacos in Farmington. There's no future here, Rachel. You can't argue with that."

Rachel didn't have an answer. She never thought about the future. Up until now, she lived each day as it came, comfortably clinging to the past, the one embedded in the house she loved. She cherished its sense of comfort and safety, starting with its solid walnut, front door with its center panel of leaves and birds. She admired too the heavy, hand-hewn wood ceiling lintels carved to resemble curling vines. A massive plank table with a trestle base graced the dining room. It could seat a dozen people easily, and often had.

A vintage baby grand piano occupied an entire corner of the parlor. Her mother told her it came from Spain, long before, from Toledo, in fact. The sound of that piano used to echo off the walls when played, but she couldn't remember the last time anyone sat down to touch its keys. Memories of family gatherings that took place when she was a young girl were fading like old photographs; groups of people she hadn't seen in so many years, she very well might have imagined them.

But the house held her fast—inside and out. Simple things, like the tiled kitchen with its warm, sun-baked floors, and the view upstairs of the pine-covered hills and the river beyond. She especially adored the small stained glass window above the front door in the foyer, a square panel with a red, six-petaled, wild rose in its center. The window's origins remained a mystery—but its brilliant light, in the evenings when the setting sun shone through creating streaming rays of crimson and gold, seemed magical.

Rachel couldn't let go. She couldn't explain why she thought they still had the right to refuse; protest, write a letter to Congresswoman Fernández—something. Maybe just stall, a few more years. How could she tell Gerry that the move seemed like a confrontation with everything unresolved between them, especially their rocky relationship, and her family's past?

She even knew of graves in the cemetery with familiar names like Morales, from decades earlier on her mother's side, and Martínez, on her father's, dating as far back as the eighteen hundreds, maybe even before that. She'd been meaning to study them and work out a family tree, maybe find some history—explain who they were to the children, to her troubled Ángel and little Juan—if only she herself knew. But didn't.

Just going to the cemetery seemed difficult, the very idea, painful. One of her ancestors, a great-great-grandmother, had made sure that at least she would not be forgotten. Right in the front yard, not more than twenty feet from the door, the largest of the town's old walnut trees bore the name *Rebeca* carved into its base. It was still clear enough to read, although a part of the letter *R* had swollen into a bulbous scar, as if a bullet had grazed the injured bark. Centuries had helped heal the wound, but Rebeca's spirit somehow lingered in the branches to this very day.

* * *

Gerry paced, impatient, his temper simmering for no apparent reason. It was almost dinner time and Rachel was about to bring the children in. "I'm cutting out," he called as went out the back door and climbed onto his Harley. "Need to clear my head."

"Okay, bye." Rachel watched him as he disappeared down the road. How long would he be gone this time? His rides took him away for hours. At home, he was moody and restless. They hardly ever talked about anything personal any more, and he hardly ever touched her either. Maybe she just didn't matter.

She brooded. With each passing day, Rachel knew that when it came time to move, she'd never be able to go. She'd play along until the time was right, and then tell him it was over. Done. One loss at a time.

The thought of leaving festered like a sore, the pain no less real. Some nights, she was certain she could hear the old house moan and sigh, just as sure as she could hear the wind in the foothills sweep through the sleepy town, then wrap itself around the old adobe walls in a timeless embrace. She could barely endure the thought of a bulldozer wiping it off the face of the earth. No cash payment could replace the sense of herself she felt within its frame, as well as the deep hold it had upon her.

Although her mother and father were both gone, Rachel held on to their memory and the stories they used to tell. She needed to write them down before they were forgotten, weave them into her present life. Tearing the house down might somehow take her family's entire history as well, as if it had never even existed. For a moment she thought about the horror of her parent's wreck so long ago, that sudden empty feeling of losing everything, of having no family to love anymore, of not belonging to anyone. That pain had taken a very long time to heal.

"I'm sorry," she said, whispering to the ancient walnut tree in the courtyard, knowing it too would be destroyed. "Forgive me, Mother," she said to the piano and the timeworn table in the dining room. "I'm sorry, for letting you down. There's simply nothing I can do."

Why did she feel their presence so closely now? The overpowering feeling enveloped her. Perhaps neither of parents' spirits had ever left, lingering among their possessions over the many years. Whatever it was, she knew she owed them some loyalty, and the house deserved some respect. She'd give it to them, any way she could.

CHAPTER FIVE

Coming Undone

ÁNGEL TURNED TO HIS brother in the dark. Their beds lined up barely a foot apart, just enough space for their mother to squeeze in and change the sheets. The small bedroom, with smooth plastered walls and an angled ceiling above the twin beds had been Ángel's alone before Grandpa Héctor moved in. Then everything changed, but little Juan gladly gave up his bed for their Papa and moved in with his older brother—together at last, like two explorers on a quest.

For most of Juan's short seven years, he and Ángel had been inseparable until Ángel went to boarding school. Now that he was home, Juan clung to his sibling more than ever, thrilled to have him back, and in the very same room! A month had passed since Mama told them about the house being sold. He didn't really understand why but, whatever the reason, felt sad.

Ángel felt pissed, way more than sad. It was grown-up business and it stunk. No way would he move with his dad to Farmington, and he didn't want to stay with his mom in Estrella either. No one would call him a mama's boy. He was old enough. They'd see. It was time for him to do his own thing, once and for all.

* * *

This night would be the last night in the only home the boys had ever known. By Wednesday afternoon, both of them and their *abuelo* would move to Old Pine Road and share the spare rooms at Auntie Carmen's while the family's adobe and everything around it fell to the wrecker's ball. And all this, Rachel assured them, "while Dad finds a new house for us to live in somewhere else."

Much as she hated repeating it, the explanation was a way to tide things over until she found the courage to say she wasn't going—and neither were the boys. Somehow, she'd find a place for herself and her children to stay in Estrella, with or without her husband.

* * *

"You awake?" asked Juan.

"Yeah."

"We're gonna move soon. To a new town," Juan paused here, as if searching for the next word, then started again. "I'm gonna miss my swing and my fort and the crawdads in the creek. But I'm glad we're moving to Auntie's house. Papa Héctor will be there and there's an apple tree with a swing and a big screen TV. *Tia* Carmen cooks real good too."

Ángel didn't answer. He could feel his little brother sitting up in the dark, hear his voice cracking, and knew he was on the verge of tears.

"*They're* gonna move," Ángel said, breaking his silence. "*Them.* Not us. At least, not me. I'm not going anywhere."

"Not you? Why?" Juan asked. He grasped the edge of his favorite blanket and lay down, facing his brother. He pulled the blanket up, scrunched under his chin. Anxious, he started to rock from side to side, causing the bed to creak. His eyes narrowed and he stared through the dark at Ángel who lay on his back, an arm's reach away. "Whatcha mean, you're not going?" he asked in one short, forced explosive breath.

"Just like I said. I'm not goin' *nowhere.*"

"But Mama says they're going to tear down the house and Dad said we're going to be rich and go to Farmington. And Papa Héctor said we're going to live in a brand new house and start a new school and have lots of new friends," Juan confirmed, his voice quivering with a newfound, false bravado. "He's gonna' go with us, too. But not Noche and Lucía. Mama says they don't like goats in Farmington. That's not fair. What will Poquito do without Noche and Lucía to play with? I don't want to go there. Do you? I don't want new friends."

Juan stared even harder at his older brother, squinting in the dark. The bed seemed to spin, the floor disappearing. Fear turned the edge of the blanket into a giant knot. He couldn't imagine losing Ángel again. Instinctively, he started inching towards his older brother's bed. The jab of a foot under the sheets jutted out, warning him not to get any closer. In his faintest voice, Juan dared ask, "You're not going to stay here by yourself, are you?"

Ángel didn't answer. He had been scheming all day with the Ramírez brothers, Ronaldo and Ramón, who were fifteen and seventeen years old. Ramon didn't live at home anymore and had finished high school with a diploma, whatever that was. He worked at the print shop and had a sweet car he resurrected from a wreck: a custom, black '81 Camaro Z28 with a double-barreled Hemi. He could come and go whenever he wanted, at least when he could afford some gas, and already had his own place. It wasn't much—a converted garage behind the shop, but he told Ángel months ago that he could move in with him for a while if he wanted.

Ángel hadn't told Juan about it yet. "Go to sleep now," he answered. "Don't worry, *Pinto.*"

"Can I stay here with you too? I mean, if you're not going? Can I? Please?"

"Shhhh," said Ángel putting his finger to his lips.

Juan twisted his mouth into a worried frown and rolled onto his side closing his eyes. He wrapped the edge of his blanket around his thumb and rocked some more. The floor settled, the room quieted once again.

Ángel flipped on a pair of earphones plugged into his MP3 player and selected Tejano rock. He cracked the window, then fired up the stub of a half-smoked cigarette he'd stashed behind the headboard and lay on his back, staring into the night thinking of the new life he'd have when he was free.

* * *

Morning dawns early in an empty house. Sunlight streams cold and unobstructed through windows without curtains and bounces hard off rooms stripped almost bare. The boys awoke early and dressed for school while Rachel prepared the very last breakfast to be shared in the tiled kitchen.

By eight o'clock, the bus arrived and the brothers ran to its open door, quickly climbing aboard. Rachel waved goodbye and turned to the task at hand, emptying the kitchen cabinets and fridge. The day before, she packed up the boys' toys and clothing and moved them all to her sister's. Almost everything else worth keeping was already in boxes; a cluster of assorted cartons sitting in the middle of each room, ready for the moving van that would take it and the furniture into storage until they were ready for it again. Tonight, after dinner with the kids, Rachel would sleep in the house alone. She didn't want Héctor or the children to witness the wreckers who would arrive within forty-eight hours for the demolition.

Gerry had already left Estrella, to "search for some place to live," he said, in spite of Rachel's protests. "I'll scope out what's doin' in Farmington and get me a lease on that warehouse," he assured her. "You just watch. Then I'll set up the bike shop. I got to find me someplace to live meantime, find a bank, get us a mortgage, and get the new business up and running. You'll see. It's gonna be big."

Gerry left the day after the government reimbursement check arrived, assuring Rachel she could handle the remaining packing by herself. "Yeah, just relax. I'll be back for the rest later. Get your stuff and the boys' things together. Not to worry."

That was over a week ago. Incredible. Since Gerry left town, he'd only called once to follow up. Whenever Rachel called him, she got his voice mail. Damn. Was he avoiding her? Why?

Rachel arranged to move into a motel near the diner, the *Casa del Rey*, the day of the tear-down. No point staying with Carmen; not enough room, and, besides, she needed to be close to work. She promised the boys she'd see them every afternoon and join them at night for dinner. Luckily, Carmen lived near the bus route on the edge of town and the school bus could pick up the children per usual. They'd be fine, even though Ángel seemed crushed, more sullen than ever.

Gerry promised he'd be back the day before the demolition to help load the furniture. The day he left, he barely hugged the boys goodbye, got into his car and backed out of the drive. Unrolling the window, he stopped briefly and waved at Rachel. "*Adiós,* babe."

"*¿Adiós*? That's it? Not even a hug or a kiss? Oh well, what did I expect?"

Exhaust poured out of the tailpipe as Gerry gunned the motor and sped away.

"Son of a bitch. Why did I ever…?"

* * *

The wreckers were scheduled to arrive early Friday. Rachel wanted to be ready. By Wednesday afternoon she'd packed up every last thing but her bedding and toiletries and forced herself to do a final check. Nothing left.

After dinner, she returned to the house alone, counting on Gerry to arrive first thing Thursday morning as previously agreed. Just in case, she phoned, leaving this message: "The house has to be vacated by noon on Thursday at the latest. You'd better be here by eight, *pronto.*"

Late afternoon would be okay, too. But telling him to come so early gave her some leeway in case he was late, which he often was. She lay down, exhausted, but struggled to fall asleep, counting the minutes until morning, dreading every one of them.

CHAPTER SIX

Moving Out

UP EARLY, RACHEL OPENED a thermos of coffee, and sat at the kitchen table, to no avail. Eight o'clock. came and went. No Gerry. By eight-thirty she started dialing his number on her cell. Again and again. Still no answer. Where was he? At nine o'clock, someone knocked at the front door. Finally! She opened it to find a man she'd never seen before.

"*Buenos días, señora.*" Behind him on the driveway sat a beat-up van with an open trailer. "*Mucho gusto. Me llamo Octavio.*" He extended a hand.

He explained in Spanish that Gerry was really busy and couldn't come, and besides he owed him a favor, so here he was instead. "Ready?"

Rachel fumed, cursing under her breath, but showed him the pile of boxes in the front room and started to help him load the assortment up the tailgate ramp. She could barely lift her half of the dining room table, which seemed to be made out of stone, not wood. The queen-size mattress weighed more than she imagined as well. In no time, sweat stained her T-shirt and dripped down her neck.

But by noon, Octavio was back in the truck cab and heading off to a storage warehouse near Taos with all their worldly goods. Rachel proceeded to check every closet for the last time, just in case, and packed her personal belongings and bedding into her car. That was it. Done. The house felt like a morgue.

Earlier that month, Rachel loaned the rosewood piano to the church until she knew for sure where they would live. The local cleric, Father Núñez, accepted it kindly—*gracias, gracias,* such a fine instrument, just needed tuning—a piano would add much to their weddings and festivals.

For Rachel, the move flew by too fast. In less than a day the house had turned into a hollow shell, echoing when she walked on its bare tile floors; the empty rooms, meaningless, as if no one had ever lived there. The old adobe walls looked naked without the bright *Chimayó* weavings she had collected, or the many relics that had been in the family for so long, especially the small silver crucifix affixed above the front door and the painted *retablo* of Our Lady of Guadalupe in the hallway. Those had been in the family for ages.

Most of all, she missed the silver-framed photo taken at her parents' twentieth anniversary celebration the year before they died, packed away days ago. Now, a dark square of plaster on the entry wall served as testament to the many years the image hung there. Eight people once gathered for that picture. She could identify a few of them, but always wondered who the others were. Aunts and uncles, cousins, maybe? They were all a lot older than her parents. They didn't live in Estrella, that much she knew. Party guests, perhaps? How was it they just disappeared? Why did she never think to ask her parents before it was too late, or her sister for that matter?

Wherever she turned, the house seemed to shrink before her eyes. Once Octavio drove away, a chill crept up Rachel's spine. The house felt suffocating, like a tomb. Open the windows—get out, get some air. Locking the front door out of habit, she left and headed for work. The rest of the afternoon dragged as she thought of the destruction scheduled for the following day. The horrific image of the walls and tile roof flattened to dust turned into a headache that wouldn't subside. Two Advil did nothing to help. She couldn't wait to be with her children; she wanted to cling to them, hold them tight. Before long, she and the boys would be homeless and it hurt.

* * *

When the bulldozers arrived the next morning, Rachel stood by her car, still hoping for a miracle and wishing for some way to hold on. She'd closed the diner until noon with apologies and a sign on the door, while Carmen got the kids off to school. Héctor stayed behind with the dog. Rachel didn't want any of them near.

She walked through the house one more time, then waited by the door, clinging to the handle as if to administer last rites. The men began unloading their heavy equipment from a semi-trailer flatbed, but Rachel could tell right away that something was amiss. Several of them were arguing. The big backhoe sat on idle, grumbling in its tracks. She approached the foreman.

"*¿Qué pasa, señor*?" she asked. "Is something wrong?"

"Sí," the operator answered. "We are missing the release form from Public Service; you know, gas and power. Signed by you, yes?" He needed the inspection document certifying the house had been unhooked from all services, officially.

Rachel had never seen it. Maybe Gerry had. But the work couldn't begin without it. The wreckers were on a schedule and argued loudly with the inspector over the delay. Someone made a phone call, then another, and by nine o'clock. a deputy from the County Sheriff's Estrella sub-station drove up and pulled over.

"*Buenos días. ¿Cuál es el problema?*" the officer asked, stepping out of his patrol car and greeting the crew. He lifted his hat, smiled at Rachel, then walked over to a group of men standing next to a truck. A few minutes of conversation and the deputy flipped open his cell phone. He returned to the man in charge. They walked through the house and back outside to the electric and gas meters. The lines had been flagged as disconnected. It all looked good.

With a wave of his hand, things began to move. Both the backhoe and a menacing bulldozer kicked back on, engines rumbling. They roared slowly up towards the house, crushing the picket fence like toothpicks, then stopped, waiting once more. The foreman signaled the officer again.

Deputy Flores headed over. Another short discussion and he decided to hold off until the courier arrived with the paperwork. Something about liability. "*Sí, sí. No problema, señor*—we'll just wait. *Por favor.*"

José Flores had a smooth way of getting things done. Six-foot-two in stocking feet and roughly 190 pounds, he kept himself in good shape for a man past forty. His strong profile and deep-set brown eyes, framed by a thick shock of black hair, graying slightly on the temples, gave him an air of authority. He had been posted in Estrella for two years and was respected by the community as fair but tough. Well-liked by locals, many still wondered why he was single. Some heard he was divorced; unusual for a Catholic.

Some also heard he had a girlfriend in the area, but if he did, he kept her away from the prying eyes of the town where he now lived. Everyone knew he had close family nearby: a married sister in Espanola who had a three year-old son, and his mother who had moved there from Socorro. Being near them is what made him ask for the transfer from Santa Fe in the first place. Besides, small towns had always worked best for him. He liked the closeness.

Deputy Flores knew Rachel and Gerry Ortega only slightly. Working in a town of eleven hundred people, he pretty much thought he knew just about everyone, one way or another. Just recently he'd been involved in breaking up a fracas near the elementary school. He'd hauled the Ortega's bruised teenaged son back to the *Taco Stop* in cuffs, the only way he could get the boy to quit flailing at everything he saw. Before that incident, he stopped by the diner occasionally for some of the *sopapillas* Rachel turned out each day at noon. And her tamales, he swore, were the best he'd ever tasted.

Flores liked Rachel. She worked hard and cared for her kids. Anybody who could tame a boy like Ángel even a little bit had his respect. She wasn't too bad to look at either: about five-foot-eight with fair skin, shoulder-length brown hair that fell in natural waves, and luminous dark eyes … the kind of eyes you could lose yourself in if you looked too long. She seemed quiet, but determined somehow as well. Sure had a classy look about her.

Many of the people in the small towns of northern New Mexico prided themselves on being direct descendants of the original Spanish settlers. He assumed Rachel did too. She was probably Castilian, with her creamy complexion. In fact, some of the residents proudly considered themselves more Spanish than New Mexican; related to the original families that came with the legendary Juan de Oñate expedition following the Conquistadors, way back when. He didn't know much about Gerry though, who came out of a mixed marriage: half Hispanic, half Anglo, from somewhere near Trinidad, down in southern Colorado. But then, nobody knew much about Gerry, other than that he liked to drink.

* * *

Flores attempted to set Rachel at ease. She looked anxious about the delay. "Sorry to hear about your house, *señora.* I know your family had been there a long time. And too bad about the back-up here. It happens. But Public Service over in Santa Fe is sending somebody with the paperwork right over, probably on the road right now. You'll need to sign it though. You're the legal owner, right?"

Rachel nodded, glad that the awful throbbing of the loud machines had stopped. "Yeah, sure, I can do that." She smiled at the officer and tried to look calm. She wished the whole thing was over. "But, *señor* … uh, Deputy Flores—would you mind staying around if there's any more difficulty?" she asked, wondering what else could go wrong, but sure that something might. "Gerry was held up in Farmington, and I, just, well …"

Rachel had come to rely on Flores' ability to handle whatever came his way. She still owed him for saving Ángel from the thrashing he got earlier that year when the kid lost his temper and challenged a group of older students all at once. Bad idea. The boy had quieted down by the time Flores brought him to the *Taco Stop*, especially since he left him with a stern warning: "Shape up or go back to Roswell, *tipo duro*."

Ángel heard that threat, loud and clear. It stuck, for a while. She felt comfortable asking the officer for a little more time.

"You bet, *señora,*" Flores answered, scanning the road "I can stick around. I need to make some phone calls anyway."

* * *

The document arrived, Rachel signed off, and the wreckers started in earnest at the back of house. The backhoe driver drove right through the goat yard to begin the attack. Earlier, the goats had been moved to the neighbor, Señor Mendes, who put up a makeshift pen. One day, Rachel promised the children, they'd be with their pets again.

As the exterior adobe walls crumbled and caved, the original interior support beams lay fully exposed, rugged timbers still strong. They wouldn't give up as easily. Rachel studied the procedure from a distance, like watching a hanging. Her head ached. She winced at every snap and crack. Each chomp of the monster backhoe's giant claw tore at her gut. Finally, she looked away, overwhelmed by her loss, bitter and angry.

How could this be happening? How could I have given up without a fight?

CHAPTER SEVEN

An Unexpected Find

FOR TWENTY MINUTES THE work continued uninterrupted. A front-end loader followed in the wake of the two bigger machines, scooping up plaster, mud brick and debris and dumping it into a waiting truck. Thick walls disintegrated into pulverized adobe and time. Then everything stopped, only the huff-huff of giant machines at rest. The backhoe operator stepped out of his cab and waved a gloved hand.

Flores opened the door of his car. Again? He approached the driver to see what could be the matter. A few words were exchanged and he motioned for Rachel to join them.

"Come on over here a minute, would you?" he called. "Around back, okay? Looks like they need you."

With the back porch and kitchen torn away, Rachel could see they had come to the center of the house, the dining room, a large rectangular space with a storage closet on one wall and an open walk-in pantry with three long wooden shelves. Aromatic wood planks lined the closet on one side and gave off a strong scent of freshly-split cedar.

The closet wall had been gouged first from the kitchen side where a ragged hole now gaped. But strangely, the blow didn't show on the dining room side at all. Instead, the hole revealed a second, smaller closet, about four feet wide by eight feet in length and just as high, just large enough for three, maybe four persons, to stand in. Rachel had never realized anything was there. To someone who knew about it, the secret closet must have been accessible from inside the larger one, or maybe from the kitchen at one time. It had to have been part of the house since the very beginning, at least one hundred and fifty years earlier. To have added it later would have been impossible.

"What's this?" she asked, peering into its bare interior.

"I'm guessing it was either a hiding place, or a kind of safe room for whoever built this house in the first place," said Flores. "Back in the day, there were no security deposits in local banks. Where else would you hide your valuables? Whatever it was, when the men broke through the kitchen wall, they found this."

The bulldozer operator, a man with a sweat-soaked bandana wrapped around his head and thick plaster dust all over his black mustache, stepped forward.

"*Tenga, señora*—it looks old. *Muy viejo*. Maybe *muy importante.*"

Rachel stared. His gloved hands held a dusty wooden box, its lid carved in a beautiful floral design that reminded her of the hand-carved front door. She could see ornate brass hinges and an iron latch under the heavy layer of dust.

"*Gracias*," she said, taking it from him, surprised by its weight. She stared at it, filled with wonder.

Flores grasped her shoulder. "Hey, you might want to open that over here," he suggested, motioning to his vehicle. "It's nobody's business. Maybe something Mom and Dad left behind?"

"Hardly," she answered. "At least, I don't think so. I never saw it before. It looks … so much older …" Rachel wrapped her arms around the box and followed him back to his patrol car. He opened the door and she climbed in. Flores pulled a chamois out of the glove compartment and wiped the dust off as best he could.

"There."

Rachel opened the latch and lifted the heavy lid. It stayed upright as she looked inside. In one corner of the plain wooden interior was a Bible bound with a cracked and darkened leather cover. She opened the book and touched the fragile yellowed pages gently. The edges fairly crumbled at her touch. The Bible was written in an alphabet she didn't recognize. Dozens of inscriptions on the inside cover bore family names in a fine hand, some in Spanish, like Velásquez, Mendes, and Martínez. Others she only guessed at, like Abravanel and Pereira, and there—Morales, followed by what she assumed were birth dates, or perhaps death entries.

Next to the Bible, wrapped in a piece of brittle, yellowed muslin, lay two heavy silver candlesticks no more than seven inches tall, deeply tarnished. One bore dents along its flared base, but both were etched around the bottom with the same pattern: a simple floral motif encased in beaded ropes of silver—a design like nothing she had seen before in the shops or homes in Río Arriba county. Most curious of all, however, was a five inch-long, flat and narrow silver case with a hollow interior, a relic of some kind, perhaps. Black with oxidation, the fanciful design on the front was obscure, but looked to Rachel like two twisted columns on either side of a tree. Above this was a strange silver letter. The top of the case bore a small silver crown.

"And what's this?" she asked, picking it up and holding it in her palm. She peered through the open bottom of the case into its hollow cavity, turning it around.

Flores watched intently as she picked up each item and examined it. "What do you think it is?" He looked at her, his head tilted.

"I have no idea."

"Well then, I don't know either."

Rachel sat upright, puzzled by his response. What could he mean by that?

Before she could ask another question, the second bulldozer hit the front porch of the house from the side, knocking down the support posts, whacking the carved door to pieces, and destroying the mud-plastered entry portico with a deafening crunch.

"*Oh no!*" Rachel screamed. "*Madre de Dios*, my window!"

In the hurry and hustle to get everything done, and with the chaos of moving, she had forgotten her precious rose window in the foyer. Why didn't she think of taking it out? She should have called someone … rescued it! Could have, should have—was it too late? Oh please, wait!

The leaded panes cracked and split as the walls shuddered around them. To Rachel, the impact sounded like a jet plane had fallen from the sky. She closed the lid of the box with a snap and looked out the car window in horror. As the bulldozer backed up and rolled forward one more time, the rest of the house surrendered, imploding into a pile of fallen adobe chunks, clouds of pink-colored dust and slivered shards of shattered glass.

CHAPTER EIGHT

The Runaways

FLORES RETURNED TO HIS office, deeply moved by the cache found in the hidden pantry of the Ortega house. *Who would have ever thought?* It puzzled him. *You just never know what you'll unearth in a demolition.*

He didn't know why, but he felt the loss of Rachel's house as if it was his own. He knew what it was like to lose someone or something you love. Knew it well. But when she broke down there at the end … *hijolé*, he had never seen anyone so distraught over a broken window. It tore him up too. She actually burst into tears. And she just didn't know what to think about the old box and its contents. Frankly, neither did he.

No need to tell anyone what he assumed was the story behind that find. Why should he? When he realized that Rachel had no idea what she held in her lap, he figured it was better to say nothing for the time being. She'd had enough surprises lately.

* * *

Thursday mornings usually kept all staff members at the sub-station filing paperwork. Flores typed up a weekly report on his laptop to send out by Friday noon. Staff Sergeant Carruthers down in Santa Fe demanded everything on time and was a stickler for detail, whether it was the summary of a domestic dispute or a crime report. The Junior Deputy in Estrella, Roy Hubbard, couldn't spell worth a darn—in English or Spanish. No sense trying to delegate the job to him. He'd only have to do it over again.

Flipping up the tab on a can of ice tea from the vending machine, Flores took a long swallow and started to review his notes. The phone rang. He picked up the receiver while continuing to scroll.

"Estrella Substation—*Hola. Buenos días* to you, *Señor* Vega. What's that? A long-haired kid walked out with a six-pack? Bud Lite? He ran when you asked for his ID. OK, got it. What time was that? Can you give me a description of the vehicle he got into, please? Uh huh. Right. Big muffler in the back. Got it. I'll get back to you. Thanks."

Flores looked at his watch. *That car belongs to the Ramírez boys. I'd know it anywhere. The kid ... don't even want to think of who that might be. Oh well, he's her problem, not mine.* He closed his laptop and looked out the window, then tilted back his chair, folding his arms. "*Diablo*," he muttered. "Little troublemaker."

* * *

Rachel scraped down the griddle after the last diner paid up. Then she counted the receipts and bills and stuck them under the change bin in the cash drawer. The safe could wait. Thinking back, the food business was what she was best at and she intended to stay with it. After all, she still held the lease for the restaurant for another twelve months—if she could just buy some time and figure out what to do, maybe she could keep everything status quo. Then again, who was she kidding? Nothing, it seemed, was ever going to be the same. It had only been a few hours since the house went down and already she felt disembodied. Alien. Alone.

She cleaned the counter, turned the coffee pots upside down, emptied the garbage and called it a day. It was only a quarter 'til three, but she couldn't stand being alone another minute. Besides, Principal Torres had called her around noon with the news that her older son never showed up to school that day. Did she know where he was? Swallowing her surprise, she pretended she knew. "Oh, he's home sick today. Sorry, I forgot to call in."

How in the world? Where could he have gone? Pleading a mother's neglect, she begged Torres not to put the absence on Ángel's record, as long as she made sure he was there on time Monday morning. Furious, she hung the *Closed* sign on the door and headed across the street to the motel, thinking she'd drive over to Carmen's and pick up Juan, then go looking for Ángel. She'd find him if he was hanging around in town. Estrella wasn't that big. She still hadn't been able to get hold of her husband. But maybe Gerry had come down from Farmington and picked up Ángel on his own. That would make sense. The boy was probably with his dad.

She had a hunch she might find them at *El Rodeo*, the bar Gerry used to hang out at. Ángel was underage, but he went there sometimes with his father to play pool. Every once in a while Gerry let Ángel have a beer too, behind the bartender's back.

That had to be it. Of course. But why wouldn't he call her if he was here? No, that would be way too considerate. Then again, if he was back from Farmington, why would he take Ángel out of school? Gerry knew how much trouble Ángel had been in. He wasn't a great father but he still didn't want his son back in juvenile hall. It wouldn't take much.

"Oh crap," she said. "Crap, crap, crap! *Madre de Dios sálvame*." She stopped at the motel reception office to see if anyone had left a message. Something. Anything. Not a clue. By God, when she found that boy, he was going to get grounded for an entire year.

CHAPTER NINE

Don't Look Now

"HOLA, MAMACITA!" CALLED FLORES as he pushed open the front door. It was one o'clock and he'd already had a very full day. He tossed his jacket over a hook on the hall tree and put his cap over that. His mother had been waiting for him since noon, happy to be back in the role she loved—providing for her children, in this case, a full-grown man. She adored José and doted on him every way she could.

The piquant aroma of simmering *sopa de albóndigas* filled the house. Rosa Flores knew the savory soup was José's favorite dish and Deputy Hubbard's too, ever since he tasted the sample José brought down to the station one night. She made enough for them both.

When Rosa Flores moved to Estrella after her husband passed away, she bought a small house on Toma Road knowing José was scheduled to move to town a year later. He took half of a duplex just two doors down from her. She could keep an eye on his place when he was gone and cook for him too. It gave her great comfort to know her son was nearby.

Flores sniffed the air with gusto. "*Bueno.* Smells good. Don't have much time to eat, though. I need to follow up on some calls. All kinds of trouble out there today. Save some of that for supper—*¿sí?*" He reached for a tortilla on the counter and rummaged in a drawer for the long-handled spoon.

"Not so fast, *mijo.*" Rosa stopped him, pulling the spoon away. "Don't I get a hug?"

At seventy-four, Rosa's health was still good and her mind as sharp as ever. Flores ignored all the guff his partners gave him about living next door to his mother but, frankly, he enjoyed it when she pampered him. Hers was unconditional love, something he could count on. Laughing, he hugged her hard. "Now, let's eat."

Rosa set the plate of tortillas on the table, her face serious. She waited until Flores finished his first bowl of soup and then began. "Tell me more of this unusual find, José," she began. "The box you told me about on the phone. *Señora* Ortega must have been very surprised."

Flores suddenly regretted spilling the morning's news. But ever since his move to Estrella, he and Rosa had grown so much closer. She'd become his closest confidante. And although Rosa was glad to be there for him when he needed her, most of all, she wanted nothing more for him than to find the right woman and settle down. He deserved someone to share his heart with.

Flores had phoned her immediately after the demo and told her in detail about the dusty wooden box. "You would have found it interesting, all right," he confirmed. "Real old stuff. *Sí, sí.* She was surprised."

"José, those items have meaning for all of us," said Rosa. "Everything there has survived for a reason. It's like a sign from above. Has *la señora* asked you anything more about it? Would she mind if I shared the news with the padre? He would want to know, to see it for himself."

"No, she hasn't asked," he answered, filling his bowl once more with the succulent broth. He took another tortilla. "Besides, it's private property. I shouldn't have even told you about it." He looked at his watch, dipped his tortilla in the last drop of soup and took a final bite. "And I'm not sure *señora* Ortega has much curiosity about it either," he continued. "If she wants to know more, she's going to have to ask. I just told her to put the box somewhere secure for now."

Flores picked up an apple from an earthenware bowl, regretting that he ever brought his mother into the matter, although he knew she would appreciate the discovery more than anyone. *When Rachel Ortega is ready,* he thought, *if she ever is, there's plenty of time to help her understand. If not, that box and everything in it will probably end up in some pawn shop somewhere in New Mexico.*

"Too bad," Rosa sighed. "Those treasures have come a long way. Her ancestors would be saddened to know such things were lost. They should stay with her. Or at least, somewhere secure, until their meaning becomes clear. This is no accident, my son. She must be made to understand what she has inherited, from who knows how far back."

"Mama, please, it's not our problem. If she is to know, she must come to it on her own."

"Ay, José, *por favor.* Her past has emerged out of the darkness. I can feel it. You were a witness, *mijo.* We have to help her."

"Me? No way. And I don't think you should either. Besides, don't talk to me about helping women. You know my luck there. If it's really as important as you think, one day she'll find out what she needs to know. Right now, I have a liquor store theft to investigate; one more petty crime."

* * *

After finding no word of Ángel at the motel office, Rachel walked briskly toward the plaza. She'd parked her car behind the *Santuario del Renacimiento*, an old adobe church, which stood at the north side of the square. She stepped onto the stone porch and through the wooden doors, opened wide in the heat of the day. The building was empty, her footsteps echoing as she walked, the pews abandoned. But its cool dark space gave her a sense of peace. She needed some now. Rachel bowed her head, knelt before the statue of Our Lady, and crossed herself.

"*Por favor, madre,*" she asked. "Feel my heart. It is so worried. I need my son to come home. And I ask you to help me be strong."

The Virgin Mother offered no comfort to her this day. The statue seemed immutable, uncaring and cold. Rachel stood up, the prayer unanswered. Who was she kidding? This would never work. She felt empty. Perhaps she should talk to Father Núñez about Ángel? Maybe he could help her in some way. Walking to the back of the church, she knocked on the door of his office but no one answered. No matter. It would keep.

Fishing the keys out of her sweater pocket, she started up the old Impala. But searching the floor of the car and the seat beside her, she realized she'd left her purse back at the diner. Driving around the plaza, she pulled up moments later at the back entrance. The door stood ajar. Impossible! She'd locked it herself only minutes earlier! Then she noticed that the glass above the door handle was smashed. In the short time she was gone, someone had broken into the *Taco Stop* and fled.

Rachel rushed inside and found her purse upside down on the pantry floor and the register open, the cash drawer bare. She dialed Carmen's number and waited impatiently while the phone rang over and over, to no avail.

"Dammit, Carmen. Answer the phone!"

Suddenly her sister's voice came on the line. "*¿Hola?*"

"Carmen, it's me. I've been robbed! At least two hundred dollars—gone. I can't believe I didn't put the money away before I left. Damn, I swore I would never do that. And my purse, wouldn't you know it?—left it here and all my cash is gone. At least another fifty."

"Oh, I'm so sorry. What can I do?" Carmen asked.

"I don't know exactly. Could you come over and help me clean up this mess? Patch up the door? There's glass everywhere. You can leave Juan with Héctor for thirty minutes. He'll be fine."

"Sure. I'll head right over. Listen, Juan's been acting real funny since the bus dropped him off from school a little while ago. Says he hasn't seen his brother all day. He seems real upset."

"That figures. The principal called and said Ángel was truant today. I lied and said he was sick at home. I don't know where the hell he is. Just what I needed, on top of everything else."

"Listen, Rachel, don't you think you should call the police?" Carmen suggested. "You need to report this. It's a break-in."

"You're right. I will. Just tell my little *Pinto* that Mama's coming as soon as she can. I promised him I'd be home early. Lord, I hate to say it, but I hope it wasn't Ángel who pulled this stunt."

"Why would you say that? What a crazy idea ... Oh my God—hold on a minute. I can't believe what I'm seeing!"

"What?"

"While we're talking—two kids in a yellow Camaro pulled up here in front of the house. I think I saw Ángel in the back seat. They slowed down like they were going to park. Then, the back door popped open, the kid in back yelled something, and Juan jumped in with Poquito under his arm! Oh my God! Would you look at that! They just took off, heading up Pine to the south. Now both your kids are gone!"

CHAPTER TEN

Estrella, *Nueva España,* 1809

To Build a House

REBECA MORALES MARTINEZ REACHED up and set the last mud brick into place, helping to make the closet behind the big *cocina* a perfect rectangle, twice as long as it was wide. The small space would be adequate to store water jugs, seeds for planting, wine and oil, as well as those things prying eyes had no reason to know of—personal things, belongings of value, and special sacraments as well.

Rebeca's husband, Captain Moisés Martinez, told her so. This hidden pantry would provide needed privacy for two, maybe even four—up to six persons. She would understand why in time. Cool, well insulated, and extremely well-hidden behind the kitchen, she was made to understand that such a space was a necessity.

Rebeca wiped her hands on her long apron and stepped back to admire their work. Moisés set down the wooden bucket filled with straw and mud and stood next to her to get a better view. He tilted his head this way and that, checking the support beams for soundness, a smile upon his lips.

"*¡Qué bonito! Muy bueno.*This will be the finest house in the valley one day," he said. He ran his fingers over the well-chiseled niches in the struts designed to hold the shelves. In winter, many provisions could be held here. He was anxious to fill them.

Arm-in-arm, they walked together following the inside perimeter of the great room on all four sides. Door and window openings were in place and the floor smooth and ready for the clay tiles to be set. When finished, this fine adobe would be roomy, airy, and durable: two stories high, with a kitchen, a central staircase, two bedrooms below and three above, as well as a spacious courtyard. He hoped for many children.

The couple returned to their task, moving quickly, layering the mud walls with sure and steady hands. Rebeca stopped to rest, often short of breath. "It's nothing," she insisted, when her husband stopped to help her. "I'll be fine."

She found herself improving at laying bricks. One by one, practice makes perfect. Soon the thick interior walls would mask the secret storage area behind the kitchen completely.

"Rest now. *Es suficiente.* Enough for today. Don't push yourself." Moisés took Rebeca's hand and bade her sit. Her bulging belly held the promise of their first child. He hoped it would be a son to carry on the family name. From his limited experience, he knew his wife was almost too old for pregnancy and it worried him. He rubbed her shoulders. Not much time left. If all went as planned, they would move in and harvest the ripening fields before the infant's first cries filled the air.

The hidden room served as the heart of this outpost high above the Rio Grande, the place he had chosen as home after discovering his wife in a convent behind the local church. Perhaps the God of Abraham himself had led him to find her: a woman who shared his history and whom he could love with all his heart—Rebeca Elena Morales. He could rest in her eyes—deep brown, accepting and trusting. This house promised a new world for them in so many ways, a stronghold, and a place where it was safe to be oneself.

From the top of the rise where Moisés laid the foundation, looking south, he could see the entire valley below—the green belt of cottonwoods along the river, the gentle hills on both sides beyond, and the majestic mountains, the lavender peaks of the *Sangre de Cristo* with slopes covered in mesquite and tall bristlecone pine rising farther behind. His fields were rich with buffalo grass and his livestock fattened easily. Each day with Rebeca by his side brought new blessings. And, although he could not prove it, ever since she became his wife, even the stars in heaven high above their village seemed to shine much brighter than before.

* * *

Captain Moisés Alejandro Martínez had been sent by General Antonio Vega of the Viceroy's forces three years earlier to secure beef and grain for the Spanish militia. Managing such a vast empire as New Spain took many men, many strong horses and supplies. Within a short time, Moisés found himself running a brisk commissary and entrenched himself in the settlement, surrounded by rich pastures and abundant water nearby. He requested permission to buy land there and was so granted.

Over time, he drew up plans for a house and a stable beside the river. While in service, he brought six mares up from Santa Fe to be served by his fine Spanish Barb, to breed and train good horses for the cavalry. He would lease the rest of his land to sheepherders to produce the fine wool that local weavers made into blankets. The only thing missing from his dream was a wife and children. Although several comely *señoritas* were available, he dared not take just anyone. Until the right woman should appear, his needs and prayers would have to go —as they had thus far—unmet.

Shortly after he arrived in the valley, he heard about the scandal of the former *alcalde*, the once powerful Don Ricardo de Córdova, whose appointment as governor was terminated after a "personal embarrassment." The truth was difficult to determine; no one cared to explain the matter to him in great detail. But he knew that the head of the archdiocese in Santa Fe did not countenance episodes of public disgrace and reassigned de Córdova back to the capital. That much was fact. It was recorded officially that, "the Don had attempted to wed an orphan girl, raised by *Las Hermanas del Sagrado Corazón,* the local convent. She was exposed at the altar as a heathen and heretic—a Jewess, in fact." The *alcalde* was said to have departed for Mexico City immediately after the debacle and was never heard from in the Northern territory again.

Moisés' heart raced when he first heard the tale. Could it be true? He feigned disinterest but couldn't believe the facts. It seemed miraculous to learn that one of his own could be here—hidden in plain sight. He and his parents had been members of the Church in good standing, but never forgot what their grandparents believed in—or who they were. Like many New Christians, they had survived years of suspicion in Spain, living outwardly in perfect Christian piety, yet secretly following the laws of Moses any way they could.

But even here, in the New World, in the new capital of *Ciudad de Mexico*, the Church continued relentless pursuit of anyone suspected of such behavior, in fact any form of heresy and witchcraft as well. No Jewish convert was ever really safe. At the first opportunity, Moisés inquired about assuming a post far to the north. He was not the only one seeking assignment away from the Inquisitors. With hope, they would never reach that far.

This way, many day's ride from the capital, he hoped he might be able to fulfill some of the obligations of the Covenant without being discovered. As long as he was able, he would recite the prayers of his people privately as his father had taught him, and teach them to his sons and daughters, should he be so blessed.

It was with much happiness that he submitted his request for the hand of Rebeca Morales in marriage. With little discussion, the good Sisters accepted, intending to handle the matter quietly.

* * *

Following the debacle of the failed marriage to de Córdova, Rebeca had been informally baptized in the waters of the Río Grande by the Sisters,(for appearances), and returned to life in the convent as before. They denounced the accusation regarding Rebeca's heritage and had her resume her former place among them, as if nothing had transpired. Her father, Enrique Morales, however, was accused by the local priest of being a Jew himself, and therefore a candidate for the Tribunal in Mexico City. Were he guilty of hiding his true identity and that of his daughter, as well as feigning the Catholic faith, his life was in grave peril.

Morales soundly denied that either he, his first wife, or Rebeca were of Jewish blood, yet had no way to prove otherwise. A physician was summoned to examine him by military order. If he was a Jew, the suspected proof of circumcision would betray him with no further argument.

Rebeca worried about the outcome. What would they do to him then? But before the local doctor could bring him in for questioning, Morales rode out of Estrella on his best horse in the dark of night, abandoning daughter, land and home.

* * *

"I was allowed to stay at the convent," explained Rebeca, leaning back against her husband's shoulder as they rested, admiring their progress. "I suppose they kept me out of pity. I'd been raised a proper Catholic, after all, but never invited to take my vows. I was doomed to remain a novice all my life. Then, God looked down upon me. The good news came when you arrived. Ten long years following that first betrothal and humiliation, I learned with happiness that a stranger had inquired about me. You. Someone at last asked for my hand."

"*Sí*, my beloved," Moisés reassured her. "*Dio me bendijo.* Finding you was God's work."

"The Lord finally heard my prayers," she continued, her eyes filled with light. "Perhaps I could start a new life somewhere else, I believed, but the thought of wedding a stranger frightened me. *Verdad*. Now, thinking back to the first time I saw you, I felt such relief. Your countenance pleased me. You were so handsome; your eyes so kind. I found you much to my liking."

Moisés came originally from Barcelona, the capital of Catalonia, one of the great communities of Jews in Spain during the Middle Ages. He had deep-set brown eyes and dark hair, high cheekbones and a slender, long nose. He bore the tall frame of so many of those from that region. At their first introduction, clad in high leather boots and a dark blue gabardine coat trimmed with silver buttons, he appeared a man of comfortable means.

Rebeca blushed when their eyes first met. A tiny glow sprang up in her heart. Perhaps he really was the one. This time, there would be no congregation, no wedding festivities, only an official consecration from the priest before the nuns and Mother Superior. Rebeca felt humbled before a man who would willingly take her as his bride. She celebrated her good fortune in silence while the priest pronounced them husband and wife in Christ.

Walking together toward the door of the church, Rebeca bubbled with excitement, bouncing with each step. She clung to her new husband as if to a raft in a stream, for he had indeed rescued her from a life adrift. Now she had a course to follow, as long as he led the way. She took nothing but the clothes on her back, a pair of silver candlesticks left to her by her late mother and the old leather-bound family Bible her father had given her as a child. The name of its first owners, Velásquez, still glinted in gold on the cover.

* * *

The first months on the *rancho* with Moisés unfolded with joy. The couple lived in a temporary dwelling, a small one-room adobe, while their future home went up, one story at a time, nearby. Rebeca helped her husband feed and water his fine brood mares and cultivate the land. The hard work and fresh air invigorated her, lifting years of sadness. She cherished her role as his helpmate and confidante. And to her surprise, she relished their time together in bed at night. The Sisters had never given her any idea.

Lying side by side one evening, looking up at the stars through the bedside window, Moisés took his wife's hand and turned to her. "Far away, in the country of my parents, in Spain, many of our relatives died horrible deaths just because of who we were and what we believed in. Those who are left are still in grave danger, to this day. We are suspected of heresy, hunted, tried, and sometimes tortured. Here too they pursue us; in fact, wherever the Church is strong."

He sat up and took her in his arms. "Look at me. You must promise never to reveal the traditions and rituals I will teach you. Even if we find others like ourselves, outwardly we must always be part of the Catholic community, for safety's sake. For now, we are a community of two. It is enough. But we will dedicate our life to one God, *el Dio*, god of the patriarchs."

One night as they sat together for their evening meal, Moisés recited a prayer in a language Rebeca had not heard before. "*Barukh ata Adonai*," he said, trying to remember. The exact order of the words failed him. "Blessed be the Lord, our God" would have to be enough. He taught her the few sacred words of the Hebrew people introducing the Sabbath prayer, to be recited weekly over a shared cup of wine on Friday nights, the commencement of the *Sábado*.

"We will keep the laws of *kashrut*," he continued, "and always separate milk from meat. Only those animals with split hooves are allowed to be eaten, except for swine, which are forbidden. We may partake only of fish with scales. We will take each animal's lives as respectfully and painlessly as we can, and always, remove all blood. Privately, we will honor Saturday as the day of rest, as we are able, but on Sundays, we will attend mass in the Church as well."

Moisés taught Rebeca all that he knew; in fact, all he could remember of his father's teachings and of the special days for fasting and prayer. In the blossoming of his love, he carved her initials into the young walnut sapling that grew in the clearing before their new home. He intended to add his own initials at some point; perhaps after a child was born.

A mere two months following their marriage, the pregnancy made itself known. Rebeca felt nauseous and terribly tired. Over the last years in the convent, she had been undernourished, having eaten little and languishing there, with hardly a reason to live. Her thin body was not prepared for the rigors of child bearing. But with each week, as the new life swelled inside her, she tried to grow stronger. She ate more, and slept in the afternoons. She continued to help her husband as best she could, milking the cow and preparing the foods he taught her to cook according to his tradition. She was determined to deliver a healthy child.

CHAPTER ELEVEN

Estrella 1810

La Revolución

BEFORE LONG CAME NEWS of the revolution, of Mexicans rising up, led by Father Hidalgo, a respected Catholic priest, and General Ignacio Allende, a turncoat in the Spanish forces, both determined to throw off over two hundred years of Spanish rule. Rural armies assembled to protect their homeland. Local resources were commandeered and a new militia formed, bent on storming the capital. Thousands rallied to march on Mexico City. Under the inspiration of Hidalgo and General Allende, now members of the new Revolutionary Army, the looming Mexican War of Independence was about to change the landscape of *Nueva España* forever.

Moisés received orders to bolster the provision of meat and horses while Estrella became a defense post in the north. In the shifts between religion and politics that followed, it was decreed that the convent be repurposed as a military stronghold, and the Sisters reassigned to safety in Santa Fe. The entire contents of the small chapel of the *Santuario* were to be emptied. Even the leaded glass rose window was to be taken down, the opening sealed for security; the window offered for sale.

Moisés could not believe his good fortune. He offered a decent sum and secured it for their dwelling; no other takers made any offer. The window would be installed as a finishing touch in their welcoming *entrada* in a niche above the front door; a surprise for his beloved, a way to mark the birth of their first child.

Within four months, the adobe was nearly complete, as sound and beautiful a dwelling as any in the Rio Grande Valley. A fine rosewood piano was brought north by ox-cart from Albuquerque. Produced by a famous workshop, it had come all the way to New Spain by ship many years before. On the very day it was to be installed, Moisés awoke to a desperate cry.

"*¡Ven!* Come quickly," Rebeca called to him. She stood outside the entrance to their bedroom, gripping the doorpost, her eyes filled with tears, her face a ghostly white. "Something is wrong, *querido*. Terribly wrong. I have much blood."

"*¡Híjole!* he cried at the sight of his wife's terrified eyes and crimson-stained nightshirt. It couldn't be—it was too early for the birth. "*¿Qué pasa?*"

"*¡Yo no sé!*" she cried. "Inside—like a knife. And the pain, Moisés. So much pain." She held his shoulder, then slipped to the ground, gasping. "*¡Se va! ¡Ay!* It leaves me. Our child!"

The miscarriage tore her womb with a force so great it left her breathless. She lay in her husband's arms. "Our child has left me, beloved. God takes it too soon!"

Moisés helped her back inside, changing her soiled garments and washing her body before carrying her to their bed. Afterward, Rebeca slept for many hours. Neither the sound of the hammer used to make the small wooden cross for the grave, nor the chinks of the iron spade against the earth could wake her. Moisés wrapped the fetus in a clean shroud, according to Jewish law, grateful that no eyes but his would ever see it. As the sun set amidst fiery red and copper clouds, a heartbroken father whispered the sacred lines of the *Tehillim* or psalms customarily recited before burial, then covered the small grave with earth and bowed his head, wiping the tears from his eyes.

He installed the rose window the very next day, dedicating it as a memorial to their lost babe, to their sorrow and their love. Perhaps it would help console his wife. *When she is ready,* he thought, *we will try again. We must never lose hope.*

The God of Abraham provides.

CHAPTER TWELVE

He Who Does Not Judge

GRANDFATHER HÉCTOR SAT IN the swing chair on the porch, slowly rocking back and forth, listening to the afternoon—leaves falling, the wind undulating in the trees, and far away, the shrill call of a cowbird in the oaks. He enjoyed staying at Carmen's house while they waited for Gerry to find a new home for the family. His son said it wouldn't be long. Meanwhile, things would get better. They had to. Maybe the move would be good for all of them, starting over, coming together.

For the time being, Héctor liked Carmen's cooking, and especially the area where she lived, out on the edge of things, far from the traffic and village noise. He enjoyed the sounds of the neighborhood—the children when they came home from school; the calling, shouting and singing out; the creak of school bus doors opening and closing with that strange clap at the end, and the beep of bicycle horns. When the *niños* weren't around, he savored the balm of silence, and the endless hum of his thoughts.

It was nearly supper; the street noise gone. Héctor clenched his weathered hands in his lap. *¡Ay!* Sore today. The right one, especially. Usually they didn't hurt this much until winter.

Heat wilted the afternoon. Perspiration dripped down his temples as he rocked to and fro, his shirt visibly damp. Carmen approached the porch with a glass of lemonade. Héctor looked up when he heard the ice cubes tinkling against the glass and the turn of the handle on the screen door.

"Hola, cariño," Carmen said, so as not to startle him.

"*Hola, Carmen.* Tell me. *¿Ónde están Ángel y mi Juanito*?" he asked, slipping into the old, archaic form of Spanish so many from southern Colorado and northern New Mexico still used. "Where are the boys?" He had not seen Juan since lunchtime when he came home from school. The older one rarely hung around much these days. But his Juanito? The house was too quiet. Something didn't feel right.

Since news of the move weeks earlier, he and Juan had begun a ritual. After lunch, the boy would sit on his grandfather's lap and tell him about his morning at school. He would describe events with his small hands, fingers working excitedly, and sometimes, just for fun, grab his grandfather's grey curls, bursting into giggles. Their time together made the sale and demolition of the house and the move to Carmen's more bearable. The boy's affection had awakened his old heart like nothing before. He laughed occasionally, slept better and developed something of an appetite. He had become a recluse since his wife's death, after all. Life without her had been so hard, especially since his vision deteriorated and finally disappeared altogether. How long had it been? More than ten years already. What a blow; a terrible loss. But now, he could almost see again, through Juan's young and eager eyes. The world had a new kind of color once more.

"*¿Ónde?*" he asked.

Héctor spoke English well enough, but didn't use it very often. He was born of Hispanic parents in Alamosa, a town located in Southern

Colorado in the San Luis Valley, in a culture that had long accepted Anglos and Hispanics equally. He never questioned life there, had even married into the Anglo community once he moved farther north to Trinidad. His wife, Bettina, raised in the Midwest, had accepted him fully and cared less if he spoke Spanish or English.

But their son Gerry never accepted either. Critical of both Anglos and Latinos, Gerry resented both his mother and father, never forgiving either for not being more like the other. Héctor thought that Gerry's marriage to Rachel Martinez seemed to aggravate his son's difficulties, although he'd hoped that committing to a local woman with deep roots in the Hispanic community might make them dissolve. But Gerry only got worse, drinking more as the years wore on. He behaved like an outsider, avoiding the church, feast days, and local events, although he might show up at an outdoor fiesta once in a while, mainly for the food.

"Carmen, where is the little one?" the old man asked.

She sat down next to him and placed the icy glass in his hands.

"I don't know," she said, trying to hide her concern. "Probably at a friend's. I'm not sure."

She had no more idea where the boys were than Rachel did; whether they planned on coming back, or were still out on some road headed away from town. But she didn't want to tell Héctor the truth. It could be that Ángel and Juanito just went for a joyride with the older teens. It didn't feel that way, though, when she saw Juan hop in with his dog. It looked more like a kidnapping, but that had to be her imagination.

Ángel would never hurt Juan, at least not on purpose. Meanwhile, she was not about to tell Héctor what happened until Rachel got back. She'd let her sister explain it. The old man had been napping at the time when the pickup occurred, thank goodness.

Héctor took a long slurping gulp of the lemonade. He smacked his lips. "*Ah, esta limonada está muy buena. Muncho sabor. Gracias, Carmen.*"

"You sit tight, Héctor, okay? Juan will be along soon, I'm sure. I'll get some supper ready. We're having chili." She returned to the kitchen and turned on the radio, drowning her thoughts with the raucous sounds of *Mexicana, Tejas*, and the news.

The old man drank half the glass and continued to rock. His vacant eyes stared into the afternoon sun. "*¿Ónde está Juanito*?" he asked again to no one in particular.

CHAPTER THIRTEEN

Reality Check

RACHEL SAT AT A table in her diner, still furious over the break-in. She waited for the police to arrive and make the necessary report. Meanwhile, Carmen came over, helped her clean up the debris, found a usable piece of cardboard to replace the broken glass, and then left. It was almost three o'clock. Apparently it took Deputy Hubbard longer than usual to answer a call.

Whatever was keeping him? He finally showed up, checked the handle of the door for fingerprints, and took down her information, noting the time of the break-in and amount of money missing. Nothing more to be done.

Rachel called Gerry's cell phone for the fourth time that day. What an aggravation. Every single time it went to voice mail. Since Gerry carried his cell with him, she couldn't imagine why he wouldn't pick up. He had to know it was her. She needed to tell him about the boys, the theft and the damage to the *Taco Stop*, and the two hundred and fifty dollars in cash, gone, although she was sure he wouldn't care about that. But then there was the door. They might even need a new one. They still had a half-year lease on the building and they'd have to cover the repair. They were probably insured against flood and fire, but not theft. Hardly anyone got robbed in Estrella. Gerry looked at her incredulously when she asked about it once, saying, "Who would ever rob a two-bit operation like that?"

Rachel had a pretty good idea who might have broken in, but with a sinking heart, chose not to mention it to the deputy. Hubbard asked her straight out if she had reason to suspect anyone, but didn't question her further when she said no.

Once Gerry answers, maybe I'll just tell him the boys are missing, Rachel decided. *Nothing more. Not yet. Besides, bad news would just make him angry. Now that I know who the boys were with and what time they took off, the other details can wait. Damn. Those Ramírez kids are wild sometimes, but not criminal. Maybe they'll all be back before I reach him. Maybe I should wait. Gerry will be furious when he hears what Ángel's done.*

The teenage boys' father, Alejandro Ramírez, didn't seem concerned at all when she called to inquire about his sons, or if he had seen them.

"Yo no sé," he replied. "*Sí, sí,* I spoke to the police. I told them, they go for a drive. They'll be back, sooner or later; *no es nada*—not to worry."

If the boys were still gone by nightfall, Deputy Flores would certainly get the police on their tail and find them. She never thought Ángel should be out with the Ramírez boys in the first place. Meanwhile, her guts were churning. Nothing but good news would calm them.

Where the hell is Gerry? Ever since that letter came from the highway department, nothing had gone right. As soon as the big check arrived, he dumped everything straight into her lap and disappeared, like they never existed. The more she thought about him, the more she wanted to hit something—hard. She called his number one more time.

"*¿Sí?"* A woman answered. The sultry voice erupted in laughter.

"Here, gimme that phone—what do you think you're doing?" Gerry's voice covered hers.

"*Hola,*" Rachel said.

"Hey ... Rachel?" Gerry answered, sounding surprised. "Hi. Great to hear from you. How's it going? I've been meaning to call." He sounded tipsy.

"Oh, sure you have, Gerry. Did you get my messages? All one hundred of them? Why haven't you called me back? And who the hell was that?" Rachel asked.

"Oh, her? Nobody. I ... hired her as a receptionist. You know, answer phones. Only she answered the wrong one. I mean, um ... here—say hi. Lucita, meet Rachel."

Laughter again. This time more raucous than the first.

"Hi. *¿Cómo estás?*"

Rachel felt the heat rise in her face and her heart quicken. "Just fine, thanks. Hey, maybe I'll call back another time, okay? And do me a favor, Lucita. Take a memo. Tell Gerry to go to hell."

CHAPTER FOURTEEN

Never Trust

"WHERE ARE WE?" JUAN asked, rubbing his eyes. He'd fallen asleep in the back seat of the Camaro next to his brother and his dog. The car rumbled onto the gravel parking lot of a dilapidated convenience store twenty miles south of Estrella. The sun sinking over the distant mountains signaled that night was closing in. Ángel peered curiously out the window, checking out the store.

"Where *are* we?" Juan asked again.

"At a Stop N' Go," Ángel answered.

"I can see that. Come on. Like where?"

"I don't know exactly. Just shut up, would you, *Pinto*?"

Juan's Chihuahua slumped onto the boy's lap, its pink tongue lolling, and lay panting, thirsty from the long afternoon in the hot car. The dog's head darted back and forth, bouncing as he looked inquisitively from boy to boy.

"Poquito needs water. Me too. An' I gotta pee," Juan squirmed. "And I'm hungry."

"Yeah, I know. Just wait."

Ramón Ramírez steered the car around the front of a two-pump station and turned to Ángel in the back seat. "I need some cash." He knew the teen had money, because he was with Ángel when they broke into his mother's place. "We need gas and you're paying. We got a long way to get back."

"No problem, man. Um—whattaya mean, *back*? I thought we were going to California. That's what you said."

Ramón didn't answer.

"Okay, uh, well, before we leave, can we get some food?" Ángel asked. "My brother's gotta go to the bathroom. And he needs some water." He glanced at the dog. "Him too."

"Sure kid," Ramón said. He looked at his brother in the passenger seat who looked back, not saying a word.

The older pair got out of the car. Ramón unscrewed the gas cap. "Okay, get out. But make it fast."

"I'm gonna get Juan some jerky or a burrito or something and a drink. You guys want anything?"

"Sure. We could eat," said Ramón. "Give us a couple twenties and we'll get some food—for the kid too. How 'bout you?"

Ángel shrugged and reached into his pocket for the bills. "Get me five hot dogs, okay? And, some water and two Cokes. I'll take Juan to the bathroom. Be right back."

Ángel picked up Poquito and tucked him under his left arm. "Come on, squirt." The key to the restroom hung inside the store's front door. Ángel grabbed it and headed around to the side of the building. He didn't notice Ronaldo following them.

* * *

Flores fidgeted at his desk; three-thirty already. *Thank goodness it's Friday. This sure has been one hell of a week and maybe the longest day … ever.*

Twice, he dialed Rachel's cell phone and then quit before it started to ring. He couldn't even remember why he was calling her; just wanted to hear her voice. Too bad about that break-in. She sure had some bad luck. He knew what she wanted was some good news, but he had nothing to tell her yet. Thinking about her all afternoon made him edgy. He almost jumped out of his chair when she walked into the station earlier that day carrying the old wooden box.

"Got a minute?" she asked. Not waiting for an answer, she continued, "It's over. The house, the courtyard, the patio—everything. Just rubble and dust. It all went so fast. Listen, I've got to get back to work and I don't know what to do with this box. I can't keep it in the diner and there's not a square inch of space left in the trunk of my car. I sure don't want to leave it lying in the motel room. There's no safe in there. Would you store it for me until I find a better place?"

Flores looked up into her tired face. *Sure is pretty, even when she's upset.* Rachel had such a look of weary exasperation he wanted to put his arms around her and hug her until she relaxed and smiled and all the worry lines melted away. Then again, maybe not—what was he thinking?

He cleared his throat. Cops, ministers, doctors: they all had to keep emotions in check and merely be of service, right? At least, that's what his conscience told him. Weighing his options, he answered. "Well, it's not regulation. I really shouldn't. But maybe I can make an exception this time. You'll need to find a better place for it soon."

"Thanks," she said with a sigh. "I will. Maybe at my sister's. Anyway, one less thing to worry about for the moment." Her grave expression gave way to a smile. "No news yet about my truant son?"

"*Nada*. Sorry."

"I am so worried. Ángel's in so much trouble already." She ran her hands through her hair, combing it out of her face. She looked distracted, and stared past him, embarrassed somehow. "Sorry to be such a bother. I didn't know what else to do, where to turn."

Rachel turned to leave and cast a glance his way, the look in her eyes more anxious and sad than thankful. "*Gracias,*" she said and left as quickly as she came in.

That worried look came back to haunt Flores for hours after she left. Did he do the right thing? Should he have allowed her to entrust him with her newfound valuables? Cops weren't safe deposit boxes after all.

Lots of things lately made no sense. For one thing, José knew he was old enough to know better than to get involved with a married *chica*, but was also intrigued by *señora* Rachel Martinez Ortega. She sure had her burden. What with the demolition, the kids, the husband, the break-in—it was almost like that old adobe was avenging its demise on her. And while her beleaguered life was coming apart at the seams, he felt as if somehow he had been summoned to watch the fall. Catch her even. His mother was right; she needed help.

Flores tried to concentrate and get back to work. Emails needed answering, schedules had to be filed—but he wanted to find those boys first. Where to start?

He read over the break-in report Roy left on his desk, trying to decipher that Texas scrawl. More than likely Ramón Ramírez had talked Ángel into robbing the diner. Probably told him they'd just borrow some cash. He'd heard that kind of thinking before. Peer pressure can make younger kids do just about anything.

He leaned back in his chair to consider what to do next and closed his eyes for all of sixty seconds, just to clear his head. Then he opened them, ready to dig back into his work again. Routine reports and local incidents; one computer file after the other. Then, there was her name again—Rachel Ortega—on the Public Service release document. How did he end up with that? It needed to get back to her. He looked up at the clock, 5:40 already. Where'd the time go? If that souped-up black Camaro wasn't spotted by midnight, he'd make sure the whole state got to looking for it.

Flores couldn't focus. Rachel again. She sure seemed like one smart woman; definitely holding her own. *Wonder what happened there? Why would a man leave a good woman like that? Why in the world?*

He got up to make some coffee and, as if on cue, Rachel pulled up, parked her car, and walked in. Her face was drawn and her tense lips suppressed a smile. Dark circles shadowed her eyes.

"Hi. Sorry to bother you. Just checking in before I head over to my sister's."

"Yeah, sure. No problem. What's up?" José asked. "And—how'd you do that?"

"Do what?" she answered.

"Uh, never mind. I was just thinking of calling you. Got your paperwork here; I think you need this copy. So—Hubbard is out cruising, searching the drive-ins, the rec center and the pool hall, asking around. We'll find 'em, don't worry. Four kids don't just disappear into thin air. How are you holding up?"

"Actually, I think I'm having a nervous breakdown," she said with a thin smile. "I can't think straight. I'm glad you're on duty and not Hubbard. I need to talk."

"Yeah, well, it's my night on. And Roy ain't so bad when you get to know him. He's a good listener really, if it ever gets to that. But so am I—so lay it on the table, *señora.* I am here to serve." He jerked his thumb toward his badge in proof.

Rachel's eyes began to fill with overdue tears. She grimaced, trying to hold them back.

"I'm just so worried about Juan. He's never been out this late without me. Ángel's tough, you know that. He can handle anything. He's run off before. And my husband … he's no help at all."

"Hey, hey—get a grip, *cálmate.* Sit down. Let me get you a cup of coffee. It's fresh, but nothing special."

"That sounds good, thank you." She sat down and searched her purse for a tissue. Flores poured them both a cup. The phone rang. Rachel startled, spilling coffee on the desk.

"No matter," he said, grabbing his handkerchief and mopping it up, then turned to the phone. "Flores here."

"Hey José, how goes it?" Headquarters, calling from Albuquerque.

"Fine. *¿Qué pasa?*, Masterson? What's up?"

Rachel leaned over the desk top, hands clasped around the cup.

"The name Ramírez mean anything to you?"

Flores turned on the speaker phone. He nodded his head.

"Speak of the devil," said Flores, his eyes meeting Rachel's across the desk. "Yes, why?"

"I've got a black Camaro here. No registration, no license. Driver: Ramón Ramírez supposedly, says he's from Estrella. A kid about seventeen, eighteen. Says it's his car."

"And ...?"

"We caught him speeding, DUI and serving a minor, if he ain't one himself. Says the kid he's with ... brother's ..." The signal broke up for a second, then returned. "Those damn kids got enough booze in this car to party for a week. Can't reach any parents at the number he gave me. You got room up there? I'm bringing 'em in."

"Hold on a minute, will you, Bill?' Flores turned to Rachel and put his hand over the phone. "Good news, Rachel, they found them!"

"Oh my God!" Rachel's eyes lit up with joy. She reached for Flores's arm and gave it a squeeze. "Where are they?"

"Okay, yeah, sure ..." Flores continued, holding his palm up indicating that Rachel wait with her questions. "You bet. I got plenty of room here. Deluxe accommodations. Bring 'em on over. So where exactly are you?"

Before the trooper could answer, Flores stopped. "Hang on a sec, Bill. How many kids did you say there were, total?"

"Two."

"Just two?"

"What did he say?" interrupted Rachel, her smile disappearing as she heard the question. She blinked hard, catching her breath.

Flores put the phone on hold and turned to her again, his face grim. "Looks like I spoke too soon. Sorry, but I think we got trouble."

CHAPTER FIFTEEN

In the Dark of Night

"QUICK, GET DOWN, *PINTO*!" Ángel shushed his brother. "Duck!"

The headlights of an approaching vehicle cast a broad light on the curving road, throwing a bright glare on the pavement and ghoulish shadows across the sagebrush. Ángel and Juan huddled by the side of the road trying to stay out of the headlights. After the car zoomed by, they got up and loped on in the dark. The hum of an engine beyond the rise alerted Ángel. Danger! He pushed Juan to his knees again and sat down beside him. Together they knelt close to the ground once more. Poquito struggled in Juan's thin arms, whining softly.

"Stay down," hissed Ángel.

"Ow, you're hurting me. I can't get …"

"Quiet. Here comes another one."

When the second vehicle had passed, Ángel let his brother stand up briefly, then plunked him down on the ground again. "Get over here," he said. "Close to me."

The earth was cold and hard. The younger boy wished he could snuggle into his brother's lap but was afraid Ángel would bop him. He knelt by the older one's side, leaning against his shoulder.

"Ángel?" Juan asked, teeth chattering. "Where are we?" He shivered in his jean jacket. Poquito shivered with him, held tight against his chest.

"I don't know," said his brother. "I don't know. Just let me think."

"Why did you have to start a fight with Ronaldo when he came into the bathroom?" Juan asked, even though he knew Ángel wished he would shut up. "Why didn't you just give him that stupid money? He was mean! He scared me. I want to go home. Now!"

"Stop it!" Ángel yelled. "I don't know, I don't know, it just happened. And I still don't want to go home, understand? I'm not going home and I'm not moving to Farmington, ever."

Juan stopped asking questions and sat still, stroking his dog's head while it cuddled close. Ángel was older. Maybe he knew what was right.

Ángel had no intention of spending the night in a wild darkness of sagebrush, snakeweed, rocks, and scary shadows. They needed shelter. Besides, lightning had started to streak the sky over the distant mountains. All he had with them was a pack of cigarettes with just three left, some matches, two twenty dollar bills in his sock, and half a Snickers bar.

At least those no-good Ramírez brothers could have left us the hot dogs, thought Ángel. *I'm starving. Maybe we can find a barn or a shed or something to sleep under and some food somewhere. That's what we need. And water, especially for Poquito. We better start walking.* Ángel felt his split lip and the swelling over one eye tingle. His lip hurt, but at least it stopped bleeding. He hated Ronaldo.

With nothing in sight but a single illuminated casino billboard rising into the night sky a quarter mile away, Ángel sighed and told Juan to get up. The sign read "Paradise" with two giant white dice cubes rolling in space and the words: "Twenty-five Miles." He gave Juan the Snickers and took his hand. "We're gonna walk some more, OK? Till we find a place to spend the night."

Faint stars peppered the sky as the two boys walked hand-in-hand down an empty country road. Intermittent currents of cold air rose from gullies like wraiths, causing goose bumps on Juan's arms to rise. Neither boy said a word.

Ángel had grown up with the legends of ancient Indians who once lived in these parts: Navajo, Pueblo, and Zuni. The Taos pueblo was practically in his back yard. He knew the brush-covered hills and arroyos were home to the Trickster or El Coyote—a devilish being apt to do anything to anyone, at least that's what he was told. The sound of real coyotes howling somewhere in the distance added an eerie feeling to the night. *Juan better hold tight to Poquito*, thought Ángel. *Maybe I ... nah. It's his dog.*

Wrapped tight against his chest, the short-haired Chihuahua now trembled inside the boy's jacket, his head and front paws hanging out over the zippered front. Juan stuck his hands deep into the jacket's flannel-lined pockets to keep them warm. Poquito pivoted his head this way and that, his triangular ears perked hard to catch the sounds of the night; nose in the air, sniffing.

Time dragged on as the boys trudged north along the pavement. No shelter anywhere, just open land and a flat two-lane road. A three-quarter moon rose, illuminating the white line down the middle and adding a faint airbrushed glow to the mountain tops. Brighter stars pierced the sky like bullets passing through to another world. Nothing felt familiar, everything ominous, everything so far away from home. They might as well have been on Mars.

Juan started to sniffle. "I'm scared," he whined. "And cold—I'm freezing, Ángel."

"I know, *Pinto*, me too, and I'm sorry. But we'll be okay. Trust me, you'll see." He took Juan's right hand in both of his own and rubbed. "Don't be scared. Please don't be scared. And don't cry. Everything's gonna be all right, I promise."

Juan stopped, sitting down abruptly. "No, it's not! And I'm tired! I'm not walking any more. We're lost. I'm going to sleep right here, next to this dirt."

Juan plunked himself backwards against a small mound. Heaving a big sigh, he laid back, arms wide open. With a yap, Poquito shot out of his half-zipped jacket. The dog barked wildly and skittered off into the brush, gone into the void.

"*No!*" screamed Juan, jumping up. "Come back, Poquito!" But the dog was already a shadow among shadows, invisible; the deep dark expanse of fenceless land swallowing him whole. His barks grew fainter as he ran.

"Oh, *no*!" shouted Juan. "Poquito, come back!"

"Aw crap," said Ángel. "What'd you have to go do that for? Why didn't you hold on to him?"

Juan leapt off the mound and started to run, disappearing into the gloom.

"Hey!" Ángel ran after him, cursing. "Damn you. Come back here!"

Like two crazed drunks, the boys jumped and ran, Juan weaving and Ángel hopping, around and over the ragged bushes and rocks—stumbling, getting up, shouting and calling, chasing a phantom dog that appeared only when it leapt into the air. Ángel grew more anxious about losing Juan than Poquito. The moonlit landscape of undulating ruts and gullies along an old washed-out riverbed seemed to go on forever. Juan kept running like a wind-up toy, chasing and calling out "¡*Poquito*!" over and over at the top of his lungs.

Then suddenly they were out in the open, by the road again. A speeding truck appeared around the bend, headlights gleaming. Ángel stared and froze, then screamed as he saw Poquito running toward it, except it wasn't Poquito—too big! A coyote loping along the roadside held the small dog tight in its jaws. The animal, startled by Ángel, jumped, then dashed straight into the light beam of the oncoming truck and cringed down. The driver hit the brakes, tires squealing, rubber burning. But it was too late. The animal's blood curdling yelp pierced the night.

"No, no!" screamed Ángel, turning to catch his little brother before he ran straight into the road.

Juan shrieked when he saw the vehicle hit the coyote, tossing the animal like a beanbag to the side. Released from the clench of the coyote's jaws, Poquito flew through the air and landed in the brush. The truck stopped, then backed up slowly, almost in front of where the boys hid, and squeaked to a halt, motor idling. The bright headlights made everything else turn black. A door creaked open slowly, then slammed shut. A man's voice cursed strange words in the dark.

Ángel's heart beat like a million native drums, every nerve taut. Juan shook and sobbed, hiding behind Ángel's back, too afraid to look. "Is Poco dead? Is Poco dead? Is he dead?" drilled Juan, hanging on to Ángel's jacket like a shield.

"Shhh, I don't know, *Pinto*. There's the driver—quiet." He stepped back, pulling Juan with him farther into the shadows and held him by his hand with a strong protective grip.

A tall Indian appeared, illuminated by the headlights of his vehicle. He approached the coyote and raised a booted foot to nudge it a couple times. It didn't move. Then he cocked his head as if he were listening.

"Ángel tha ..."

Ángel clamped his hand over Juan's mouth. His hand was shaking.

The man walked past the front of his truck and knelt down in the darkness. When he stood up and reappeared in the headlights, he held Poquito in his arms.

"Where did you come from, *łééchąą'í*?" he said, cradling the dog, his stooped shoulders a stark profile in the beam of the bright lights. The man's long hair, hanging down under a wide headband tied at the back of his head, riffled in the night wind. He stared out into the darkness and remained still for some moments while the two boys held their breath, not moving a muscle. Then the man turned back.

"Don't hurt him! Please!" Juan shouted at the top of his lungs, popping up. "He's mine! He's my dog, he's *my dog*!"

Juan ripped away out of Ángel's grasp and ran toward the vehicle. He threw himself at the Indian like a wild thing, then wrapped his arms around the tall man's legs and sobbed, begging for him to save Poquito—begging for him to save them all.

CHAPTER SIXTEEN

Missing

THE ROAD UNFOLDED IN silence, dawn's pale light still a vague promise far to the east. The truck traveled another seventy-five miles in its journey toward Socorro, south of Albuquerque. Frank Yazzi headed up Highway 65 toward the Alamo Navajo reservation another thirty miles outside of Magdalena and pressed hard on the gas. It was late. He had to be back by six o'clock at least to catch an hour of sleep and make it to work at the sports center on time.

The weekend up in Dulce at the Council meeting had not gone too well. Call it unexpected trouble. Tribal committee meetings could get pretty rowdy sometimes, but usually didn't end up in fist fights and this time it really wasn't his fault.

He glanced over at his strange quarry. Poquito lay panting on his side on the floor of the cab, neck and shoulder swollen, the puncture wounds coagulating into scabs. A cut paw looked sore, but functional. *That was one lucky dog.*

The boys lay curled around each other on the passenger seat, the older one's head against the door, the younger with his head in the crook of his brother's arm. They were sound asleep like two worn out pups, both snoring softly. According to the elder boy who'd answered a few of Yazzi's questions when they first climbed in, they had nowhere special to go. "Anywhere's OK. For sure though," the boy added, "not home."

Frank didn't probe. One look at Ángel told him all he needed to know. They were runaways.

He would have to see about getting them wherever they belonged, and soon. Two lost boys in an Indian's vehicle was a red flag in these parts. He didn't want to be stopped and have to answer any questions from the fuzz. He headed straight home. Yazzi turned onto his gravel drive just as the sun lit up the horizon, and honked twice lightly to wake Della who would still be sleeping. That was their sign, to let her know when he arrived at odd hours. She still slept with a rifle next to the bed. He'd brought home unexpected guests before, but a pair of white boys for breakfast? Definitely a first.

* * *

"Oh my God, only *two* boys?" Rachel gasped when she heard the news. Flores hung up the phone and remained silent, tapping the desk with his left hand, his lips pursed as he thought about his next move.

Rachel pushed her chair away from the desk and sat, motionless. Then stood up and leaned toward him, her face drained. "So where are my kids?" she asked, her voice barely audible. "Where are my sons? Please tell me they found them, too."

She looked down at her watch and then back to his face, her eyes filling with tears. From a stoic persistence that had enabled her to watch her husband leave, see her household goods hauled off, her home crushed to rubble and her restaurant vandalized, she finally caved in. "Oh my God … where are they?"

"I don't know but we'll sure as hell find 'em. Meanwhile, we've got to get you out of here. You're a wreck. Maybe I should take you over to your sister's."

"She's not there now ... works late Friday nights. No, please, I just want to stay here until you find out where they are. Is that all right?"

Flores looked at his watch: nine-fifteen. A bad start to a long shift. "OK. Just sit tight for a minute."

This was not how he wanted things to go. It had been more than eight hours since the boys took off. He phoned Carruthers at headquarters to put an Amber Alert out for Ángel and Juan and send the information to the FBI in Albuquerque. Then he faxed the photos that Rachel had in her wallet for statewide distribution within the system. Deputy Masterson would arrive soon with the Ramírez brothers. He definitely wanted a sit-down with them, no monkey business.

Rachel slumped back in her chair, her face in her hands. "I'm sorry," she said, vainly searching for more tissues in her purse, "but I can't handle any more. I just can't."

"You're entitled to a few tears at this point, maybe a river in my book." He offered a box of tissues. "Look—we have good people in our Missing Persons department. They're already on the case. Meanwhile, may I suggest— you really should call your husband?"

"I keep trying. I can't reach him."

Rachel walked over to the door and stepped outside. She dialed Gerry's number on her cell and stood, staring blankly into the parking lot, rubbing her left temple, listening to his recording.

"Call me—now," was all she said. She hung up and went back inside. Fury burned in her eyes.

"Um … would you like some more coffee?" Flores asked, keeping his distance. Women in tears had a way of making him unravel. It never failed.

"No, but thanks anyway. Hey, I better call my sister at least," Rachel said. "And leave her a message." As she punched in Carmen's number, she began to pray in silent supplication. Tears flowed beneath her closed lids.

"*Por favor, tráemelos a casa,*" she whispered. "Bring my children home."

The shrill ring of the office phone on Flores' desk startled them both. Rachel spun toward the sound. José picked up the receiver.

"Estrella substation—Flores here. What's that?—oh, you're not? Damn, I wanted to talk to those two punks myself. Yeah, I know. Let me know if you hear anything. Thanks."

He hung up and folded his arms across his chest. A weariness clouded his eyes.

"What?" asked Rachel.

Flores shook his head. "They're rerouting the Ramírez boys to Santa Fe for interrogation there. I guess they don't trust us small-town cops. OK. Plan B. We do what we can here. But I need to take a quick break, get something to eat. It's almost nine-thirty. There's nothing I can do right now anyway—and Hubbard will be in any minute. My mother usually keeps some food warm for me most nights; likes to have me join her. What do you say? Want to come? I'm sure she'd be glad to have you. And I, uh, told her earlier I've been looking for your sons. So she knows about the case."

"Yes—thanks, I'd appreciate that, even though I doubt if I can eat a thing."

As if on cue, Hubbard came through the front door. Taking his chair behind the desk, he punched in. "Take a break, boss. My turn."

Flores got up, slipped on his jacket and extended his arm to Rachel. "Good. Then let's go. I'll let my mother know we're on the way."

Settled into Flores' squad car, Rachel could no longer do anything but breathe. As they pulled out onto the road, she inhaled deeply, exhaled, and resolved to pull herself together before she made a complete fool of herself. All these tears—why wouldn't they stop?

She watched Flores as he drove, mesmerized by his hands on the wheel, strong hands that could calm an angry boy or break up a fight, hands belonging to a good man, she decided, with a good heart.

Flores looked straight ahead as he drove, his eyes on the road. But feeling her gaze on him, he turned slightly and smiled.

Her pulse quickened to an unfamiliar beat. She smiled back. It was the first time she'd felt safe all day.

They pulled into Rosa's driveway and parked the car. Flores helped Rachel out and escorted her to the front door. He knocked, then called out "*¡Hola!*" The fragrance of cumin, cilantro and garlic wafted like manna out the nearby open window.

Is that roasting chicken that smells so good? Rachel realized she actually *was* famished. She peered through the door's frosted glass panels. Through them she could make out two candles burning on a table somewhere inside, their bright, diffused glow as warm a welcome that anyone with a heavy heart could hope for.

CHAPTER SEVENTEEN

Sábado

"COME IN, COME IN, please, *señora* Ortega. I am so happy to meet you. But sorry to hear about your troubles, about *los niños. Por favor, entrar.*"

Rachel stepped through the door and practically fell into the embrace of José's mother, Rosa, a small woman with graying hair cut short framing a wide, heart-shaped face and deep brown eyes. Her smile held boundless warmth. She wore a full apron with a busy floral motif and smelled of lavender and chili powder, a strange but oddly comforting combination. The two women, young and old, hugged as if they had known each other for years.

"What news of the boys?" asked Rosa.

Rachel shook her head. "*Nada.* Nothing yet."

"My son will find them, you'll see—José, *chulo,* what took you two so long? *Señora* Ortega must be starving."

Rachel removed her shawl and folded it over her arm. "Please, call me Rachel."

Rosa smiled. José hung his brown police jacket on a peg inside the doorway.

"You don't remove your gun inside the house?" asked Rachel, eyeing the piece suspiciously.

"Nope. Stays right here, in case somebody wants to steal my dinner." He grinned, patting the holster at his waist. "What? Makes you nervous?"

"Yes," she answered, blushing.

Flores took off his gun belt and hung it over the hook next to his jacket. "Okay, just for you, just this once."

"Sure smells good in here, *Mamacita.* I told Rachel what a great cook you are. I …" he began, turning to his mother. But the two women were already heading toward the small dining room, arm-in-arm, like old friends.

As they passed through the wide doorway, Rachel heard an unexpected greeting.

"*Buenas noches, señoras.*" A warm, familiar and resonant voice.

The sound seemed to echo off the whitewashed walls and surround them. Standing beside the window across the room stood Estrella's parish priest, Father Domingo Núñez, the same man Rachel had given the family's piano to a week earlier. His white cleric's collar gleamed against his sun-browned neck in the glow of a bright table lamp. Two white candles burned in glass holders on the other side. The cheerful flames flickered as they entered.

Father Núñez appeared surprisingly youthful, although past sixty. Time seemed to have no effect on his boyish face, smooth, with broad cheeks and a straight, snubbed nose. Heavy brows shaded his gray-blue eyes, and closely trimmed, silver white hair receded at his temples. By contrast, overgrown ringlets curled stubbornly at his collar. Respected and much admired, the padre had led his parish wisely for many years, almost fifteen to be exact. Once regarded as an outsider, he was now more than entrenched in their close mountain community.

"Father Núñez, what a surprise—how nice to see you," said Rachel.

Rosa flicked on the light switch. A six-armed brass chandelier above the table sparked to life, creating a halo of light above the table. The priest stepped forward and clasped each woman's hands, followed by a paternal hug. His eyes, bright and lively, shone with care.

"Welcome, Rachel. It's good to see you, too. But, my goodness—I heard the news on my way over this evening. We are all so worried. Please know, I've already offered a special prayer for your children's safe return. Rest assured, God looks after all of us. They'll be found."

Father Núñez was the last person Rachel had expected to see this night, even though she'd been trying to contact him since early morning. How odd. More important, how did he already know? The Amber Alert, she imagined. No doubt it was all over town.

"Thank you," she answered. "I appreciate anything you can do. And no, there's no news, nothing yet. You know, I was going to call on you earlier before all this occurred. I'm glad you're here."

Núñez pulled up a chair at the table. "You must be exhausted. Try not to worry. I am sure the Lord will bring your children back this night. And Deputy Flores here is his best assistant."

The two men locked gazes for a moment, Núñez offering a broad smile.

"That's right, that's my job—finding lost boys," said Flores. "You just watch."

"I've alerted my colleagues at the Archdiocese," said Núñez. "We'll keep a lookout in Santa Fe and Taos and beyond. But tell me—how are you?"

Rachel didn't answer. She wasn't faring well at all and it showed. Dark circles filled sunken wells beneath her tired eyes. She wanted to share with him how she had found the church empty that afternoon and the Madonna distant and cold, but couldn't find her voice. She dared not speak of further disappointment. She wanted to curse and swear and scream and condemn her worthless husband who had still not replied to her messages and the news that their children had run off and were completely out of reach. She wanted to tell the priest exactly how she felt—angry, powerless, and abandoned. And wanted him to know too, that only by breaking down and going to José Flores did she find support and friendship, something she'd not experienced from a man since she was a kid when her father was alive. And she wanted to tell him how, at this very moment, she felt a deep connection to all of them, as if she were standing among a family she'd never known, but who suddenly felt familiar. She felt safe. How could she explain all that?

"I'm okay, I guess … I …" Rachel sat down, her voice breaking.

"I understand. You've been through a lot. You must be patient. All will be well; let us hope." A long moment of silence followed. Rosa poured wine into the glasses, then headed for the kitchen.

"Rachel?" The priest hesitated. "Allow me to ask you about something else, if I may. Deputy Flores confided in me that when your home was torn down, they found a Bible stored in a box in a hidden closet. I find this fascinating."

Father Núñez had moved on, feeling as if he might light a fuse in Rachel by talking about the boys any further—one that if lit, could explode.

"Yes, that's right. He's keeping it for me," Rachel said, surprised that José had told the padre. She wondered who else knew. Surely, no harm would come if the priest was aware of the box and the old Bible inside. He was almost entitled.

"I would be interested to see this book myself. Would that be all right with you?" he asked.

"Why certainly, of course. But, I'm not sure where it is," she answered almost apologetically. She glanced up at Flores who looked back with a mute stare. He cleared his throat.

Rachel tried a sip of the wine Rosa had poured earlier. It tasted sweet and gratifying, as calming as an embrace. She breathed deep and took a long swallow, waiting.

"Uh … it's actually in my car, in the trunk," José stammered. "I never did lock it up at the station. Had no time. Give me a minute. I'll go get it."

"After dinner, *por favor,*" Rosa cut in, placing a pitcher of water on the table. "Our guest looks like she's about to faint from hunger. The book can wait. Time to eat."

The party sat around the dining table and bowed their heads for a moment in silent prayer. "Bless this food that He has given and all who partake of it," interjected the priest. "Let us begin."

Rosa filled the glasses with water and loaded a basket of *bolillos* next to a platter of freshly-made tortillas. The crusty rolls lay under colorful embroidered linens protecting them from the dry New Mexico air.

After a home-cooked meal of tomatillo soup, garlic chicken, Spanish rice and baked squash, the priest sighed, wiped his mouth and put down his napkin. "*Mis amigos,* I beg to be excused. I must be off soon—I have an early morning tomorrow. I'm driving out to Romero's ranch to bless his livestock before the gathering for Saint Francis. Thank you for this excellent meal, Rosa, as always, and the fine company. Now, if I may, let us have a look at this mysterious holy book before I go, even briefly. I'm so anxious to see it."

Flores ducked out the front door and returned with the box in his hands. He set it on the table and opened it, revealing the pair of candle-sticks, the Bible and the small oblong case. The priest examined the candlesticks in silence. Then he carefully removed the Bible and held it with a kind of quiet reverence.

He stared at the contents as if seeing a ghost. His hands trembled. He peered down at the ancient volume, pulling his reading glasses out of his frock. Whatever gilded lettering had once been on the cover was mostly faded but he studied what remained for some moments. The name Velásquez had practically fused onto the surface itself. Lifting the leather cover and turning to the first page, he drew in a slow whistle as he saw the many entries scrawled in ink on the flyleaf. A series of dates and names spilling over to the back inside cover traced a heritage from the year 1473 all the way to August, 1925. Beyond that, the record keeping had apparently been abandoned, or the book itself hidden away and forgotten.

Núñez turned it over as if holding a fragile egg and opened it from the back to the front, then turned a few of the parchment pages, dry and brittle with age, stopping here and there to absorb what he saw. The corners of his eyes crinkled as he shook his head in disbelief. A film of tears made them mist. He turned to his wine glass, holding it up for a moment as if to toast the Almighty, then downed what was left inside in one gulp. He closed his eyes and opened them again, lost in rapture.

"This book is written in a very ancient text, Rachel—Hebrew. See here." He pointed to a page near the back, the beginning. "Look closely, each letter, so beautiful to behold, and each one, so full of meaning. And here—some personal notes with the dates have been added, on the inside of the cover, in what I think is Portuguese. Here's another inscription I cannot decipher. The language is quite foreign to me. I can't say for sure exactly what it is."

He pointed to tiny entries in faded sepia ink. "Many of the others are in an old form of Spanish I'm not too familiar with either. I recognize a word or two. In all, it's simply remarkable for it to have survived this long. I believe it is exceedingly rare."

Núñez bowed his head and mumbled something softly to himself that Rachel didn't catch. She stared at the notes in the book, trying to make sense out of the strange letters. She could feel the padre's excitement.

"My children, truly, this is a moment of grace," said Núñez. "This Old Testament is a gift from the past. *El testamento viejo*, written in both Spanish and Hebrew. A fine Sephardic Bible, a survivor of the centuries."

"What's that?" asked Rachel, looking up at him. "Sephardic?"

"Oh my. Let me pause here. A short history lesson might be in order— agreed? He straightened his cassock beneath him. "Um … where to begin? For starters, the word Sephardic refers to Jews who lived in the Iberian Peninsula, that is, Spain, and Portugal, as far back as the sixth century before Christ. They remained there until Spain became a Catholic country in the fifteenth century. Are you with me?"

Rachel nodded.

"They were a learned people who studied the Holy Book. Back then, most Bibles of course were handwritten and highly prized. The

Jews of that region called their homeland *Sepharad,* and eventually, many of the Jews of Middle Eastern or Mediterranean descent became known as *Sephardim*. That's the short version."

"Sepharad," Rachel whispered to herself. The explanation felt surreal. Hebrew? *Sephardim*? It made no sense to her. Why would a Hebrew book be in Estrella, in her house?

"OK. And ...what else?"

"They spoke a language that grew out of the rule of the Ottoman Empire, a mix of Castilian, Turkish and Hebrew, as well some of the languages of the many regions they inhabited," the padre continued. "Much later, it came to be called Ladino, or *Judeo español*. Meanwhile, even under Ottoman rule, they practiced their ancient religion freely. They maintained specific Jewish customs like keeping the Sabbath on Saturday and abstaining from eating pork. Among them were poets and writers, philosophers and merchants. Their culture thrived when Iberia was controlled by Moors, and they all lived peacefully together for centuries, a time referred to as *La Convivencia,* the co-existence, a time of intellectual creativity. The arts, poetry and science flourished, some even refer to it as the Jewish Golden Age of Spain. Back then, Jews could be found in great cities like Seville, Cordoba and Toledo—very cultured communities."

Núñez closed the Bible and carefully put it back into the wooden box. "Shall I continue?"

"Yes, please," said Rachel. "This is all new to me."

"The period of tolerance for Spanish Jews ended by the late thirteen hundreds. Forced conversions and economic restrictions were imposed. Finally, they were expelled from Spain, a sad and difficult time. In 1492, King Ferdinand and Queen Isabella decreed that all Jews and Muslims must convert to Christianity or leave. By then, Spain had become a Catholic country so both faiths were persecuted. *Sephardim* fled by the thousands to other parts of Europe and the New World rather than convert."

Rosa came in from the kitchen and sat down, listening closely.

"Then again, many Jews did convert and stayed on. Some even went to New Spain, what we call Mexico, to help build the new empire. Those converts, or *conversos,* known as New Christians, who stayed behind always remained in some danger, always under suspicion. Were they really of true faith? Or were they still secretly Jews? The Church was determined to find out. What followed was a relentless persecution of those suspected of heresy, a campaign called the Spanish Inquisition, an evil war against innocents. Thousands died for no legitimate reason. A horrific scar in our history, truly; a three hundred year stain upon the Church that I personally deplore. But forgive me—I go on far too long. I must be boring you."

"No, Padre," answered Rachel, "you're not, but then I was never very interested in history, to tell the truth." She laughed, a bit embarrassed, and tried to conceal a yawn. The Church had never taught her much beyond the rosary and Hail Mary and her favorite maxim "do unto others." Certainly not this. But as much as she wanted to know more, she just couldn't absorb what Núñez had to say right now. She kept wondering about her kids, hoping to hear José's phone ring. Besides, what could any of this possibly have to do with *her* life? Overwhelmed by the exhausting events of the day, at that moment all she really wanted to do was sleep.

"Another time, perhaps," he concluded, seeing her fatigue. "I would be glad to tell you more." He patted her arm and handed her the book. "Guard this treasure well, Rachel. It is priceless."

She nodded. "Thank you, Father Núñez. I will."

On the sideboard in the dining room, the candles burned down to pools of wax and sputtered out. It was already past ten, time to go. Rachel regretted leaving Rosa's house, so cozy, so lived in, and full of love. She disliked the thought of returning to her empty motel room, traffic passing next to her window. She felt so vulnerable there and hated the thought of staying alone, as well. Maybe Carmen was home by now. She could spend the night on her sofa. Oh, except it was Friday and Carmen worked until midnight on Friday nights. She probably wasn't back yet and Grandfather Héctor would be sound asleep. No sense waking him up.

"I'll drop you off wherever you like," said Flores, "after we swing by the substation to see what's come in on the log—if you're not too tired. Then I go back to work."

"Oh no, I'm good. And I'll probably go back to my motel after all. I'm tired but can last long enough to see what's come in, if anything. Maybe some news. Let's go."

As they rose to leave the table, Rachel turned to José's mother and hugged her tight. "Thank you for the meal, *señora* Flores. Dinner was delicious. I had no idea I was so hungry. And thank you for including me. But tell me, please," she asked, looking at the candlesticks on the sideboard, "why have you lit candles this night?"

Rosa patted her cheek. "We were celebrating being together, dear. And I ... was praying your children would be found soon and come home. I lit those candles for them, one for Ángel, and one for your little Juan."

Father Núñez, winked, and then smiled briefly. "Indeed," he said, shrugging on his coat. "Rest well, my child. With God's will, this situation shall be resolved before morning. My prayers are with you."

They hugged farewell.

Flores snapped on his holster and put on his jacket. "Come on," he said, taking Rachel by the arm. "Let's go. I still need to drive down to Santa Fe tonight."

CHAPTER EIGHTEEN

Signs from Above

FATHER NÚÑEZ STARTED HIS engine and let the car idle while Deputy Flores and Rachel pulled out of the drive. He watched them head down Toma Road. The tail lights of the patrol car disappeared into the darkness.

Good God have mercy! Núñez crossed himself, then bowed his head. *Lord be praised. What affirmation! What an absolute sign!*

He sighed a deep and resonant sigh. *So this is it, after all? What I've been waiting for, all this time? Finally, something I can recognize.* Unable to move for some minutes, he sat in the car in the darkness, needing to catch his breath.

Finding that Sephardic Bible confirmed beyond any doubt that this was precisely where he was supposed to be. *This* was where he had been sent to prove his calling and confirm his heart's long search, as well as his family's unknown buried roots. When he first arrived in New Mexico fifteen years earlier to work in Albuquerque under the direction of the

Monsignor, the message wasn't clear, and the road map, undecipherable. Back then, he really wasn't so sure.

To begin with, he didn't speak Spanish very well and was perceived as an obvious outsider with his soft, Northeastern accent and formal New England ways. People were too polite, distant. They seemed cold and very private, keeping him at bay. Some were cordial, others just civil. He was rarely invited in.

But by the time he transferred to Estrella, he spoke Spanish like a native and understood the local customs better. Even priests, he discovered, had to earn respect. He learned not to be intrusive and instead, patient to the extreme. His parishioners taught him that good things come to those who wait. So, wait he did. Over time, he was gradually accepted, developing close ties to the community, one family at a time. Once they knew he was there to stay, the real work began.

Building a parish and creating a passionate love for God—that was his mission, and the heart of his struggle as well. He lived in the space between the demands of the Church and the hunt for his family's past, as well as his own conflicted sense of himself. Who was he, really? That was the question that drove his search, and therein lay a certain measure of guilt; that he'd abandoned one generation in the desperate search for another. But seeing Rachel's Bible gave him a soaring measure of hope.

CHAPTER NINETEEN

A Homecoming

PADRE DOMINGO NÚÑEZ HAD been raised in one of the many ethnic neighborhoods of New Bedford, Massachusetts, thirty miles south of Boston. His family lived in an area once founded by Portuguese immigrants who'd settled there in the mid-nineteenth century, an enclave that had grown into a solid part of the city over the decades. Early on, most had been involved with shipbuilding and whaling, at least until whale oil was preempted by electricity a few decades later.

His parents had only moved there after World War II. Núñez's grandfather on his father's side, Señor Emmanuel Alonso Núñez, had been born in New Mexico, somewhere near the Mora Valley, south of Taos, nearly one hundred years earlier. Domingo was but a teen when the elder Nuñez died at eighty-nine, back in 1960, but knew that he'd served in World War I and returned home disillusioned and troubled, never to recover fully. What he'd seen over in Europe stayed with him for a lifetime. He was a reclusive old man who lived with his memories and rarely spoke of his past.

Like many soldiers who had left their loved ones behind before they went to war, he had returned, taken a job in ranching, and married his high school sweetheart. They celebrated the birth of their son, Núñez's father, Arturo, in 1925. Now eighty-one and still working, Arturo was determined never to retire.

A younger Arturo was but seventeen when World War II broke out and America mobilized her troops. He enlisted in the U.S. Army straight out of high school and headed overseas to help bring an end to Hitler's regime. Surviving two years of ground battle, he and hundreds of other foot soldiers in the Allied Forces helped open the gates of Dachau to confront firsthand what the Germans had done. The sight of the skeletal survivors and the stiff, cord-like heaps of the dead stole his voice for months afterward, leaving an irreparable wound to his soul. The horrors of the camps seared a deep emotional scar, one he would carry for the rest of his life. In a thousand years, he never imagined the injustice one human being could levy on another. He was deeply traumatized by what the Nazis had done to the Jews.

Upon returning to New Mexico in 1944, following his discharge from the service, he found himself restless and troubled, as if danger lurked everywhere. He didn't know why, living in a state of mistrust that wouldn't subside. He married within the year and Domingo, their only son, was born in 1949. But life back then was hard and the local economy in rural New Mexico depressed. Arturo convinced his wife they had to move away, to a place where they could have a better future. An Army buddy had told him about New Bedford and offered to help set him up if he ever wanted to try. Before long, he and his wife moved to the New England coastal town with everything they owned and established a small grocery in the heart of the old Portuguese neighborhood. Selling fruit, freshly caught fish and homemade sweets, the store was an instant success.

Núñez remembered the arguments he had with his father as a teen, mainly about his future.

"You'll stay here and help us with the business," Arturo told him. "I'll need you for deliveries and warehouse work so we can grow. I can't afford to hire anyone. You're our future."

"It's not what I want," Domingo dared refute him. He was by then already an altar boy and deeply drawn to the Church. "I hope to serve the Lord. You sent me to Catholic school and I have learned well what the Church means to our people. It's our salvation, Papa, I was born to guide. I beg you to send me to seminary."

In the end, Arturo relented and Domingo left for Boston after graduation with a troubled heart. Even as he served his first parish in nearby Arlington at twenty, the sense of having failed his father grew; a feeling to follow him all the way to New Mexico, only to grow darker over the years.

Reminiscing now, all the tumult seemed eons ago. Following ordination, and anxious to serve the Church, Nunez sought to quell a growing curiosity. He began to do research. Why did his family leave New Mexico and choose to live so far away, divorced from their familial roots? How long had his grandfather been there? Where was he born? Why was he, Domingo, the only one in his family to have blue eyes? These and other unanswerable questions plagued him.

"Your grandmother came from somewhere in old Mexico," his father told him. "Sonora, I think, or Monterey. Maybe Nueva Leon. Your grandfather—from Zacatecas. He worked in the mines." He couldn't help him go back any further, try as he might. His memory for family history had grown dim.

All that Domingo Núñez knew was that he, a Catholic priest working in a suburb of Boston in 1994, had a powerful yearning to return to the land where his grandfather and father once lived. It drove him to distraction. Finally, he put in his request for a transfer if there ever was an opening. Within the year, he was heading west.

Fate brought him to the small hamlet of Estrella in the upper Rio Grande, founded, he first thought, in the mid-eighteen hundreds. But the small church at its core still bore its keystone with the date etched upon it—1750. After this night, he had every reason to believe that the community he was serving was probably much older than that. Rachel's Bible was proof enough. He couldn't wait to follow its trail. And what of the tarnished silver case therein with the raised Hebrew letter, *shin,* meaning guardian or protector soldered on its front, and those elegant, hand-chased silver candlesticks, so obviously well-used and exquisitely made? What was their story?

CHAPTER TWENTY

Nueva España, 1754

Guarding the Light

SNUFFING OUT THE TALLOW candles, María Sequerra smothered the still-smoking wicks with her fingers and tucked the two silver candlesticks under the base of a large, footed earthen bowl in the center of the table. Here in their home in *Nueva España* she had learned quickly that an unexpected knock at the door was not a good sign. Her parents had taught her that the secret rituals they observed on Fridays were for their eyes only. How many had perished because of them?

She slipped the Holy Book with the gold letters on its cover back into the secret pocket under the seat of her father's chair and pushed the chair under the table so nothing would look out of place. Then she opened the window to clear away any smoke and ran into the *cocina* to hide. Another loud knock and gruff voices told her they would all be in grave danger should either the book or the candles be found. That much she had already learned from the look on her mother Catalina's face whenever she dared ask why they were always hidden away.

"Good evening, Father Rincón," she heard her father say. "God be with you and welcome."

The padre stood at the door, a foul-breathed, hooded menace clothed in black. Behind him, waiting on the path to the Sequerra family *bodega*, two mounted horsemen held the reins of the clergyman's mare. They were the priest's mercenaries, no doubt, paid by the Church to help expose the suspect, the criminals, and above all, heretic Jews—those whom the tribunal in Mexico City suspected still practiced their forbidden religion in secret.

"What brings you to my door this Friday evening?" Ephraim asked. "Please, come in. The weather is perfect for mid-September, is it not?"

Fall had not yet begun to chill the low ridges of the Sierra Nevada Mountains and the bustling village of San Miguel el Grande, an outpost of the Church and a strategic Spanish settlement. It was well placed along the *El Camino Real de Tierra Adentro*, a trade route heading north toward the silver mines in Zacatecas and beyond, and the most far-flung settlements of New Spain. Here, in the area of Guanajuato, more than four hours away from the capital, Mexico City, the weather was more clement. Enough rain fell to nurture vegetation through the early summer and fill the shallow rivers so necessary for cultivation.

On the plateau where Ephraim and his family lived, an hour's ride to the village, the summers lasted long enough and the winters stayed rainy and mild, perfect for the Madeira grapevines planted in the valley behind their house. The land was much like the hilly Iberian coast of Portugal where he'd first learned the vintner's craft. The stepped landscape of San Miguel was more akin to the mountainous area of Belmonte, not far from Lisbon, one of the great centers of Jewish life in the late sixteen hundreds and the place where Ephraim spent his childhood.

Ephraim Velasquez Sequerra had come to New Spain as a closely guarded employee of the Church to plant vineyards for sacramental wine. He had served thus at his home in Portugal. He planted his cuttings with pride the first season of their arrival more than a decade earlier, and finally, after so many seasons of vigorous growth, expected his best grape harvest this fall. The fragrant Santo Madeira grapes bursting with flavor would guarantee their future.

"We are not interested in the weather, *señor,*" said the cleric. "We are interested in you. You have been until now a trusted servant of the Church, but we have reason to be concerned."

"Me? But why?"

María peered cautiously into the front room and was surprised to see the priest enter their door. He had a flat, uneven nose, which seemed to divide his face in half, thin lips beneath a sparse mustache and a thick unkempt beard. Coffee-brown, reptilian eyes with heavy lids stared blankly. The cleric did not smile. His stiff personage frightened her, wrapped in bulky, dark robes anchored by a heavy belt. María shrank farther behind the door.

* * *

This farmhouse in San Miguel de Allende was the only home María Sequerra had ever really known. She'd been born just prior to their escape from Portugal when, according to her father, the persecution of suspected heretics in Lisbon drove him and his pregnant wife to leave. Enlisting with those who sought to help build the colony in the New World, they joined the many shiploads of migrants headed across the sea.

Ephraim had never once been charged with any crime. He was unknown in Portugal's large community of *Marranos,* the original name for Jews there and those in Spain. The word in Spanish meant swine, filthy pig in fact, its reference more than clear. His family had converted some thirty-five years earlier becoming *Cristianos nuevos* and he had been raised a pious Catholic all his life. Or so it seemed. Like many, his parents fled Spain in hopes for a better life and settled in Portugal; others from Andalusia went to Turkey, Greece, and as far away as Morocco, even farther into North Africa.

But the Inquisition came to Portugal as well, and over one hundred and fifty years, countless innocents were sent to their deaths by burning at the stake or even more hideous means. Torture was the main instrument of the Inquisitors; heinous means to extract a confession. Entire families disappeared in the fiery persecutions, or *autos de fe*, where crowds gathered in public plazas to watch Jewish men and women staked, garroted, torched and consumed in diabolical purges of flame.

A witness to these atrocities, Ephraim had been shaken to the core. He believed that in *Nueva España*, in the new colonies, they might find peace and make a new life. He had heard that one could almost disappear into the mountains far from the city and live as one pleased. He prayed in secret to the God of his forefathers to lead them there. The village of San Miguel seemed ideal.

By then, the far-ranging borders of the Spanish empire ran from the tip of the Yucatan all the way to the interior of the *tierra conquistada*, to just above the trade center of Santa Fe in the Sangre de Cristo Mountains and farther west to the great ocean. Settled more than four hours from the capital of *Ciudad de Mexico*, he began anew. But now, after precious years of peace, he could hardly believe a new wave of persecution had arisen, and here in San Miguel el Grande, too. The cruel arm of Spain's despotic rule reached so very far. How he regretted disappointing his wife whom he had promised such terrors would be left behind.

CHAPTER TWENTY-ONE

Accused

MARÍA HELD HER BREATH. By the time she'd celebrated her fourteenth birthday, only a week earlier, she had learned what a New Christian needed to know in order to survive. She finally understood that those Friday night blessings her father bestowed upon her and her infant brother were not something approved by Church doctrine. Indeed, quite the reverse.

And now she knew that the book with strange letters was forbidden too. Her father, never formally schooled in Hebrew and raised by parents who had converted to Christianity, had never known what the letters meant. But like many others, he memorized important passages, prayers, and chants that had been repeated over the years. The importance of those sacred words seemed to grow dearer to him after he left his homeland.

When Maria's little brother was born, the adults held an important ceremony she was not allowed to attend. But she understood from the assembly gathered that day—supposedly to help with the grape harvest—that it would be something to set her brother apart forever as well, something to bind him to their people. As she hid now, fearful of what might come, she listened carefully.

"Enter, please. You are most welcome to come into my humble abode, *Inquisidor*," Ephraim repeated, entreating the cleric. "Have a glass of wine with me, sir, in your honor and in the name of Jesus, forgiver of all sins."

María's father offered a special wine this night; the last of a rich and fragrant Port, distilled from his own vines grown in Portugal, and brought with them on their journey. The product of the sweet grapes found around the city of Porto Santo was renowned. The few casks Ephraim had brought with him had opened many doors. Now, all he had was this final jug. He hoped it would buy him some lenience at least.

Catalina scowled at the priest from behind her shawl. A woman of thirty-seven years, she ran her household strictly and kept her children close. No matter how much promise the New World offered, she'd fled Portugal in terror and never got over her fear. Seeing one's relatives burned at the stake teaches a special kind of caution.

"Thank you, no, *señor* Sequerra," said the cleric. "I did not come here to drink. The Church has reason to suspect you are keeping some truth from us. This is no social call. We have no patience for those who tell falsehoods or defile our sacraments. We have been told two lights were seen shining through your window this night. Observing the unholy Sabbath perhaps?"

"Not at all, good sir," Ephraim answered, trying to remain calm. "We are the most devout servants of Christ, I assure you. Besides, we are poor, we cannot afford the luxury of candles. It was an oil lamp to see by, or perhaps a reflection of the setting sun. We live by the light our Lord Jesus provides. Whoever spoke against us must have seen the surface of my crucifix here shining in those last rays."

He pointed to the small silver cross, a few inches in width and length, which hung on the dining room wall across from the window, still barely illuminated by the twilight outside. "Surely, but a rumor."

Ephraim turned to uncork the bottle of wine and poured two glasses, his hands unsteady.

"The Church will not be deceived, *señor* Sequerra. Kneel before me. Kneel before a true Messenger of God and swear upon your very life that you are not guilty of heresy. It is said you came here in a ship with many who practice Judaism in secret. Are you a Jew? Because if you are, or if you are hiding even one faithless Jewish dog, then you and your family shall suffer." The crack of a heavy whip splitting the air caused María to jerk in terror. She peered around the doorway, then screamed when the second lash cut across her father's back. Its snake-like end snapped loudly and the crucifix hanging on the wall fell to the floor.

Ephraim collapsed, facedown, and lay at the foot of the cloaked priest standing over him, a bright stripe of blood oozing through his shirt. The cleric rounded the braided leather into a coil under his arm and stepped back. "There shall be no further reports of such blasphemies, do you understand? Remember, the guardians of the Mother Church are watching you."

Ephraim rose, shaking, and watched through the door as the men rode back down the path toward town. His wife and daughter ran to him in tears. His nightmare had been realized—they'd been identified. Some treason in their midst? A jealous neighbor or cleric, even a suspicious friend. Who knew?

CHAPTER TWENTY-TWO

On the Run

UNBEKNOWNST TO EPHRAIM, THE Inquisition had established itself in Mexico City in 1571 to ensure that all Jewish converts were good Catholics, proven to have *limpieza de sangre,* or pure blood. This was determined by grueling investigations into distant parentage, as recorded through birth records. Males were checked for circumcision; women observed closely to see that they did not practice Jewish dietary customs or rituals within the household. So many of the *anusim* or forced ones attempted to flee to Mexico during the Inquisition in Spain that the Spaniards passed an edict forbidding entry to anyone who could not prove Catholic ancestry for four consecutive generations.

Ephraim, employed by the Church in Spain, and now in the New World to secure the wine they needed, felt safe enough—in fact, certain that they were beyond question. Jewish ancestry preceded his great-great-grandmother, such a very long time ago. But after this debacle, he understood their safety was at stake. Turning to his wife and daughter, he spoke softly. "Gather your things, *mis queridas.* Take the infant in your shawl, Catalina; secure him well. We are leaving this place. I feared in my heart this day would come, and have already made plans."

"How shall we escape?" she asked.

"We'll load the mule and saddle the mare. Bring only what will last —grains and dried fruit. We have little time. There is a way north, beyond the reach of those who might pursue us. We will walk at night and hide where we can, sleeping by day. Tell anyone who asks we are only pilgrims on our way."

"But how shall we know which way to go?" asked Catalina.

"I've been told that one of our own waits each evening at the outskirts of San Luis to take people through the mountains to safety. From there, we'll travel to Monterey, to Coahuila, Mata Moros, then on to El Paso del Norte. North, always north, to Santa Fe and even beyond. We will go farther, past any contact with the Holy See. I would rather perish on the journey if God wills it, than by their hand."

"With luck," he continued, "we shall find others like ourselves, far away from their bloodthirsty tribunal. We will change our name, Catalina, start anew. We'll leave our surname Sequerra behind and become—Garcia perhaps. Or Martinez, something more common, more like them. We shall settle deep in the mountains to live as we wish—and observe God's commandments as our ancestors did. We must leave now. Pack up, my darlings, hurry."

"What else shall we take, Ephraim?" she asked, tearfully attending to her husband's bleeding back with shaking hands.

"Only essentials. Waste no time. Stay calm. The others often see us watering the animals at sundown and will think nothing of it. Let us go in pairs. María will take the donkey. And you, Catalina, with the boy, come with me, guiding the mare. Lead her slowly, as if to graze. When the animals have drunk their fill, we shall continue by the light of the moon. I will not wait to be caught by these zealots."

"What will become of us?" Catalina implored.

"I do not know for certain, *mi amada,*" said Ephraim. "But the future is in our own hands. The map to the northern territory will be in your care." He handed her a folded piece of leather from a pouch at his belt. "Hide it well. I know it by heart. If we get separated, follow the way up the Rio Grande. Ask where the river flows. Continue north to the settlements from there, with or without me."

Ephraim's wife sat down at the table, numb. "I am so sorry you have to leave your precious vines, my husband."

"As am I," he answered. "But I take the next generation with me. The cuttings are already bundled as we speak."

Per her mother's instructions, María rescued the silver candlesticks from their hiding place under the bowl. She quickly sewed each one into the folds of her underskirts. They would never be detected there. The Bible went into the lining of her coat. Confused and worried, she picked up the small silver cross from the floor where it had fallen in the fray. She held it in her hands.

But where to hide it? Something of such value cannot be left behind. We might need it someday. Reluctantly, she cut open the back of her old fabric doll dressed in layers of lace like a bride, now worn and tattered, and buried the cross deep into the stuffing in its back and arms, then sewed it shut.

Father need not even know. Not yet. Surely, he overlooked such an important thing. He will think I am most responsible. I hope so. If nothing else, it might protect us somehow from further harm.

CHAPTER TWENTY-THREE

On the Rez

AFTER OPENING THE PASSENGER door, Frank Yazzi gently picked up Juan in his arms. The boy still slept, dead to the world, as did the wounded dog curled on the floor of the truck, snoring loudly. Suddenly alert, the animal was up on all fours, clawing at Juan's arm. Yazzi picked the dog up too, then motioned with his head for Ángel to get out.

The boy jumped down to the gravel drive and rubbed the sleep from his eyes. He pulled up his baggy jeans, searched through his pockets for a cigarette, fished for some matches, then lit up. He took a drag, exhaled, then he combed his long bangs out of his eyes with his fingers.

Yazzi's woman stood waiting for them at the back door, a curious expression on her face. When she heard the truck pull in, she went straight to the kitchen to start coffee. Wearing a long, light blue terrycloth robe, her black hair pulled up into a loose knot, she peered out of the doorway, then opened the screen door, shaking her head.

"What the hell you got there, Frank?" She stopped short when she saw the children. "Hey now—you win those two in a poker game or something?"

"Not hardly,"Yazzi answered."They found me. Long story.You better make some breakfast, Della, and lots of it, cause I guarantee you, they gonna' be hungry. Somethin' for this dog too."

The Navajo carried the younger boy, still sleeping, into the house. Ángel followed. Poquito trotted alongside.

Yazzi lay the child down on a threadbare, three-seat sofa in front of an old console television turned to the morning news. Juan moaned, murmuring *"Mama, Mama,"* in his sleep, then turned over and buried his face in a sofa pillow.The dog hopped up and lay beside him, panting. It licked its wounded paw until the cushion below him was soaked. Ángel dragged on his cigarette stub some more and sank onto the couch beside his brother, scanning the room, looking for a way out if he needed one. His stomach growled. "Thanks, mister," he said. "So now what?"

"Not sure. Breakfast maybe. You tell me. But hey—son of a gun! Look at that!" said the Navajo, pointing to the television screen. "I think I just saw you on TV."

CHAPTER TWENTY-FOUR

A Sixth Sense

HÉCTOR SAT UP, ALONE in the dark. Something awakened him, something unknown, a sensation so strange and fearful that it shook him out of a deep sleep—almost a cross between a premonition and a memory, as if whatever was going to happen had happened before and would certainly happen again. It gave him an eerie chill. He lay back, sucked in a deep breath, and rubbed the sleep from his eyes. It had to be close to midnight.

He was sure the feeling had to do with his boys. All day he believed what Carmen told him—that the kids probably left for a school field trip and might be gone until supper. He'd accepted her assurances like a gullible old fool until he heard last night's newscast. Did they think because he was blind that he was deaf too? The sound of Juanito and Ángel's names on the evening news shot through him like a lance. His *nietos*, missing? Amber Alerts were very serious. He might be old and blind, but he knew that much.

Héctor confronted Carmen when she called him to the table for dinner. How dare she lie to him? He cursed her for making up stories and then, ashamed of shouting at her, begged her forgiveness. This was no time for a family to be fighting.

The next morning, Carmen asked Héctor to stay close by the phone in case anyone should call while she was at work and apologized over and over for not telling the truth—said she just didn't want him to worry. Besides, she thought the kids would be back by now. She was just as concerned as he was. She gathered her jacket and keys to head over to the Senior Center where she helped out on Saturday afternoons. But first made sure the old man was comfortable.

"Please, just be here for them in case they come home," she said, as she straightened the quilts around his bed. "Or if they call, or if we get some news. We need you to be here for us too, Papa. For Rachel and me. She needs you to be strong for her boys and for her."

"*Si*, I will be here for them, always. *Para los dos*."

The old man rubbed his forehead as he sat in the dark, thinking back about what had transpired, worrying about the boys and worse, regretting his son Gerry's selfishness and apparent infidelity. *Personas* were talking. Maybe there was another woman. *!Hijole!* It wasn't his way to meddle, but as a father, he could feel the scandal coming, the heartbreak too. He knew a wall had grown up between Gerry and his wife. It was tall and thick. He could feel it. Now Gerry had turned his back on the whole family. Perhaps their separation was the devil's hand; a punishment for Gerry behaving in such a godless and ungrateful way. He had never held much respect for the Church. Shameful. In Héctor's mind, such contempt had consequences.

Héctor wrapped his hands around a *santo*, a wooden statue kept near his bed. It was his favorite, one that he often held these past few days and cherished. It was a figure of Saint Joseph, carved in his youth. Roughly hewn of cottonwood, he could see it clearly in his mind as he felt the outlines of the face with his sensitive fingertips. Even blind, he understood now just how he might have done it better.

When he was only thirty, he had been the best *santero* in the state, sought after for many private commissions. In his talented fingers, beloved saints came alive. His finely chiseled-and-shaped faces detailed features in a way few could match: planes of cheekbones, brows and rugged chins. The carvings of Héctor Ortega could make a person laugh or cry, humble themselves, even coax a painful truth from a regretful mouth. Most of all, they brought comfort to the suffering, as did this one to him now, its wooden hands clasped in prayer.

He turned it around and around, remembering exactly how it looked years ago. This day he prayed many times already for Saint Joseph to help the police find his grandchildren. He prayed again, gripping the sculpture tightly. "*Por favor,* lead the children home."

As he felt himself nodding off to sleep, he remembered the small church in San Cristóbal. The priest had commissioned him to carve a three-part *retablo* of Santa Teresa d' Ávila. It was said that Saint Theresa had been born of Jews who had converted to Christianity centuries earlier in Spain—and was raised a Catholic. Pious, even as a girl, she wrote many works about her love of God and the essence of prayer, and eventually was canonized in 1640. She became a revered patroness of Spain. Famed for her spirituality, she was a queen among saints. Some also said she could speak to God directly. Héctor adored her. The commission of this nine foot-high altarpiece was by far the most important assignment he had ever received; an unexpected honor.

Héctor knew he was a capable carver, but had never done anything near that large before: only single *bultos* and *retablos*, and dared not admit he had no conception of how to adorn the two side panels of the triptych. Angels? Clouds? Birds? Other saints? Images of Holy Jesus himself? He could see the center panel in his mind's eye: an image of his beloved Teresa in her crimson robe and halo, a dove hovering over her left shoulder, according to tradition. But she could not stand alone. What to put around her?

The priest said not to worry. The design would come, all would be revealed in time. But pray as he might for inspiration—nothing did. He hoped that with enough devotion the images would arise, yet over the two months he worked obsessively on the center panel—he never once received inspiration from above no matter how hard he tried.

Three months into the commission, while finishing off Saint Theresa's crown, Héctor continued to muse upon the subjects he would carve onto the panel's wings. Distracted, he stepped wrong, lost his balance, and fell backwards from the scaffold. He lay stunned on the floor for some time, head throbbing, but eventually got up on his own. At first he seemed fine, but then felt dizzy, so he went home early and straight to bed, complaining of a headache. He awoke the next morning, pain-free, ready to begin again. But by the end of the day, the headache had returned, even worse than before. His head began to throb.

Each day for the next few days was the same thing, and although the headaches grew more severe, he was driven to work by the baffling triptych. He ignored the pain and persevered. Then, one morning he woke up, completely unable to see. A dark veil had settled over his eyes. In despair, he was forced to abandon the commission and hire a young assistant to complete the job. Recycling favorite subjects in local liturgical art, the carver copied the design of an older triptych featuring scenes of the Ascension. Héctor reeled under the disappointment. The altar to *Santa Teresa* no longer reflected her glory. His masterpiece belonged to another.

From then on, both Héctor and Bettina struggled, living on her salary alone. He never carved another thing. She worked as a nurse at the local hospital, and they were just able to make ends meet. Their only child, Gerry, still a teen at the time, took Héctor's disability badly. In Gerry's eyes, after the blindness came, Héctor simply ceased to exist.

CHAPTER TWENTY-FIVE

Magic in His Hands

"RACHEL! WHERE ARE YOU? Rachel!"

Héctor startled, jerking upright in bed. He heard Gerry's voice calling out his wife's name, over and over. It had to be late. He sat still, saying nothing, but listening carefully to the angry sounding phone conversation audible outside his bedroom door.

"What do you mean, you don't know where they are?" Gerry asked. "You're their mother, aren't you? And why aren't you here at your sister's? I don't know why in the hell I ever trusted you … all right—geez, settle down, all right, all right. So I'm here now, okay? Of course I heard about it! I just wish for once you'd quit holding everything that goes wrong against me. For Pete's sake, I'm your husband—remember? I told you I'd be back and I'm back!"

Héctor heard him pause and then continue.

"You're at the police station? Oh—that's great. The cops—that figures, the freakin' cops. Okay … so leave. Get over here now." He sighed heavily. "We need to talk. I'll be waiting. Don't make me come over there, OK? You'll regret it."

Gerry clicked his cell phone closed.

Héctor heard steps. The refrigerator opened: ice rattled in a glass, then a television announcement for rubber tires. Then Pepsi. Then *Telemundo*. The channel changed again and again.

Not much of a gentleman, his son. Impatient, as always. Héctor heard him pop a can, then switch the channel some more. The annoying chatter of random surfing continued until Héctor fell back asleep.

* * *

Carmen came home after midnight and found her brother-in-law passed out, snoring on the couch. Héctor heard her open the linen closet in the hall, talking to herself in Spanish, cursing the day Gerry Ortega ever married her sister.

The old man lay awake and mused on the strange vision he had seen in his mind before his son burst into the house that night. He hoped he could conjure it up again. He had dozed off, drawn to a comforting scene from his past with a red-gold sunset sinking behind indigo mountains; colors he could still envision vividly although he had not seen them in years. For some unexplainable reason, Héctor felt at peace for the first time since the boys disappeared. He was glad Gerry had not come into his room or disturbed him, for he had nothing but reproaches to offer. When the brilliant sky in his mind started to darken once again, he fell into an even deeper sleep.

Héctor tossed and turned. In the wee hours of the morning, his dreams carried him to a place where the carved altar panels for the Church of San Cristóbal appeared, now finished, a luminous gilded halo around the blessed head of *Santa Teresa*, glowing brightly above her red robes. The side panels were flung wide open, and to his surprise he could see the triptych completed by his own hand at last. Carved on either side were images of cherubim with the worried faces of two children—faces he had never actually seen with his own eyes, but always imagined. He knew exactly who they were. Juanito and Ángel, each chiseled in great detail and fine relief, staring balefully into his eyes. Blessed God! They were so beautiful. He loved them so much. *La Santa Teresa* would guide them home, sooner or later. This he truly believed.

CHAPTER TWENTY-SIX

Saved for the Time Being

"OKAY, *MIS AMIGOS*, HOW did you two end up out in the middle of nowhere?" Della pierced Ángel with a steely look, tapping her fingers on the kitchen table. She may not have measured much taller than the teen, but she was tough. Kids were not her favorite thing.

The boy stared back, expressionless. Mute.

Yazzi winced. He could hear it coming.

"All right then, you little brat. Pull up a chair and sit down," she added, nodding to Ángel. "And I mean right now! Breakfast's ready. Better wake up the little guy, too. And don't you dare smoke that white man's cancer stick in here! Give it to me this minute!"

Della grabbed the cigarette before Ángel could hand it to her and snapped what was left in half, tossing the pieces into the sink.

Tantalized by the wafting smell of scrambled eggs and tortillas, Juan woke up on his own, ready to eat as soon as his eyes popped open. He sat upright on the sofa, hugging the blanket that Della had tossed over him. He looked around, confused, then glanced down.

"Poquito!"

The dog barked sharply, wagging its tail.

"Oh, you're not dead, you're not dead!" He pulled the dog close and hugged him, trying not to hurt any obvious wounds. "That mean ol' coyote could never get you, boy, huh? You showed him. You hungry? I sure am. Ángel, where are we?"

In seconds the younger boy slipped off the sofa and climbed up on to a chair at the table. He eyed Della for a moment, decided she was safe, then grabbed the waiting glass and swallowed a huge gulp of milk. He took a couple of deep breaths, attacked the glass again, then wiped his mouth with his arm and went after the platter of scrambled eggs—first grabbing a tortilla off another plate and dropping it on the floor. Poquito limped to the offering, sniffed, and tore in.

Della shot a look of compassion at Juan, then sat down across from Ángel and continued the grill. "So, where you two runaways from, anyhow? And what in the world were you doing out in the *llano* by yourself last night?" she demanded, giving Ángel a dark-eyed, up and down stare.

The teen glared back at her and didn't say a word—just ripped a big bite from his stuffed tortilla and munched. His eyes narrowed.

"You don't speak up, boy, she'll have *you* for breakfast," said Yazzi, taking a sip of his coffee. "I'd answer her. Now. She may be small, but she's strong." He pulled his chair closer, then turned to Della. "This one don't talk much," he said, flipping his thumb at Ángel. "Like I said—roadkill. They were in the brush. Sure was a cold night out there and they were pretty scared."

"What happened to his cheek? And that eye?" Della asked. She held Ángel's head in her hands, lifting his chin and turning his head, squinting at his purple face as if it were a bruised eggplant.

Juan looked up, seeing his brother's injuries as if for the first time. He squinted. "I bet that hurts," he said, making a sour face. Turning to Della, he added matter-of-factly, "He got punched."

"Whoever ditched 'em, roughed him up some," said Yazzi. "He says they stole his money. By the time I picked 'em up alongside the road, they looked like desert rats after a day-long cougar chase. And that little runt-dog just about got gobbled by a coyote. It was the darnedest thing. I saw the dog between its jaws before I hit him with the truck. Couldn't believe my eyes."

Juan stopped eating as he absorbed the details of the story, his own eyes round as saucers.

"Man, I hate to run down an animal on the road—anyway, it's a miracle the dog's not hurt—what saved him was my front grill, I think. *Tőbájíshchíní* must like that little fella."

Yazzi turned to Ángel and said, "OK, boy. Time's up. Enough bull crap. You better tell me what's goin' on and I mean now, because I'm gonna guess that the state and the FBI are both out looking for you. I got no friends in the FBI. Don't want trouble I didn't go looking for. For the record, white kids don't hang out much here on the Rez, you know. I need some answers and this minute."

"I ain't white. I'm New Mexican," Ángel answered, sitting up stiffly.

"You look white to me. You ain't Diné, whatever you are."

"Listen, can't you just hide us, mister? Ángel asked, risking co-operation with a stranger and suddenly taking charge of his own defense. "Please, just for a day? I can't go back there. I can work. I can work for you!" he pleaded.

"Where is *there*, son?" Yazzi asked.

"Um, up north a ways, I think," the boy answered. "I'm not sure. Don't matter where anyway. Could you maybe just let us stay here until they stop looking? We didn't do anything wrong."

"They won't stop looking. Funny thing about a manhunt—longer it goes, bigger it gets. More men, bigger search, for a while anyways. They ought to be letting the bloodhounds loose right about now. You sure you ain't done something bad?"

"No. I mean—yes. Well, I don't know. Sort of maybe, I guess, but not that bad. It's complicated."

"Mmm-hmm. It always is." Yazzi frowned, rubbing his chin.

Della, picked up the empty plates and laid them in the sink with a clatter. "I'm not liking this. Not one bit."

"Okay *muchachos*, this is what will happen," said Yazzi, ignoring her. "One of two things: either I take you home or turn you in. So what'll it be? You're not staying here."

"Oh no, please, no. We can't go home. We have no home. Please don't turn us in, mister—I can't tell you why. Isn't there just someone who could hide us for a few days until I figure something out?"

Yazzi pondered. In light of his problems with the Council lately, another headache like these kids was the last thing he needed. Still, maybe they could just disappear.

"No. Yeah, well, there is someone I know, maybe. You kids got any money?"

"Some," said Ángel.

Della stood up, shaking her head and glaring at her partner. "I have no idea what's going on in your head right now. but don't you include me, Frank Yazzi," she said, her hands on her hips. "I see that look in your eyes. Whatever the hell you got planned, get on with it. And when you're done, don't tell me about it." She stomped out of the kitchen.

"Some days she's just like that—touchy. OK. Whatever you got, hold on to it. And here's a little more, just in case."

Yazzi pulled two twenties from his wallet and laid them in Ángel's palm. "That's what you get. Don't spend it if you don't have to. And don't tell nobody where you got it. I don't know you; you don't know me. And if you get found, or go home, don't ever tell anybody I helped, understood?"

"Yes sir, Mr. Yazzi," said Ángel, taking the stranger's money, realizing for the first time how his leaving home affected people—even people he never knew. He wondered with a gulp how his mother was taking this, what with Juan gone now, too.

"He's my brother," Ángel said, pointing to Juan, as if it was time for a formal introduction.

"Figured as much," said Yazzi. "Do look alike."

"But he's not old enough for all this," Ángel said. "It's not his fault."

"You're right there."

"And I can't leave him here."

"Right again."

What bothered Ángel most was that he couldn't just run off into the sunset like movie heroes do. He had wanted freedom so bad, so awfully bad, and now all he had was responsibility—Juan trailing after him like a big fat tail. Why did they pick him up? What was he thinking? Ever since he and those damn Ramírez brothers had picked up his brother at the house, the burden had grown heavier by the hour. He could not make whatever this was into a grand adventure any longer—or a great escape, either.

"I wish he wasn't here," said Ángel, a deep sadness in his eyes.

"Who?" said Juan in a thin voice, jerking his head up. "Me? Me? You wish I wasn't here? That's not fair! You brought me, butthead." He glared across the table at Ángel, his mouth curled down in a pout-like frown, tears welling up. Then he shrugged, folding his arms across his chest, and huffed.

"You brought him, you protect him, son," said the Navajo, glancing at Ángel as he downed his coffee.

Frank Yazzi doubted his own sanity—but maybe things could just cool off for a while. Then the kids could show up at home, wherever that was. Was he really thinking of taking these two children to his uncle Tomás? Tomás Begay? A contract shepherd who worked for a rancher with twenty thousand acres southwest of the Rez, Tomás was his mother's older brother; a vet, retired on a Navy pension, a man who spoke Navajo like the old ones and who knew many of the traditions and secrets of the Diné nation. A healer of sorts, a good man.

Tomás followed the ancient ways, from long before the white man came. He liked to spend the mild seasons outdoors, on his own. He camped alone with over eight hundred woolies in a small valley east of the Mogollons, wild mountains unfit for man or beast. Seventy-nine years old, the lone shepherd loved his solitary life and lived in a battered trailer with no electricity. Once in a long while, visitors came to his valley to request his services as a medicine man. Most of the time, it was just him and his sheepdog, Shelter—an Aussie shepherd mix who knew as much about sheep as a real woolie, or so it seemed. Tomas could hide anybody out there if he had to. And make some good medicine while he was at it.

Yazzi mused on the possibility. Why not? Uncle Tomás could always say no, but for now, it was worth a try.

CHAPTER TWENTY-SEVEN

A Hideaway

CROSSING A BRIDGE OVER the Río Hondo in the mid-morning heat, Ángel and Juan gazed at the glittering water below. Yazzi's pickup crossed over and rumbled along the rocky road for some time, spitting up gravel and clouds of brown dust as it lurched back and forth between gears; up and down, but mostly up, spiraling into the short-grass hills of sheep country and the timeless world of the Diné. The morning started before dawn, driving two hundred miles south and west toward the Mogollon Mountains.

Across the front seat from Frank Yazzi, Ángel watched through the dusty windows, rays of sunlight streaming, Juan slumped up against him, asleep and drooling on his sleeve. This isn't at all what he had imagined running away would be like. For sure he would have been someplace good by now if he'd been alone. California couldn't be all *that* far. He saw it plenty of times on Mrs. Carlson's globe, and it was like barely one inch from New Mexico.

But now, for all he knew, it might just as well be as far away as New York City. Not that he knew for sure what he would do when he got to California—be a movie star or something, maybe a rock star, or a race car driver maybe—but he'd promised Juan they would go to Disneyland, first thing. Then, after they were done with that, they'd just have to see.

Frank Yazzi sat silent, driving, flooded with memories of the last time he ran away as a kid—and the punishment that followed. He was thirteen when it happened. He spent two nights in a jail when he was caught, then spent a month grounded at home, hardly leaving his room. That was the worst month of his life.

"Why didn't you turn us in, Mr. Yazzi?" asked Ángel. Adults were so unpredictable. He was beginning to feel nervous about their long ride up into the mountains with this strange Navajo man. He could not figure out why Mr. Yazzi was helping them—gave them money even. During the morning newscast the lady on TV said a reward was posted for him and Juan: five thousand dollars for any information! He wished he had some of that.

Ángel had learned long ago most grown-ups could never be trusted. Why was this man different? Because he was an Indian?

Yazzi cast him a sideways glance, forfeiting an answer. "You thirsty?" he asked. "Water bottle in the glove box. Help yourself. So tell me somethin', kid...ain't you got somebody back home you care about? Somebody who might be worried about you? Your mom, maybe?"

"I do, I do!" shouted Juan, bouncing awake. "I got someone, yeah—my *abuelo* Héctor. He's pretty old and don't see so good. But he cares a lot."

"What's his na...?"

"Héctor," Juan blurted. "Héctor Ortega. He's my best friend. He watches TV with me and we eat Frito pies on Saturday morning. He's at *Tía* Carmen Trujillo's house in Estrella right now. He likes her porch."

"He's none of your business!" Ángel shouted, trying to drown out his brother. But it was too late. Juan had blabbed.

Yazzi nodded. That was all he needed.

About eleven o'clock, the truck descended into a deep sandy draw, well-protected from wind and sight. There, at the bottom of the dried-out riverbed, a dented aluminum trailer sat gleaming in the sun. As Yazzi's truck thumped and squeaked to a halt, the screen door of the trailer swung open with a loud, tinny slap. A rifle barrel protruded carefully from the opening. Then, in the dim light of the interior, a shadowy silhouette emerged holding the firearm.

Ángel's eyes widened. "Watch out, squirt!" he yelled to Juan, who sat bolt upright and clutched his brother's arm with both hands. "A gun!"

An inquisitive Poquito stood on his hind legs and peered out the window too, his uninjured front paw pressed against the glass, the other limp.

"Uncle, it's me," Yazzi called as the truck rolled to a stop and the Indian stepped down. He waved at whoever was on the other end of that rifle barrel, then called out something the boys couldn't understand.

A much older man, wearing a cowboy hat, boots, and a shapeless *serape*, stepped out of the trailer, lowering his rifle. He stepped down and greeted Frank with a stone-faced hug. "Boys, meet Uncle Tomás. Tomás Begay."

The elder listened to Yazzi's disjointed explanation that followed, nodding his head as the facts piled up, his face solemn.

Once Yazzi finished, Tomás reached forward and shook his hand. "If you weren't my favorite nephew, Frankie ..." he said in Navajo, chuckling softly, "I wouldn't touch this. But for you ... what the hell, I'll do it."

Tomás knew such a crazy situation could not last. He might hide a couple of runaway white boys for a short time, though. He was pretty far away from anything or anybody, way out east of Deming and tucked in above the wildlife refuge. But the United States of America's Federal Bureau of Investigation – New Mexico Task Force had a lot more power than he, and long, white-man's fingers, too. He had no truck with them and wanted it to stay that way.

The old man shook the dust off his *serape* and gazed serenely at his new, two-legged lambs. Out of the open door of his trailer bounded a brindled sheepdog. It ran up to sniff Ángel and investigate the new canine on the ground. Poquito hid behind Juan's leg in fright, whining. Juan picked him up.

The gazes of old and young met: two pairs of worried, hesitant eyes, and two sets of older, wise ones. No one said a word for what seemed minutes. Then Juan turned to Ángel and pulled his sleeve, jerking it a couple times to get his brother's attention.

"We're gonna stay *here*?" he whispered. "I don't want to stay here, Ángel. It's too darn hot. And that man is weird." Juan pointed at Uncle Tomás.

"Don't worry, Juan," Yazzi reassured the little one, hearing his complaint. "You'll be fine. Your big brother will take care of you." The Diné looked Ángel straight in the face. The young rebel looked back with his usual sullen stare.

Slowly Frank strode back to his pickup, resisting the temptation to turn back and hug the boys goodbye. Over his shoulder he added, "No funny business and I'm serious. You do whatever Uncle Tomás tells you—understand? If you don't, he may turn you both into coyotes. Be good. See you 'round."

He got in, gunned the motor, and drove away, watching the blank faces of the children in his rearview mirror as they stood staring, speechless, while Uncle Tomás and his dog headed back toward camp.

CHAPTER TWENTY-EIGHT

Losing It

TRYING TO SLEEP THAT night after the dinner at Rosa's seemed futile. Rachel paced the motel room, her thoughts tumbling. The unexpected discussion about the Bible left her curious for more information and she couldn't explain why. It tugged at her, as if something she'd lost had just been found.

Out of nowhere, a strange treasure from the past had come into her life—unfortunately, at a time when she had more important things to deal with. She could hardly wrap her mind around it. She knew one thing. Family Bibles are usually records of history—she herself had one in a box in the trunk— her parent's New Testament filled with family details going all the way back to her great-great Aunt … what was her name? Maybe the 1950s. Anyway, she hardly ever looked at it. But this, an ancient Bible written in Hebrew? That part really confused her.

On top of everything else, Rachel had not expected Gerry's phone call. He rang her on her cell phone while Flores was driving her back to Carmen's—wouldn't you know? He asked her to come over to Carmen's house, immediately. Fat chance. Then he called back and started in with the blame. His angry voice and his empty threats pushed all the old buttons. She just exploded at him, right there in front of the deputy. Months of anger and resentment poured out of her. She didn't know she could be so crude. Hanging up on him, she snapped the Samsung down afterward with such force she thought she broke it, and practically ordered Deputy Flores to head to the motel after all.

The stormy conversation left her shattered, cringing with embarrassment in front of the officer. He heard every screaming hateful word she yelled in self-defense. Although Flores didn't say anything at the time, he obliged her with care, helping her out of the car the same way he might handle a terrorist's briefcase.

Rachel simmered when she thought of Gerry again. How dare he blame her even one bit for all of this? He was at the root of everything that had gone wrong after that damn letter came. He not only took part of the money from the sale of the house, he robbed her of their future. Who would want to live in Farmington?

As far as their marriage was concerned, she knew the end had come. In her mind, as a married couple they had no future. These past few days proved it. At least not the kind she wanted—ever again. As far she was concerned, their relationship wasn't really worth saving. He brought out the worst in her.

Sometimes Gerry could even get vicious. She had gotten more than one bruise from him to prove it. The last time he got physical she left the house, she was so afraid. He just didn't behave like the same man she had married, once, so easygoing and fun. Everything had changed. He said he was coming back and he did all right. But, now, after that phone call, she would never allow herself to be alone in the same place with him—not ever.

After Flores walked her to her motel room door to wish her goodnight, she remembered how he stood before her, hesitantly, looking somewhat abashed. "You gonna be okay?" he asked.

"Yeah, sure. Don't worry about me. I'll be fine." She wished she'd been truthful and asked him to stay, just a few minutes longer.

"Get some rest," he told her. "I'll call you in the morning—or right away if we hear anything. Otherwise, you call me if you need something, you hear, Rachel? Anything at all. You've got my number, right? I'm not far."

She hated watching him go, returning to his car, his gun belt clicking softly at every step. She wanted so much to follow him, lay her head on his shoulder and hold him close. Everything about José Flores felt right to her. She needed him more than she wanted to admit.

After he left, she locked herself in the motel room and took a quick shower. Then she turned on the television. Nothing but static on every channel. What did she expect? Then she opened a Coke she'd purchased from the vending machine earlier that day, sat down on the bed, and tried to figure out what her next step might be. Sleep was out of the question. Now that she could finally relax after a long day, she felt wide awake. She could thank Gerry for that.

Where else could help come from? Could they call out a door-to-door search, or should she hire a private investigator? So many questions she couldn't answer. But her heart ached just the same. Perhaps a visit with Father Núñez was in order, in part for a better explanation of that old Bible, but more important, to ask if he had any ideas for searching the Archdiocese. Priests know everyone.

Surely someone had to have seen the kids. Núñez would hear of it if they were hiding somewhere. But she felt embarrassed turning to him now, especially after all those years when she had skipped mass and avoided communion. And yet, it didn't appear that the priest held it against her. He was always cordial and forgiving.

Maybe it was time to seek help from a greater power if there really was such a thing. And back on the ground, if the state troopers didn't turn something up soon, she could hire a private investigator to follow every single clue. She'd interrogate the Ramirez brothers until they begged for mercy, even drive up and down the entire state of New Mexico herself, putting up flyers in every single town. But all of that was for tomorrow, or the next day. Was it fair to ask for divine guidance right now? To ask the almighty God for help? Even to beg? She had never asked God for anything before, but prayer seemed to be the only option left.

Prayer. How did one go about it? Whatever it was, she knew one thing—she couldn't do anything more on her own.

CHAPTER TWENTY-NINE

What the Heart Wants

HÉCTOR SAT IN HIS wooden rocker on the porch. He leaned back, pushed down with his toes, and made the chair tip back and forth slowly, listening for the creaky hymn from the boards beneath. The rhythm helped him think. That argument with Gerry at breakfast sure hadn't helped any. His head hurt from the shouting. Héctor asked Gerry what happened to the house he was supposedly looking for. His son had no answer. It was all hollow talk, jazzed up with cheap words about websites and buying power and the next new thing.

"Later, Dad. Later," he answered, putting him off.

Héctor hadn't expected much better. Gerry had been drifting for years. In a way, his wayward son had already made a break from all of them—and simply wouldn't come clean about it. Nothing but excuses and lies. Héctor knew that Gerry was a coward as well as a bully. He never understood how to be a father, and the children had suffered.

¿Qué había pasado? What did he not teach him as he grew up? Was this somehow his fault? And should the grandchildren have to pay the price? Surely they deserved something better. When does a man become a man?

Héctor remembered the wonderful dream he had the night before, the one where his grandsons' faces peered out of the wings of the altar-piece. That was his only confirmation that somehow they were safe; that somehow, everything would turn out all right.

After Gerry left that morning, Héctor retreated from the kitchen back to his room. "*Por favor Santa, Santa Teresa,*" he whispered, "Bring us back together. Give us peace."

* * *

Rachel sought out Father Núñez the next day and found him in the church sanctuary reciting his prayers. Per usual on Saturdays, the *Santuario* was quiet and almost empty. She knelt and remained on her knees in the pew behind him. Finally, he crossed himself and sat in silent devotion. Assuming that he was finished, Rachel asked if they could talk.

"I've been thinking," she began, "maybe you could ask other priests around New Mexico to help look for them."

"I've called everyone I know," he answered. "There is nothing else I can do in that regard. As for you, just—be of hope. Don't lose faith."

At this, Rachel blinked back tears. "What would you say if I told you that I think I already have? That maybe I never had any faith at all?" She got up and walked around the row of pews to join him, sitting down by his side.

"What? How so?" replied the priest, facing her.

"Look," she began, "on top of everything else that's happened, yesterday Gerry finally called me, full of accusations—that the boys running away is my fault. Then he tells me he wants a separation. He's in a big hurry all of a sudden. I think he has someone else. Not that I didn't feel it was coming. I'm not sorry. My only regret is that he beat me to it.

We're done. So, I would say up until now, my faith hasn't helped me a bit. My whole world is coming apart."

"Perhaps. Or so it only appears. Perhaps there's another plan in store for you, my child. Your world is changing, your eyes opening to another truth."

"What truth? I don't know what you mean."

"Only this— what remains to be understood may change your life from here on, forever."

Núñez studied her face to see what effect his words might have. How much he wanted to tell her what he suspected about her family's identity, something he was sure she needed to know.

"Don't seek answers just now. Just trust. You're at a crossroads, Rachel. The path ahead may be different from the one you've walked. All this change around you must be for a reason. Trust that the boys will be found and returned home safely. Everything else—is but a sign. I feel it from the bottom of my heart. Remember, from the broken shell of an egg, a new being emerges, a new world is born. Your story is being rewritten even as we speak."

Rachel got up and paced before the pews. Núñez watched her, afraid to lead the conversation toward the once-hidden box, toward exposing her family's roots. Yet, one day he knew he must. Before he could think of where to begin, she started.

"What do you make of that old Bible, Father?" she began, as if reading his mind. "It seemed to surface literally out of nowhere. And why was it hidden in my parent's house? Do you know?"

"I think so," he answered.

"Then tell me."

"The answer lies in your family."

"What do you mean, 'my family?' Except for Carmen, they're all gone."

"Your ancestors—here in Estrella. It could be that the answers to all your questions lie in our town cemetery; a place you told me yourself was full of relatives, but people you knew little about. The records of the

Santuario del Renacimiento hold their tales—at least outwardly. I think that would help. Are you interested?"

"Yes, I guess so, but right now?" answered Rachel. Her mind tumbled with the distraction of it all. Too much. Not now. She looked at her watch. Suddenly, she felt a sense of panic. What was she doing here having this conversation? She had planned to spend the morning posting "Missing Children" flyers that the sheriff's office had prepared. Her goal was to drive the length of the High Road all the way to Santa Fe and get them up at every intersection. Carmen promised to help her.

"Honestly, I have so many things I need to do. I am interested, but can we save it for another time?"

"Of course. Whenever you like. Just remember this, we can't always understand what we have been given, or why."

CHAPTER THIRTY

A Medicine Man

THE FIRE BURNED BRIGHTEST at the core of the coals and then sputtered away to pale orange and blue. Whatever was cooking in that big black pot made Juan's stomach growl. It smelled amazing. He could hardly wait for Uncle Tomás to put some of it on his funny tin plate.

Juan hated waiting for dinner. He had never been any place that didn't have a TV before. It sucked. He spent the afternoon counting rocks in the hot shade and watching Poquito chase lizards. Never caught any, but he sure had a lot of fun trying. Just watching his dog play was almost as good as TV. Boy was it hot. He made sure his four-legged buddy had lots of water and kept his sore paw wrapped up. That was Tomás's idea. He seemed to be getting over that coyote bite finally. Still limped though.

Ángel just sulked; annoyed with the way everything turned out. *Why, oh why, did I ask the Ramírez brothers to go back and pick up Juan? Was I nuts*? He took a slow stroll around the Indian's camp, wondering if the old guy had any tobacco. *What a dump. At least the shepherd had a decent size dog—not rat-size like Poco.*

By mid-afternoon, Ángel had managed to teach the spotted sheep-dog to roll over. The dog was smart and willing. After several tries, the animal was covered with dust and shook its coat all over him. Ángel coughed, then sneezed. Staying occupied in the most boring place he'd ever been took every ounce of patience he had. He knew for sure he wouldn't be able to take much more of this damn sheep camp. No way.

"Gave the dog the day off; he's all yours," said Tomás as his boots crunched the grit next to Ángel. He squatted next to the boy.

"Where'd you come from?" Ángel stared at him in astonishment.

"Figured you kids could use some entertainment—no white man's idiot box and all."

The Diné didn't answer further; just ruffled the head of his dog and gazed off into space. The two stayed that way, side by side, both silent for a long, long time. The sun moved farther west into the sky. The wind picked up a notch.

Geez, who is this guy? Ángel asked himself. He never knew anybody who talked less than him. Juan was right, this man *is* weird. Mr. Yazzi said his Uncle Tomás was a medicine man, but Ángel didn't know what that meant exactly, some kind of doctor, he imagined, maybe a sheep doctor.

They stayed silent some more.

"Uncle Tomás?"

"Yeah?"

"Yazzi said you're a medicine man."

"Wouldn't go that far."

Silence again.

"So ... so how's it goin?"

"Good. Good, real good."

They remained seated, looking down the shallow draw towards Little Dry Creek, and watching Juan as he sat beneath a *piñón,* laughing at Poquito. Juan had dust all over his bare feet. He coughed, then picked his nose.

"Dry," said Tomás.

"Huh?"

"The air."

"Oh, oh yeah, yeah, right."

Ángel cleared his throat and flipped his hair back with a snap of his head.

"Uncle Tomás?"

"Yeah?"

'I'm not sure what to do."

"Hmmm. I'm not surprised." Tomás looked at Ángel and pursed his lips, turning his head slightly. "You ever been lost?"

"No." Ángel looked downcast. "Not really."

"Well—seems like you're lost now."

"Nah, I just don't know what to do."

"Same thing—know how that goes."

They sat in silence again.

"Try this. Ever pretended you were somebody you're not?" asked Tomás. "Like maybe an explorer? Or a warrior?"

"Maybe," replied Ángel. "I think so. When I was a kid. " His heart beat faster. Tomás smiled.

"So it's time to pretend again. Then believe."

"Oh. And then what?"

Silence, and the wind kicking up more dust. Juan giggling under the *piñón*.

"Believe, and then you have to act. You got your brother over there to worry about."

"I know."

Tomás turned his head and squinted at Ángel. "Whatever you do now, it's about him. Not you. All about him."

Ángel listened for more but the conversation had ended. Uncle Tomás stood up and whacked the dust off. Then he walked over to his trailer and went inside, the metal door swinging in the breeze.

After dinner that night he gave each boy a thick bedroll and told them to make themselves comfortable, outside near the fire. The night was unusually warm. "Don't you kids go runnin' off anywhere now," he warned. "The ghosts of outlaws and dead Comanche roam all over out there. I kid you not. But you're safe here. " He looked up at the stars and said something in Navajo, sweeping his arms upward as if offering the whole wide world to the sky.

The campfire died down to a flickering glow. Ángel and Juan sat by the coals, staring at the orange flecks. Just for fun, Ángel spit into the core and listened to it hiss. Tomás, smoking his pipe, crouched beside the trailer a few feet away, his dusty dog curled at his feet.

Ángel climbed into his bedroll at last. Juan did the same, then snuggled over as close to his brother as the sleeping bag would allow. Within minutes, he slumped over onto Ángel's chest, snoring softly. This time, Ángel didn't push him away.

CHAPTER THIRTY-ONE

Seeing in the Dark

"AND WHAT MAY I do for you this morning?" Father Núñez asked, as he walked beside Rachel toward the courtyard of the *Santuario*. It was the third day in a row that he'd found her inside the church by nine o'clock on her knees in a pew. The morning sun warmed the cool fall air. It was already Tuesday and nothing had changed. No news. No word of Ángel or Juan.

Deputy Flores had organized a posse to canvas the region, all the way to the Colorado border, hunting for the lost boys. Rachel posted flyers for miles in every direction the day before and all day Sunday too, and was bleary eyed, exhausted from driving.

The priest carried a copy of the Holy Bible in one hand, having just finished morning office hours. Bright sunlight lit the courtyard, and the surrounding hills brindled with fall color, rust orange leaves against deep olive green. To anyone but Rachel it would have been a beautiful October day.

"I just need a place to regroup," she said, turning to Núñez. "I've closed the diner for now. I can't deal with people, problems. I'm running on empty, I swear. I can't work. I can't eat. I can't sleep. I don't know what to do."

"Four days is a long time," he said. "I can only imagine how your heart hurts."

"No, you can't," she answered. "No one can. It's like there's a knife in my chest and I can't pull it out. I keep imagining the worst. But people have been so kind, Padre. I think everybody in town has called out of concern. And on top of the kids gone missing, this thing with Gerry is killing me. We can't work together on anything, not even when our family is at stake. I have so much resentment. I have to let it go or I'll make myself sick."

"Go on ..."

"Last night he called again and said that now he intends to go find our boys himself. All of a sudden, he cares. Said he was going to cover the whole state if he has to, by motorcycle, no less. Him and his "gang," some guy he rides with. It's a joke."

"Why do you think he's finally getting involved now?"

"Oh, I'm sure it's because he's angry that they're gone, more than worried. Makes him look bad. It's finally kicked in. He's pissed that they've run off. I'm really afraid of what he'll do to them if he finds them—it's as if he wants to catch them as soon as possible so he can punish them for running away. How crazy is that? He said something about organizing all his biker buddies."

The padre nodded, shaking his head.

"The state of New Mexico seems very big to me now. The kids could be anywhere. Across the state line, even. Oh hell—excuse me—across the country for all I know." Rachel stopped, awaiting some response from the clergyman, but Núñez had none.

"Listen," she began again in earnest. "Tell me something else. Do you believe in miracles?" Her eyes bored into his. "I've been thinking about what you said once. 'God looks after all of us.' Do you really think the

Lord intervenes? And if I asked the right way—somehow, I could get some help?"

"Of course I do, Rachel, miracles happen all the time."

"But I feel so guilty, unworthy. Maybe I don't deserve a miracle. I hardly ever took the kids to church. I hardly ever went myself. Perhaps this is my punishment. I worked a lot and left them on their own, you know, with their grandfather."

"Now, now. Don't be blaming yourself."

"Well, I can't help it. Do you believe God is watching over my Ángel and my Juan right now?" she asked, hands clasped tight. "Please, tell me that you do."

"Yes, let us say I choose to," Núñez answered. "I believe it with all my heart."

Rachel stopped before the stone fountain where a statue of Our Lady of Guadalupe stood above on a pedestal in quiet repose. The sound of falling water echoed in the courtyard, a soothing babble. She turned away from the carved image.

"Then, please, tell me something to ease *my* heart."

Núñez sat down on a bench in the shade of a linden tree and opened the worn pages of his Bible to a favorite Psalm, Number 121. He began to read aloud:

I lift up mine eyes to the hills—
where does my help come from?
My help cometh from the Lord,
the Maker of Heaven and Earth.

He will not let your foot slip—
He who watches over you will not slumber;
indeed, He who watches over Israel
will neither slumber nor sleep.

The Lord watches over you—
He is your shade at your right hand;

the Sun will not harm you by day,
nor the Moon by night.

The Lord will keep you from all harm—
He will watch over your life;
The Lord will watch over your coming
and going, both now and forever more.

They sat together in silence for a few moments, the sound of sacred verse fading into the fountain's song.

"I like that," she said. "Especially the last part. But what does 'He who watches over Israel' mean? Why just Israel?"

"It's a Biblical way of looking at things, figuratively, and literally, too. Back when I was in seminary we were taught that the Lord watches over the nation of Israel, the Jewish people, dispersed all over the world, but prophesied to return to the Holy Land. Their return paves the way for the return of the Messiah, Jesus, the son of God. Jerusalem is the center of both faiths. Their God is ours too, you know."

Rachel tilted her head. "Yes, I guess so. You know, most of my life I never thought too much about God. Sorry. We believed what we were taught to believe and never questioned anything. But now, suddenly—with no way of knowing whether my boys are alive or dead, here I am, trying to reach Him, asking for His help."

"Does that really seem so odd?" he asked, patting her hand.

She sighed and looked around the courtyard as in search of something. "Yes," she laughed, the first laugh in days. "Very odd. I've never asked before. I don't know how."

"Perhaps you have without realizing. He hears you without you even knowing," Núñez said, a tone of warm assurance in his voice. "*Adonai* is all powerful."

"Who?"

"Oh, just another Hebrew name for God; rolls off the tongue sometimes."

The priest stood up and walked through the courtyard into the recesses of the church. Rachel followed. As he took the final step through the door, the breviary he was carrying slipped from his hand. "Ay! I grow clumsy. Shame on me. The Holy Writ must never touch the ground."

As he bent to pick it up, he glanced at the page fallen open there. Another favorite reading—

Psalm 118. The last line on the open page caught his eye.

And I called out to God from a narrow place and he answered me from an open place. "Perhaps these words are speaking to you, Rachel. While we call out to Him from a place of limited vision, he answers from a realm of all-knowing."

He recited it again, and Rachel smiled for the second time that day. She didn't even know why.

"Or, perhaps that's just where they are," said Núñez, "your Ángel and Juan—in an open place, in plain sight—someplace safe and good." He read the rest of the Psalm. "I wonder," said the priest, "if this isn't somehow the answer you've been looking for."

CHAPTER THIRTY-TWO

A Voice Out of Nowhere

As the rest of that day unfolded, Héctor Ortega took his usual post in the porch rocker and waited, gently rocking to and fro. Time stood still. He hated Wednesdays. Nothing much good on TV. He closed his eyes and felt the late morning breeze stir; heard it rustle the dried leaves on the ground. Mid-October smelled like rain. Good. They needed rain. It had been so dry for months.

As he began to trail off into his midday nap, he was jolted by the abrupt ringing of the phone. Normally he didn't answer Carmen's phone but since the boys ran away he answered it every time. Worry made him move even faster. The phone continued to ring as he groped his way to the kitchen. On the fifth ring he picked up the receiver. He fumbled for the pad and pen on the kitchen table so he could write down a message, hoping Carmen could read his clumsy writing.

"*¿Sí?*"

"Are you *señor* Héctor Ortega?" asked an unfamiliar voice, deep and deliberate.

"*Sí.* Who is this?"

"No matter. But Juan wants you to know he's okay. Ángel, too."

"What? Who is this calling? Juan and Ángel? Where are they? Tell me, *¡por favor!*"

"Can't tell you that, *señor.* But they are with a friend. The boys are safe." A pause, then, "Look for them near Socorro. Soon. Heading west toward Deming—Silver City maybe …"

"Socorro? Deming? Wait—who is this? Give me your name, *señor, ¡por favor! Por favor, dígame su nombre.* Give me your number!" His hands shaking, Héctor reached for the table, feeling for the pad again. "*¡Espere!* Wait—wait! *¡señor!* Please!" A click on the other end of the line ended the call.

"Oh no, no, *por favor.* Please give me more," he implored. He slumped to the table, head in his hands. "*Pero gracias, Santa Madre,*" Héctor whispered. He clasped his hands together. "*Gracias, gracias.* But no—not Silver City, not there—*desierto,* wilderness."

Héctor pushed the numeral zero on the old push-button phone Rachel had bought for him. He stabbed at it repeatedly until a woman's voice answered.

"911. Can you hold please?"

"*Sí, sí.*"

"Thank you."

While the seconds ticked by, Héctor sat impatiently in the darkness of his own world, but felt a light from within—a rising glow, coaxed up by the news that someone, somewhere, knew where his grandsons were. He said they were safe! *Gracias, gracias a la Santa Madre!* And he, Héctor Ortega, was the person that man on the phone chose to tell. But *¿por qué?,* why?

"Sorry, sir. I'm back," said the emergency operator. "Thanks for waiting. How can I help you?"

"*Sí, señora,*" he begged, "connect me with the deputy in Estrella, *pronto, pronto*. Right now! This is Héctor Ortega, 36 Twin Pine Lane, *la casa de los Ortiz. Carmen Ortiz es my familia.*"

"Is there anything I can do, sir? You sound upset. Are you all right?"

"*Si,* I'm fine, *estoy muy bien*. It's my grandsons—I have news of my grandsons!"

"You mean the missing Ortega boys?"

"*¡Sí!*, *¡Sí!*"

"I'll patch you straight through, sir. Hold on, please."

"Estrella Substation—Deputy Hubbard."

"*Señor* Roy? *Es* Héctor, Héctor Ortega."

"Well, howdy Héctor, how ya' doin' this mornin'? What can I do for you?"

"*¡Mis nietos!* My grandsons! I have news! Someone called!"

"You don't say? Hey, that's great! I'll get a hold of Deputy Flores right away, sir. Have him call you right back!"

"*¡Gracias! Gracias.*" Héctor threaded his way back outside to his rocker and sat on the edge of the seat with his hands trembling on his lap, tears of joy welling beneath his wrinkled lids.

* * *

Rachel couldn't do another thing. She hadn't gone back to work since the break-in. She'd canceled all deliveries and hung a "Closed Until Further Notice" sign on the door. She still hadn't paid the glass company who did the repair either. Mornings were spent at the *Santuario,* sitting alone.

Father Núñez found her there around noon and motioned for her to join him. "Walk with me, Rachel. We need to talk. This cannot wait any longer."

Rachel took his arm, following him to his office. "I'm listening," she said, more than curious. "What is it?"

"Well, to begin with—that Hebrew Bible of yours—I took the liberty of copying all the names down for you. It's quite a list; one that merits study someday. Yes indeed, quite a family tree."

"What should I do with it?"

"You must research the names, in time. Learn who they were. They fill in the gap between your ancestor Rebeca Elena Morales Martínez who lived here in the eighteen hundreds, and you and your two boys. Much earlier entries list the many generations before your parents' generation. Names written in Portuguese, Spanish and Judeo-Spanish link families intertwined together. This Bible passed between all their hands, safeguarded from generation to generation. I hope you don't mind if I keep it for a while longer. I'm trying to decipher some of the notes I pointed out in Rosa's dining room. Oh—and the language I didn't recognize—Dutch, of all things. Look, let me show you. Come, sit down, over here."

They stopped at a bench at the edge of the church parking lot and Núñez took a few sheets of folded paper from inside his leather satchel. He unfolded them and laid them out.

"Look," he pointed to the first page. "Here are copies of inscriptions of a few generations of Martínez, on your father's side, going back many years, starting in 1860. Then, earlier, with the family name Morales. I found dates entered from a generation who went by the name of García, long before them. One line mentions the Sequerras, dated 1690. Another lists a certain *Señor* Abravanel. The earliest entry is from a Velásquez, all the way back in 1592. Imagine!

Rachel processed the information as best she could.

"I have reason to believe that Velásquez was the original owner of the text. On the inside flyleaf are pages of more modern-day Martínez entries. Some of those names are very familiar to me, people who helped build northern New Mexico—lawyers, judges, ranchers, merchants, mostly from the Taos or Mora area."

"Are you serious? Rachel asked. "Then, all these people could be my distant relatives? If you're right, I have to have more living family somewhere. A whole lot more," said Rachel, her eyes shining for the first time in days.

"Indeed. I believe you do. Think about it. Our village Estrella—where you were born and grew up, was founded some four hundred years ago by Spanish settlers who came and built farms and ranches along the river, protected by the hills all around. They raised livestock, mostly sheep, corn and hay, and grew orchards and gardens where they found water. Some practiced weaving or embroidery or other fine crafts they brought with them from Spain. They kept precise records. That's usually the case when there's a church and much trade."

"I guess I'm aware of most of that."

"The entry here about a certain Rebeca Morales says she left the Sisterhood and eventually married a rancher who owned the property that the Trujillos own now. I was able to look up even more about her in our church records and deed file. This Rebeca grew up in the local convent, once located east of the church, in what's now a vacant lot. Apparently she was promised to a local governor of some kind in marriage, but the groom abandoned her at the altar in 1790. She did eventually marry another man, a *Señor* Martínez, and lived her whole life in Estrella—had four sons and one daughter. Their births are all recorded in the church records. Generations followed bearing various names—a tree with many branches."

"Go on."

"I looked up Rebeca's birth, marriage and death records in the archives and found some interesting facts. She's the very same Rebeca whose name was carved on the tree in the courtyard of your parents' home. You know the one, I'm sure. I remember seeing the letters there myself. There's actually a note in the records about it. I guess people in love did those kinds of things back then, just as we do now."

"That's kind of charming, isn't it?" said Rachel, smiling at the thought.

"I'm surprised your mother never told you anything about her—but then, your mother passed away when you were so young, barely a teen. Perhaps you were too young to learn her secrets."

"Secrets?"

"I am assumptive. Forgive me. Let us say circumstances."

"Why would she have hidden anything from me? That seems odd. What else do you know about this Rebeca?"

"Well, for one thing, she was never baptized."

"Really?"

"No, and it made me wonder. I took the liberty of checking, Rachel. For some reason, you weren't either. Did you know that?"

"No, I didn't. That is kind of strange, don't you think? Does that mean I'm not really Catholic?"

Núñez didn't answer. Then asked, "What do you think?"

Rachel hesitated, puzzled. "I don't know, Father. You're making me wonder about a lot of things. For one thing, those people buried in the cemetery with the same last names as my parents' families—I've always intended to find out who they were, but since my folks died I've had an aversion to that place. Last time I was there was the day before I got married. Back when I was a kid, I remember going to a lot of funerals. Can't remember whose, though. Not much was left to me, about my parents or my history. All I had for reference was my sister. She seemed to be the keeper of everything we had and she's never said anything about lost family."

"Like I said, my child, perhaps you were too young. Your turn to learn your family story never came, perhaps, due to your parents' tragic death."

"What do you mean, my turn? What story? What are you getting at?"

"Only this—that exposing more of your past may help you to plan the rest of your future. Perhaps your family history holds more secrets than you know; that much you need to understand."

"Perhaps I will, but only with your help." Rachel looked down at her watch. "Uh-oh. I'm late. The boys' grandfather is alone today. I promised I would bring him lunch. Being with him helps me function somehow. He gives me someone to care for. Think I'll pick up some tamales on the way. They won't be as good as mine, but they're still his favorite. Will you join us? Can we continue this discussion in the car?"

"It would be an honor, Rachel. Let me drive you."

CHAPTER THIRTY-THREE

Counting Sheep

ON THEIR SECOND MORNING at the sheep camp, Juan and Ángel woke up to bright skies and the fragrant smell of breakfast cooking over the fire. The bleating of many lambs in the distance filled the air. Both boys had slept soundly, straight through the night. They rolled up their bedrolls, went behind some mesquite bushes to pee and approached the fire where Tomás squatted, cooking.

"What are we going to do today, Uncle Tomás?" asked Juan, scratching his nose.

Tomás looked up and squinted. "I'm workin'. You?"

Ángel rolled his eyes. "Juan's asking if there's anything to do here—anything fun-ish."

"Fun? Hmm. Today we count sheep."

"Oh great."

"After that—up to you."

Ángel frowned, not saying a word. He squatted down on the ground then Tomás passed his plate over with scrambled eggs piled high, along with several rashers of bacon, some thick, hot pan-fried toast slathered in butter and cactus jelly, plus four fat-popping sausages. More sausages hung over the fire on sticks, smelling like heaven.

"Enjoy."

"Hate to tell you, Tomás," said Ángel after a considerable while, wiping jelly off his chin with the back of his hand, "but this place sucks, big time. We don't like it here. You don't even have a TV. And I wish those damn sheep would shut up. We need to get going. Yep, time for us to move on down the road." He took a big bite of his toast, flipped the hair out of his eyes, and chewed, gazing steely-eyed off toward the horizon, in the direction he assumed California might be.

Juan piped up, "I like it better now than yesterday. You cook real good." He burped.

Tomás gazed at Ángel, squinting his eyes even more.

Ángel had no clue what the old man was thinking.

"Okay," said Tomás.

He turned around and offered Ángel a freshly-cut cottonwood staff. Juan received a smaller one.

"Hey! Thanks Uncle Tomás. Just my size!" Juan reached for the stick, greasy butter and gleaming red jelly all over his hands and face. He banged the bottom of his stick against the ground, beaming.

"In case you don't leave—you might need these. Made 'em yesterday. Good for shepherds. Tie your shoes." Tomás turned and walked down the path toward the sound of his flock. The boys tied their sneakers and followed with their new staffs. Juan wiped his hands off on his pants. Poquito trotted behind, not limping much anymore.

Wind gusts made Juan's eyes tear up and Ángel's hair fly. Both boys zipped their jackets tight. They followed the Diné up a well-worn trail and into the junipers and *piñón* growing thick upon the hills south of the valley.

On a hillock near his bleating flock, Tomás stopped and sat down on a fallen log. He pulled out his pipe and lit up, saying nothing. After Tomás had taken several slow puffs, Ángel finally spoke up.

"What are we doing now?"

"Countin' sheep."

"Huh?"

"I sit here, have a smoke and you boys go and count 'em. That's how it works. Now go on. Don't miss any."

"You gotta be kidding," said Ángel. "That's not sheepherding. That sucks. I'm not doing that. No way."

"Suit yourself," said Tomás.

* * *

By the time the two boys returned to camp with Poquito—the dog now snoozing inside Juan's jacket—it was nearly two o'clock. Juan had finally stopped jabbering about the sheep, how many they were, and how dirty they were and how bad they smelled. He yawned, grabbed a bedroll, and lay down next to the campfire to nap. Sleep came quickly.

Ángel paced, kicked stones, and threw sticks until he couldn't stand it anymore.

"Hey, mister," said Ángel, approaching Tomás, who reclined nearby, hands behind his head. "I hate it here. Could you take us to the bus station; we need to get somewhere else."

"Maybe. Sounds like a good idea."

"I want to get out of here," said Ángel. "Now! We can't stay here anymore."

"Don't be in such a hurry. Why you so sure *there* is better than here?"

"Oh heck, well, I don't know. It just is."

"And where is *there?"*

"Not sure. California maybe?"

"What about him? What does he think?"

"I don't know."

"Okay. When you find out, let me know. Then we'll talk."

CHAPTER THIRTY-FOUR

Truth Be Told

FATHER NÚÑEZ DOWN-SHIFTED HIS old Honda to take the corner without swerving. The thought of freshly made tamales suddenly seemed very inviting. He was hungry.

"What will you do after the boys return?" he asked Rachel. He resumed their earlier conversation on a new tack, trying to stay positive.

"I really don't know. After my lease expires, there's really nothing to keep me here anymore. Nothing but my past. Gerry and I are through. But I hate to think about leaving. I love Estrella."

"Personally, I would hate to see you go."

"Well, I don't want to," said Rachel. "This place has been my home my whole life. Five generations at least lived in that old house. And you know—I feel like I betrayed a promise to safeguard it. I feel awful, even though I know it's not my fault. It didn't merit historic preservation; I even tried that. No one would listen to me on that call, seems like there are hundreds of old houses like ours. No one stands a chance when new roads are a necessity. But you've been here a long time yourself, Father. Tell me, did you know my parents at all?"

"Well, yes and no," he answered. "I moved to this parish shortly before their accident. I do remember reading the obituary. You and your sister were left to keep the house, on your own as I recall. Why didn't you go live with your grandparents back then? It seems odd to me that you girls would stay on alone."

"Oh, my mother's mother was living in a seniors' home by then; my grandfather had suffered a heart attack in his fifties and passed away. All I remember about them from when I was very little was how kind they were and old-fashioned in a way. They had a lot of strange customs I never understood, odd phrases too. Our father's parents lived more than six hours from here in the southern part of the state and neither one of us wanted to leave Estrella to stay with them. They were in their late seventies by then anyway."

"I see."

"In the end, Carmen and I insisted on staying here. The state appointed a guardian for us, my high school teacher, Sister Benitez. She needed a place to live and was such a wonderful person. It worked out for everyone. She still lives in Estrella; actually gave me away when Gerry and I got married."

"Ah yes, I know of her. Your sister Carmen must have been very brave to help raise you the way she did. How much older is she than you?"

"Five years. But it might as well have been twenty. She and I lived in our own worlds as kids, in spite of our closeness later on."

"And didn't you have some elderly relatives elsewhere, closer to Farmington?

"Yes, my mom's two older sisters—though I haven't seen either of them since the funeral and that horrible time afterwards," Rachel said. "They didn't drive, being so old. I had kind of hoped they would come to my wedding, but they didn't. They never replied to the invitation. Somehow the world I knew growing up just vanished overnight. I kind of moved on."

"Indeed. Well, it would be a shame to leave here, nonetheless. You have deep roots, I can assure you of that. I believe your family may have descended from the very first settlers. What a legacy—a founding family."

"Why would it matter now?"

"Well, there's more about your ancestor Rebeca—the one whose first marriage ended at the altar—that I think you should know. The notes we have on record at the church about the wedding were penned in 1814 by a *Fray* Adolfo Augustino, the parish priest at the time, who failed to pronounce the marriage that strange day, earlier in May 1793, for reasons we still don't understand. The whole thing was highly unusual. Perhaps he was unsettled in his mind."

"What do you think was the problem?" asked Rachel.

"One can only surmise; performing a sacrament he did not agree with or an objection by the family, perhaps? In any case, it appears that Rebeca did eventually marry a *señor* Martínez fellow, another Spaniard, later on. The notes say "*Cristiano Nuevo*." A new Christian. He was a Jew."

"Really?"

"Really. Then there's a paragraph about Rebeca Martínez's burial in 1866, and here is where it gets interesting: Following the date of her death, there was a question on how to inter the poor woman. You see, it turns out she wasn't really a Catholic at all."

"That's impossible. She was raised in a convent. Come on. What are you saying? If she wasn't a Catholic, then exactly what in the world was she?"

CHAPTER THIRTY-FIVE

Revelation

FATHER NÚÑEZ PULLED HIS Honda over to the side of the road and parked. The tamale shop wasn't much more than a storefront attached to a long trailer from which the fragrant smells of chili peppers, corn meal and seasoned, shredded pork, beef and chicken wafted into the air. Inside, two women soaked cornhusks and steamed the meat, filling the delicate tamales for enthusiastic customers. The cooked results were offered fresh or frozen from deep inside a cooler with a choice of green or red roasted chili sauce.

"Wait, Father," said Rachel as she got out from the car to get in line. "Just hold that last thought. I'll be right back."

At least three people preceded her, not bad for an early lunch hour. Rachel studied the menu, not that she didn't know it by heart.

"I'll take six pork and two shredded chicken, please," she said to the familiar face behind the counter. Her boys loved these tamales too.

"Almost as good as yours, Mom," her darling Ángel used to say. God how she missed him— her willful son, her wild child, her difficult Ángel. He loved the pork-filled tamales, but she always preferred the ones with chicken herself, ever since—well, ever since she could remember. She'd never even tasted the pork ones. After all, her mother never made them when she was growing up. Why was that, she wondered? The reality of that observance suddenly took on a new light. Why indeed?

Rachel ordered some green chili sauce and a quart of rice to go. Returning to the car, she set the steaming bag on the floor of the back seat, then took her place next to Núñez.

"OK. Please go on," said Rachel. "You were talking about Rebeca. We're not going anywhere until you make this whole thing clear to me. You said she was raised in a convent—so how could she not be Catholic, even if she wasn't baptized?"

"That's a good question, my dear. The tale of Rebeca Morales Martínez is one that fires the imagination. Evidently, her father had good reason for putting her there. It appears that his wife, the child's mother, died when she was only a tot. I discovered that the old horse stable behind the back of our own *Santuario del Renacimiento* was originally a small classroom, part of the convent in fact, and exists because of her. Church records indicate her father may have paid to build it as compensation for the Sisters' good care. I think it's possible her marriage was aborted because someone found out who she really was."

"So just who was she?"

"It appears Rebeca's mother was a *Marrano,*" said Núñez, "and probably born into one of those formerly Jewish/New Christian families who fled from Spain to Mexico and came north. Most probably Rebeca's father was too. Perhaps he wanted to protect his daughter after his wife, her mother, died and didn't want their secret to be learned. Who knows? At any rate, she was raised in the convent for protection. Such a thing was not unheard of. I am sure he hoped she would be safe there, even learn how to read and write. And then, later, she was abandoned at the altar for being who she was."

"Oh, if that's true, then it's just awful. I can't imagine such a thing. It wasn't her fault. I mean … what a shame. I can't believe my mother never told me any of this," said Rachel. "Such an amazing story. Maybe she didn't know. Did my grandmother know, or her mother before her? How could such a history be lost?"

"Maybe your mother did know and was planning to tell you when you were old enough. Or, maybe it's something she herself didn't understand or chose not to repeat. Many Catholics then, and even now still, harbor ill feelings toward Jews, especially in Latin countries and communities. And many Spanish Catholics who suspect Jewish background prefer simply to leave it alone. Why risk rocking the boat? It serves no purpose."

"That makes sense, doesn't it? I guess they have a right to protect themselves if they're apprehensive, if they have to live in fear."

"Yes and no. Denial exacts its own toll. As I have gotten to know the good people of northern New Mexico, I've learned that having Jewish ancestry was hidden for good reason. Many have seen or experienced the very same kind of anti-Semitism that lay behind the Inquisition centuries ago. Maybe not as violent, but discrimination, nonetheless. The inheritance of fear persists; the Church has not softened its stance very much. And so they go on—aware, but not making any changes, living in a kind of guarded but acknowledged and accepted deception. Privacy is crucial. That alone is a burden in my view."

Rachel unrolled the window on her side. She took a deep breath, shaking her head.

Núñez continued, "In my career as a prelate, I have learned there are those who, once made aware of unsettling facts about their ancestry, willfully choose to ignore them. Heritage is not identity after all. But it's all in how you look at it. Secrecy, in any case, was something which, for hundreds of years, was essential to survival for all *conversos*, as they prefer to be called now. Just for example, when a *converso* pair married, they often wed in secret following Jewish rituals, the night before the Catholic nuptials. Then, they would marry at the church the next day. Same thing with honoring the dead, or funerals—they conducted

Jewish rituals followed by a Catholic service. Sitting the seven days of mourning that Judaism requires was mostly impossible. But inviting people to visit and gather together for at least one night seemed safe, that's more than common."

"Remarkable," said Rachel.

"For most, the old Jewish customs faded over time, leaving only remnants of their original meaning behind—things such as kosher slaughter, avoiding eating pork, covering mirrors when a family member dies, not eating shellfish, keeping the Sabbath from sundown on Friday through Saturday night; even sweeping the dirt in a room to the center, a common habit. Something about not contaminating the threshold."

"Say that again."

"What?

"That part about sweeping the room ..."

A light went on in Rachel's mind as she remembered helping her mother clean house when she was growing up. Sweeping was like a game to her, the pile of debris or dust in the room's center, growing beneath her broom. Just a few days earlier, she had automatically cleaned up the broken glass in her diner, not sweeping it out the door or straight into a dustpan, but to the center, as she had been taught. But why? A glimmer of connection began to stir.

"Go on."

"In the end, those who adhered to the old ways, to their Jewish practices and beliefs, developed a deeply guarded life, a culture of secrecy maintained by many, even up to today. Not until the freer cultural environment of the last twenty years or so, at best, did I ever hear a New Mexican confess to having Jewish ancestry. No one ever talked about it. Yet today, for some, it's a source of pride. A great source. Many are beginning to ask and search their family trees, coming forward. I never thought I'd see it in my lifetime."

Rachel cradled her head in her hands. Then she turned slightly and peered up at him.

"So you're saying members of my family were really secret Jews? Then that means I'm one too." Rachel closed her eyes, trying to envision this new version of herself. She leaned sideways and looked at herself in the rearview mirror, staring at her reflection. "No, it just can't be."

"Oh, yes, it can," said Núñez, a determined look on his face.

"Okay, whatever it means," said Rachel. "Let's go with that for now. But tell me—what was it that so many were willing to risk their lives for and then live a double identity? Being Jewish—it's just another way of looking at the world, right?"

"No, for some, it's far more than that. Much, much more—call it an inheritance, a heritage and a relationship to God, a covenant. You know—'Obey my laws and I'll take care of you.' That, plus a deep sense of community, of connection. And that's another discussion entirely."

"Gosh, now I'm wondering if Carmen knows all this. She could never keep such a thing from me, could she, my own sister? I wonder why we've never spoken about it."

"I couldn't say, my dear. You will have to ask her."

"I will, believe me. If she does know, she's got some explaining to do. I definitely will."

Father Núñez started the engine up again and re-entered the two-lane highway. They headed toward Carmen's house where Grandfather Héctor, giddy with excitement, waited impatiently to tell Rachel the good news.

CHAPTER THIRTY-SIX

A Stranger's Voice

THE PRIEST AND HIS passenger drove on in silence, Núñez guiding the car over the curving road with easy familiarity. This was his community after all, his dominion; the families in these cloistered valleys, his precious flock, and Rachel, just one more among them he wanted to instruct and protect.

Rachel stared out at the sage-covered hills in the distance, stands of ponderosa and pine blanketing the tops of the mountains. Along the road to either side, hand-cobbled coyote fences surrounded pink adobe houses bearing colorful painted doors. Next to some of these, dried strands of deep red chili *ristras* hung. In the distance, clusters of cattle and sheep grazed on stubbled fields. This was northern New Mexico, a richly settled place peopled by the Spanish, the Anglo and by the Indian. All of this was her world too. Seasons came and went in Estrella, snows fell and melted away into spring. Babies took their first breath and the elderly passed away in an unending cycle of life. Nothing really seemed to change. But now, Rachel wondered, if maybe, all this time, she'd only seen a façade; as if the real history and substance of her life, and that of so many others, lay hidden somewhere beneath the quaint village, and behind the Church's weekly Sunday mass and yearly round of religious festivals.

She asked the padre for more.

"So, just for conversation's sake," she started, questioning him again, "If I were to accept this new version of who I am—this revised family history, where do I actually begin?"

"Oh, I think you already have, my dear," he nodded, shifting into third gear. "Trust me on that. Our current discussion is proof enough."

* * *

Ten minutes later they rolled to a stop in front of Carmen's gravel drive and parked under a big cottonwood. Rachel picked up the food and started up the walk. Núñez joined her.

"Don't ask me why," Rachel began, turning to him with a smile that surprised even her. "But at this moment, I believe my children are out there somewhere, alive and well. It's a feeling I can't explain, like the sun shining behind dark clouds. Maybe what we talked about was something I needed to hear right now and I don't even know why. But it has helped." Then, without thinking, she hugged the priest. "Thank you. *So much.*"

Núñez smiled wide. "You're welcome."

Héctor had heard the car coming and was at the front door before they reached it. Rachel stepped back as the door opened abruptly. "Papa—what's up?"

"Rachel, *mija*," Héctor said, stammering in excitement. "We have news! Just a few minutes ago … *un hombre* called! I don't know who. But he knows where the children are. *¡Verdad!* I didn't know how to reach you. The man on the phone said the kids are okay! *¡Mis nietos están bien!*"

"Who called? Who?" she asked, putting the sack of tamales down. She rushed to the phone and picked it up, a futile effort to hear the message herself, as if she even could. "Did you get his name? A number? Tell me, *abuelo,* who was it?"

"I don't know, *mi cariño.* I did not recognize his voice at all. It was a man—he sounded *muy reservado.* All he said was, 'Your grandchildren are safe.' He knew they were *my* grandchildren! He knew my name too. *¿Cómo lo sabía?* How is that? Then he said we could find them if we started at Socorro and went west. I did not understand."

"Oh! Oh my God!" Rachel gasped, tears filling her eyes at the first good news, the first sign that her children were still alive and well. "Oh, I need to call Flores right away! Maybe my boys are on their way home right now!" She grabbed her father-in-law and hugged him so hard he had to gasp.

Deputy Flores had gotten the message earlier when Héctor called 911. He'd headed straight for Carmen's house. Arriving moments after Rachel and the padre, he brought with him a recording device to capture any more calls that might come through Carmen's phone. *How did the unknown caller get her number,* he wondered, *and why Carmen's and not Rachel's cell phone?*

Once he arrived, he tried to draw out Señor Ortega for any further bit of information, but the old man had little more to give. He kept repeating himself. He definitely said the words Socorro, Deming and Silver City. The most important thing, other than the locations, was that the caller knew Héctor's name—asked for him directly. That was huge.

He couldn't be a stranger then, thought Flores. *Classic case—so many kidnappers are friends of the family.*

CHAPTER THIRTY-SEVEN

Heading West

"SHHH," ÁNGEL HISSED AS his little brother stirred and groaned, slung over his big brother's shoulder like a sack of potatoes. "Shut up."

Juan opened his eyes wide and saw the rocky ground disappearing behind them as Ángel snuck down the draw, away from Tomás's sheep camp. The sun had barely begun to light the eastern sky.

"Hey! Put me down!" Juan demanded, hitting his brother on the back with a closed fist. He raised his head, spread his arms and wiggled, kicking hard.

"Quiet! Okay, okay *Pinto*—listen. I'll put you down, but you have to shut up and swear you won't make a sound," Ángel said. He plopped Juan on his feet. "We're going to Disneyland, Juan. Today! I'll carry the dog. Just stay next to me and keep up. Not a peep, get it?"

Juan nodded, tears in his eyes. He needed to pee and was afraid to ask. Within minutes his jeans were stained all the way down the front.

It was so scary out here, early in the morning when it was still dark, in spite of being with his brother and Poquito. He was afraid of the coyotes and the bad guys, even if they were only ghosts. Still, he did his best to match his brother's strides and not complain, although he did yell once when he stubbed his toe.

Within minutes both boys were sweating. They kept up a brisk clip for a quarter of a mile following the dirt road Yazzi had driven in on. Ángel knew the main road was straight ahead—the way they had to go to get onto the highway heading west. He still carried Poquito, clenched tightly in his arms.

"I think we gotta circle around to get on the roadway out of here," said Ángel, stepping over a cattle guard. "We'll hitchhike out of this dump if we have to. Then go get some breakfast at a McDonald's somewhere and head straight to California."

"McDonald's? Really?"

"Yep."

"But I want to go home," Juan said. "When can we go home, Ángel?"

Juan kept close to his brother as they crept alongside a thicket of creosote bushes and scattered mesquite. Ángel kept looking over his shoulder to make sure that Tomás was not coming after them. He didn't see anyone, not a soul.

He stopped short when he spotted a patchwork-gray, old junk of a car parked under a cottonwood in a shady draw. The Dodge sat covered with dust; it blended in so well with the surroundings he almost didn't see it. A chipped and faded image of Kokopelli, bent over his flute, danced on the driver-side door.

"Look at that, Juan," Ángel said, eyes shining as he gazed at the car. "This is our way out of here. Please be unlocked, please, please ..." The driver's door opened easily. He let the dog in onto the cracked and duct-taped seat and grinned in delight. The keys lay before him on a rusted key-ring. The younger boy grunted as he yanked open the passenger-side door. He scrambled onto the front seat and got up on his knees so he could see out. Dust covered his hands.

"You gonna steal it, Ángel? Mama says it's bad to steal," said Juan, his eyes bright with excitement.

"Nah, just borrow it."

"But you can't drive!"

"Sure I can. Ramón showed me how once. You just turn the wheel and push on the gas right there. It's easy. There's the gas pedal, there's the brake, and there's the clutch, see?"

"Um, yeah...."

Ángel stuck the key in the ignition and turned it. The engine coughed and sputtered, then backfired a couple times. Then, with a roar the old Dodge fired up. Ángel scooted the seat as far forward as it would go, then scrunched his butt further down to touch the pedals better. He slammed the clutch down with his left foot and grabbed the stick-thing coming out of the floor with his right hand. He revved the engine. Gears ground as he fiddled with the stick and pumped the clutch. It was in!

"Are you ready to see Mickey Mouse, Juan?" Ángel shot Juan a maniacal grin.

"I guess, if you are."

The car lurched backwards.

"Hey!"

"Oops, sorry."

Ángel fiddled with the gearshift some more. Juan slapped his hands over his ears to shut out the loud grinding noises. Finally, Ángel forced the car into second gear. With a screaming roar from the over-extended engine, Tomás Begay's car came alive and sprang forward, spitting gravel and raising a cloud of dust behind them. It rumbled up the draw like a prehistoric animal come to life and on to the dirt road. The boys headed out with Ángel at the wheel, determined to drive all the way to Disneyland if they could.

* * *

Things weren't looking very good in Estrella. The whole town seemed paralyzed; Rachel's plight on everyone's lips. Gerry had come and gone, determined to succeed where the state patrol had not.

It had been five long days since Ángel and little Juan first jumped into the black Camaro owned by the Ramírez brothers. José Flores had been in law enforcement long enough to know the "forty-eight hour rule"—and the more time passed beyond that, the less chance of a happy outcome in cases involving missing children. It would just about kill him if Rachel never got her boys back. Yet, old man Ortega, their grandpa, had been called by someone who said the boys were safe. What was that all about? They had no way of knowing if the caller wasn't a prank. And why Héctor?

By Wednesday, Flores had finally received the FBI report from Albuquerque. Nothing much more to go on. Extensive copter searches of the area where the boys were last seen hadn't spotted a darn thing. Earlier, the county sheriff's department brought over a team of tracking dogs to determine the exact spot where the Ramírez brothers had shoved the kids out of the car. The eager hounds followed the boys' trail for two miles along the roadside. Then the scent led off into the brush for a ways, a strange wandering path, and ended at the roadside.

Since the trail led back to the road and disappeared, Flores deducted they were most likely picked up by someone in a vehicle. The fairly-fresh coyote corpse alongside the road made him wonder too. Road kill? Maybe that was why the driver of the vehicle stopped in the middle of nowhere? Or were the kids hitchhiking?

This was no planned abduction, just a chance encounter, obviously. But whoever picked them up was sure taking a long time to report it. Maybe a trucker, or some local who was leery of the law, or even, someone with bad intentions.

Rachel mentioned that Ángel liked California, always talked about going. The kid might have concocted some wild plan to get there. Flores held firmly to hope. He had pulled every string he knew of, calling trucking companies from Albuquerque to LA, and racked his brains for more.

When the Ramírez kids were questioned by Carruthers in Santa Fe, they finally admitted ditching the boys on County Road 344, between Cedar Grove and Golden, just east of Albuquerque. Their story checked out. A local 'Stop N' Go' confirmed selling beer to them not far from there. The lockup at Santa Fe held the Ramírez brothers on charges of battery, child abduction, and theft—plus breaking and entering Rachel's diner. They were in serious trouble. And all for what? Just dumb kids.

At first, Flores wondered about Gerry as the kidnapper—estranged husband and all. It wouldn't be the first case of abduction by a parent. He never let on to Rachel that he suspected her husband, but it did come to mind. After they surmised that the pick-up of the boys on CR 344 had to be a chance encounter however, Gerry was no longer a suspect. Besides, in Flores' opinion, the guy wasn't smart enough to kidnap his own boys. He didn't seem to want them in the first place. What a deadbeat. How in the world could Rachel have ever married him?

CHAPTER THIRTY-EIGHT

On Their Trail

FLORES RECLINED AT HIS desk with his boots propped up on its edge. Three in the afternoon on Thursday and the official search had hit a wall. Except for the call the day before, no fresh contacts, no sign. Nothing. The state patrol in the southwestern corner of the state, especially around Silver City, had been notified to be on alert. Other than that, there wasn't much more he could do. He reached into his pocket for a handkerchief to wipe his forehead. How could it be this hot in October?

Rachel sat, slouched in the chair by the window with her hands gripping the vinyl arms, eyes closed. The fan in the ceiling clicked its weary rounds. Flores had been waiting almost an hour for Sergeant Carruthers to call back; something about a sighting that morning of two runaways spotted in Denver.

Father Núñez paced back and forth between the vending machine and Deputy Hubbard's desk, his hands clasped behind him, deep in thought. The fan clicked on, like a metronome, counting empty time: tick tick tick … relentless. Rachel sighed.

Father Núñez cleared his throat. "Well, my friends, I hope we have good news soon, but I cannot wait here any longer. I really must get back. Vespers, you know."

Rachel jerked out of her stupor. "What? Oh, well—of course. Thank you so much, Padre, for your time and all your kind words and …" She looked up at him with appreciation in her eyes. "And the talk we had today. I hope you're right—about everything."

They hugged goodbye and Núñez left, wishing the deputy Godspeed. Rachel and Flores sat in silence.

"Deputy Flores?"

"Yes? Rachel, you don't need to call me that anymore. Call me José, at least when no one else is around."

"I'd be glad to. OK then, José. Can we talk?"

"I'm listening. Go ahead."

"I don't know where to start exactly …"

"The beginning works for me. Or the middle." He grinned, eyes full of intent.

Rachel laughed. He always made her smile. Just being around him made her feel warm inside and secure, as if none of the chaos in her life existed. She could barely stand to be without him lately, but didn't dare let him know.

"Well … ever since you found that box in my house—and we had dinner at your mother's—I realized I never had a clue about the truth of my own family's history. I still don't know enough to fully understand what it all means. But, after some of the things Father Núñez told me this morning, I think *you* do."

"Me? What did he tell you?" Flores asked, surprised by the reproachful look in her eyes. He had grown used to looking into Rachel's eyes, dark and usually soft in expression, sad, beautiful in their almond-shaped symmetry—framed by the longest lashes he had ever seen in his life. Now those beautiful eyes held him, like they always did, but this time, with an attraction he couldn't resist. He felt powerless.

"This sounds big; serious, anyway," he resisted. "Can we talk about it later? I'm actually kind of busy at the moment."

"Oh. Okay. It can wait." Rachel pulled out her cell phone to check her messages, then smiled. "I'm heading out then. Talk later."

Flores watched her go, reluctant and relieved. With every passing hour, he realized he was having more and more trouble keeping his personal and professional life separate. Rachel mattered a great deal to him now, no matter how much he tried to think otherwise. He pushed his chair away from the desk and tipped it back.

There's no way in hell I'm about to turn this situation into just another weekly report. No way. Whether those kids are runaways or kidnapped or what, I've got to find them. Don't know why, but they mean something to me. Her too—her life, her future. Maybe it's our future. Not sure. I've just got to keep it together while we search and somehow, and keep my distance too. Damn. It's starting to seem impossible.

Thinking about her brown eyes and wistful smile, Flores got up to make some coffee and stopped. Everything about Rachel made his head swim.

CHAPTER THIRTY-NINE

An Intuition

FRANK YAZZI SAT ON a lawn chair on his back porch, lost in thought. He studied the early morning sky, lit a cigarette. He couldn't put his finger on what was wrong. But he had a feeling that just wouldn't go away; things weren't going well. He wasn't so sure anymore he had done the right thing—taking the boys out to Uncle Tomás's trailer like that. Working on a hunch, he had asked the older man to try and gain their trust, then in a few days, get them on a bus headed home. It all seemed so logical, so easy, at the time.

Now, something gnawed at him from deep inside. The ancestors were restless. No cell phone coverage at the camp, or he would call. He got up, scrawled a note for Della and stuck it on the fridge, grabbed some water, and hopped in the truck. She would not be happy when she came home for dinner and found him gone. Too late for sorry. He had to go.

He peeled out onto the highway and hit seventy miles an hour as fast as his truck would respond. He headed southwest, wondering how he had gotten himself into this mess in the first place. That stupid coyote.

* * *

"What took you so long?" asked Tomás, squatting beside a low scrub oak. He didn't seem a bit surprised to see his nephew heading up the hill towards him on foot. Yazzi, slightly winded, knelt down next to his uncle while the heated truck steamed below in its tracks. The mid-day sun beat hard on Tomás's shoulders as he smoked his pipe, watching the clouds drift, keeping an eye on the many sheep gathered below.

"So you were expecting me?" asked Yazzi.

"Figured you'd get my smoke signals."

Yazzi laughed. "Yeah, well—next time just call. Where are they?"

"Gone. Damn kids stole my Dodge."

"No way!"

"Way."

"Oh … hell, Uncle Tomás, now I've got to go find them," Yazzi said, yanking off his ball cap and rubbing his forehead.

"You're right. 'Cause I sure won't."

"You know, I figured I would just leave the kids like I said, let you work on the older one some, then you'd drop them off near the bus stop in Deming like we planned. What went wrong? Man … this whole thing is my fault."

"Yep."

"How many miles you got on that old hunk a' junk?"

"99,389"

"Don't kid with me," Yazzi said, offering Tomás a hand as he stood up.

"Who's kidding?"

"I'm going to find those kids. That's all there is to it. When did they leave camp?"

"This morning. 6:48 I'd say, by the sun."

"Thanks a lot. Never mind, I'll find them."

"Thank Coyote, not me, nephew."

Yazzi climbed back into his pickup and headed out.

The old shepherd smiled and grunted. Squinting up at the sky, he shook his head slowly and chuckled. He knocked out his pipe on a rock and shouted, "Heya, oh—come on, Shelter boy. Let's go." The dog would know there was work to do. The flock had started moving towards the south ridge. Tomás turned down the hill toward his trailer, his steps deliberate, chanting.

Frank Yazzi drove out the way he came in. When he got to the highway, it was easy enough to see which direction they went. Dusty tire tracks along the edge of the road faded into the west. The pavement wouldn't give him any more clues from there on, but the convenience stores along the way might. He planned to stop in every one of them if necessary. But what exactly would he do when he caught up with those two rascals, if he finally did?

CHAPTER FORTY

In Time All Things

"STILL BUSY?" RACHEL INQUIRED, standing squarely before Flores' desk, eyes hopeful. She hadn't been gone but an hour.

Unable to stall further, Flores suggested that he and Rachel take a walk. No sense putting her off, or continuing this kind of a conversation with another officer within earshot. "Shall we step outside?" he asked.

"Glad to," Rachel said. A short walk might give her enough time to say what she wanted to and get some questions answered. Straight answers, once and for all. She decided to wade in gently, not pressure him at all. He must have had his reasons, not to tell her what he knew. They headed out the station door and went north, along the road.

"First of all, I want you to know how much I appreciate your help in all this," Rachel began. "Especially after that last phone call from Gerry when he got ugly and I blew up like I did. Sorry about that. You know, he actually said I would pay for it if the police didn't find his sons. Some threat. But he frightened me. It's like he's obsessed or something. He never cared this much before. I don't get it."

"Oh, he cares all right," Flores answered. "About himself. Carruthers down in Santa Fe had to listen to your husband bitch and moan about what a poor job we're doing. He showed up there and demanded a report. The Sergeant shot back and accused him of neglect. I think he got scared. Anyway, the FBI is in charge now. This search is mostly in their hands."

"Does that mean your part is done?" Rachel struggled to keep up with Flores' longer stride.

"Not exactly. We work together. Keep them informed. We're all doing the best we can, trust me. We tried to tell your husband that, but he didn't want to hear it. Sorry to say, but it appears Gerry Ortega is all Gerry cares about."

"I know."

"He doesn't strike me as the dangerous sort though, a lot more bluster than harm. Yet a heavy drinker can do almost anything if they're deep enough in the bottle, so be careful. If you see him—get out of the way."

"I will. Thanks. But look," she said, "there's something else. Something bigger than me, something that has nothing to do with my kids being lost, or kidnapped, God forbid, or having run away. Or maybe it does—I'm not sure."

She stuck her hands deep into her jacket pockets and lengthened her step. "What I do know is I can't function very well. I'm sick with worry and can't make any sense out of anything at all. A few months ago I had a life—not a great life maybe, but good enough, or so I thought— a husband, a home, two kids I adored, and a future. Now I have nothing, like it's all evaporated into thin air. Nothing left but grief, pain, and an old box full of relics that's a mystery to me, but apparently not to you. So let's go back to that—the old box." She stared at him, eyes glistening.

"Oh, wait—one more thing. Thanks to Father Núñez, as of this morning," she added, "now I also have a new slant on where my family came from. And I think you know way more about it than I do, too. Am I right?"

Rachel's lashes grew wet as tears welled up once more in her eyes. Frustration and a burning need to find the answer to at least one question forced her to break down again, much to her despair. "Sorry," she said, dabbing with a tissue. "I'm losing it again."

Flores slowed, met her eyes for an instant, then looked away again, shaking his head.

"What?" she asked.

"Just ... you. I mean, me ... it's so hard to stay objective here. I hate to see a woman cry, but more than that. You seem to have become part of my life, in spite of my best intentions."

"I have?"

"Yes, you have."

"I know what you mean. I feel that way too." She took her hand out of her left jacket pocket and slipped her arm through his.

It wasn't what she expected him to say, but she knew exactly what he meant. Next to Juan and Ángel, he was all she could think of lately. His words felt to her like a kiss, the first truly loving thoughts she had heard from a man in a long, long time. "Then I know you'll be honest with me. If it's easier, start by telling me about your life. Who are you really?" Her voice trembled, resigned but resolute.

"Rachel," he began, "my story shouldn't matter to you now, who I am, how I live."

"Not true. It does matter. Please."

"Oh, all right then," he relinquished. "My name is José Manuel Flores, son of Rosa and Ignacio Flores. Born in Roswell, New Mexico, Spanish Catholic by birth, and a devout Christian, once," he said, his face impassive.

"OK. Got that."

"And I'm also a Jew and proud of it. Yes, I am Jewish by inheritance; okay, maybe lineage and now, by choice. Those are the facts. And from the looks of things, I'm guessing you might be, too."

"So I was right! You knew. When did you learn it about yourself? And when did you change your religion?"

"Well—I grew up as a teen in Albuquerque. We moved up there when I was just a kid. My parents, me and my sister. My mom cleaned houses mostly, did ironing. You may have noticed her house is spotless. Old habits die hard. My father drove a truck until he died back in '94. He worked seven days a week, minded his own business. My mother retired in Estrella a few years ago, doting on her undeserving son." He winked at Rachel and pulled her closer.

"We kids were raised mostly by my dad's mom, Grandma Graciela, since Rosa worked long hours. Grandma Gracie we called her—tough, but she loved us to death. She could make the best ice cream float you ever tasted on a hot day. She had some interesting little habits I always took for granted though; habits my own mother had too, and brought with her here to Estrella. "

"Really."

"Five or six years ago I discovered my grandmother wasn't the only one who practiced them. A few of our neighbors in Albuquerque did too. But Gracie never talked about it. Never let on that our ways were different from anyone else's, and we never asked why."

"Different ways—like what?" Rachel urged.

"Oh, various things, like not eating pork, for instance, or keeping the Sabbath on Saturdays. Or lighting candles on Friday nights. My mother used to light *luminarias* too, nine days before Christmas. Sometimes, she lit nine candles on a special *piñata* during *La Posada* in the month of December. Around Easter time, we ate only unleavened bread—tortillas mostly. I paid it all no mind."

"Why not?"

"We did what we did because that was the way things were always done, plain and simple. The rest of the time, we went to mass like everyone else. We attended Saint Mary's every Sunday. No questions asked. I grew up worshipping Jesus and thought I always would."

"And then?" Rachel had a feeling she knew where he was going. Somehow, they had a common past. Why did it all seem like déjà vu to her? Had she seen such things before as a child and just forgotten them? How was it she felt like she knew what José was going to say before he said it?

"When I went to law enforcement school back in '91, I met my first real *converso*," Flores continued, "Daniel Gonzáles. A regular guy. One of us. But you would have never known he was Jewish without asking him. As if one could tell. He was an instructor at the Academy."

Flores paused, thinking. "A few years earlier, he'd heard about a rabbi in El Paso who offered anyone who wanted to reclaim their family's Jewish past to come and learn the about the ways of their ancestors. For those who wanted to convert, he helped them take that step, too. It's kind of complicated. They're still coming, though, by the dozens, eager to learn. Estimates are that descendants of the original *converso* settlers in the Southwest number in the many, many thousands. So trust me, I'm not the only one."

They passed a warehouse on their left and the road opened up before them with broad fields on either side. Rachel wished they could just keep on walking, out of the nightmare, and into a different life—together.

"The El Paso congregation welcomes new Hispanic brothers and sisters with open arms," Flores continued. "The awakened worshippers call themselves *anusim*—children of the forced ones— those who had been forced by the Inquisition to become Catholics against their will, way back when. Gonzáles went to services, studied, and eventually took the final step."

"Which was?"

"To convert to and actually practice Judaism, follow its customs, celebrate Jewish holidays, and especially, God's commandments. It's not really a conversion like a Christian baptism or anything; they call it 'a return.' Some go that route, some don't. Most believe they don't have to, that they're already Jews. Anyway, I liked what the guy had to say. Liked it a lot. His story hit home for me, as if this was what I was meant to do all along."

Rachel took in every word. Absentmindedly, she leaned her head against his shoulder.

"He was living a new life, one full of meaning for him. He explained that the rituals of Judaism were ways of making every day holy and every moment sacred. That they stood for something much deeper, and, like you, he started to ask more questions until he got the answers. After meeting him, there was no turning back."

"And then?

"And then it all started to click. Know what I mean? I began to meet others like myself. We're a community that shares a belief, common traditions, and celebrates together when and where we can."

As they approached a bus stop along the edge of the road, Flores guided Rachel to the wooden bench. She sat down.

"Don't get me wrong. I loved being Catholic, or thought I did. But I was drawn to the past. It reinterpreted the present for me. Judaism needs no translation, no middleman—just me and Him and the Torah, the first five books of the Bible. Its book of laws is loaded with useful guidelines for everyday living, for caring for one another. That made perfect sense. According to that book, our primary job, each and every day, is to sanctify the world. How's that for an assignment?"

Rachel smiled. She'd never seen José Flores so animated. What a difference he was from Gerry. She had always liked Flores before, when he came by the Taco Stop as a customer, before all this happened. Now—with each passing day, she felt drawn to him like a thirsty plant to water.

"Look, I can't really explain it. But if there's any magic in all of this for me, it's in the most basic connection. I feel it in the sunrise every morning and in the stars at night. It's less about believing and more about belonging—to a heritage and to each other. That's what I want, that's how I want to live. Connected. And since I've accepted it, I've never been happier in my life."

Flores took a handkerchief from his pocket and wiped his brow with an apologetic glance. He had never told his story to anyone except his ex-wife and she'd accepted none of it. When he did, all hell broke loose. That explanation cost him a marriage and a broken heart. He found it difficult to begin telling it again, even to Rachel. But now that he'd started, he couldn't stop. Rachel was the first person to hear it all, without any apologies or regrets.

"That's some story," she said. "Thanks for sharing. But why didn't you tell me what you thought when you first saw the hidden box?"

"I'm not sure," he said. "You weren't ready."

"Hmm. Maybe you're right. But I am now. Listen," said Rachel. "Carmen leaves for work at five o'clock. I promised to stay with Héctor tonight. Besides, I don't like him being alone under the circumstances. I'm hoping his phone rings again. I don't want to miss another call."

"Absolutely, let's head back," said Flores. "Then I'll drive you over." He slipped his hands around her waist and gave her a hug as they turned around. "Let's go."

CHAPTER FORTY-ONE

Don't Look Back

UPON RETURNING TO THE station, Flores signed out, promising Hubbard he'd be back within the hour. He and Rachel climbed into his car and headed out.

"OK, keep talking. What happened next? After you made the decision?" Rachel asked as Flores' car entered the highway.

"Well, I was married at the time. My wife Marina was a devout Catholic. Took it real hard when I told her my plans. I'll never forget the look on her face. She made me go with her to midnight mass, then to confession, like I was some kind of sinner."

"*Nosotros somos católicos*!" she insisted, "reminding me that our marriage was a sacrament under the Roman Catholic Church. I said I was sorry, but it was too late; it no longer mattered. Eventually, she told me to get out, even though the thought of divorce was very shameful to her. We ended it. I never expected her to understand.

"Look, Rachel," he said, turning to face her. "I don't know why your family never told you the truth. Maybe they never had a chance to, or didn't think it mattered anymore. When I saw that box—I knew. Accepting the faith of our ancestors brought me a special feeling of belonging. It might for you too."

"How many *conversos* do you know, José, people who have found out, or stopped hiding?"

"Way more than I expected. We're all over New Mexico, southern Colorado, Arizona and Texas, too. Over the Mexican border as well, I imagine. For most, it's just a matter of recognition, of acceptance, not really practice. Not in the formal sense. Outwardly, it's hard to tell. After my wife and I split up, I decided to come up here and start over, but still, mind my own business like my family did when I grew up, and just keep learning on my own. My sister in Espanola doesn't care much about it, but that's the way it goes. Some do, some don't."

"I can understand that, I think."

"My mother has joined me in keeping the faith of our ancestors alive, the very best way she can. She was thrilled to finally find out what all those old family traditions she kept really meant—takes a special delight in being observant."

Rachel nodded. "I thought she might be keeping a secret from me. I saw that extra twinkle in her eye."

"Ha! Rosa never could keep a secret worth a damn, but she likes to try." At this, Flores pulled over. He couldn't keep his mind on the road. He let the engine idle while he spoke and rested his right hand on Rachel's knee, then took her hand in his.

"So, once I moved up here, it didn't take very long before the word got around and others came to seek me out. I welcomed them. A rabbi I know in Albuquerque once said, 'We're like embers in cold fires all over New Mexico, starting to glow again.' And you know what? He's right."

Rachel smiled.

"This area was home to our people, my ancestors. You're proof of that. Based on the box and that Bible, you're a part of all this too. I want to give the box back to you today, by the way. It's time you got better acquainted with what's inside."

Rachel took his hand and laced her fingers through his. A warm flush spread through her body. She mulled over his story as if she'd been waiting a lifetime to hear it. Two lifetimes maybe. José had put a new frame around her parents who had faded into such a hazy blur—taken too soon, and helped her to see them in a brand new light. It made her rethink every detail of her life, as well as the house she grew up in—the music, the gatherings, the holidays. She even remembered the lighting of candles too, more than just during *Navidad.* All of it, as if it were yesterday.

"Look again," a voice within her called. "Try to remember."

If José Flores was right, and she was the long-lost daughter of *conversos,* how could she honor them now, the ancestors she never knew?

Rachel looked around, glancing briefly behind her before leaning closer to lay her head on José's shoulder. No one could see them. All she wanted to do was to hold him close and tell him that his story meant more to her than she could say, and that he was beginning to mean more to her every hour, as a friend, a protector, and ...

As she turned her face up towards his, she glanced into the rearview mirror. Rachel sat bolt upright, suppressing a scream. In its reflection was the last person she expected to see at that moment. Her husband, Gerry Ortega, had pulled up behind them in his faded blue Ford truck. The engine revved menacingly, then stopped. Gerry jumped out, slamming the driver's side door behind him and headed toward the patrol car. Rachel's heart skipped a beat.

Flores shifted the gear into park, turned off the ignition and pulled out the key. "Sit tight. I'll handle this." He stepped out, locking the doors with his remote, then walked around to the back of the car.

"Get out bitch!" Gerry shouted, stumbling as he approached the Deputy's vehicle. He grabbed the passenger door handle, attempting to force it open.

"Calm down, Mr. Ortega," said Flores as he confronted him. "How can I help you, sir?"

"You two-bit excuse for a cop!" shouted Gerry. "What are you doing with my wife, goddammit? I oughtta…" He took a wild swing at the Deputy's head.

Flores intercepted the fist with a quick thrust of his right, grabbed Gerry's hand, and wrenched his arm sideways, hard. The man squealed and spun around. With a practiced gesture, quicker than Rachel could follow, Flores had him in cuffs, hands behind his back.

"Calm down, and then you can talk to her. Not before. Now turn around."

"Nobody tells me what to do," hissed Gerry. "Who the hell do you think you are, you …?

"Damn, that hurts. Ow! Okay, okay!"

A loud thump sounded as Flores planted Ortega's body forward onto the patrol car, his face sideways on the hood. Rachel, in the front seat, recoiled, almost afraid to watch. The deputy held Gerry down with one hand and reached for the cell phone on his belt with the other. As he punched in a code, he answered his captive. "I'm very glad you asked, Mr. Ortega. I'll tell you who I am. In case you hadn't noticed, I'm the law around here."

CHAPTER FORTY-TWO

On the Road

YAZZI WASN'T SURE HOW much of a head start the boys had but he knew one thing for sure. They would need food and water—and gas. The older kid had some money. He'd made sure of that. That teen was a survivor— young, all right, but full of street smarts and attitude. He'd manage. But how the little guy was holding up was anybody's guess.

He pulled over alongside Highway 158 near Bayard at a strip mall. It wasn't much to look at, but the first sign of life on a fairly deserted highway dotted with tumbleweeds and sagebrush. He scanned the café, a hardware and lumber supply, a gas station, and a soft-serve Dairy Queen, its menu stripped down to the basics—ice cream, shakes, sodas and hot dogs; no inside seating, just walk-up service. Not much business to be had in the heart of sheep and cattle country out in the middle of nowhere, unless a rancher stopped by, or an occasional tourist.

"You seen two kids around here today?" he asked, stepping forward to the Dairy Queen window.

The girl behind the counter could not have been much more than a teen herself. She wore a hairnet over her jet-black pony tail. Her eyelids flashed metallic silvery-blue.

"*Sí, señor*," she answered.

"Two kids with a little dog? he added.

"*Sí, sí. Claro*."

"Great. Which way did they go when they left?"

"*En esa dirección*," she nodded, turning her head to the south.

"When?"

She looked up at the wall behind at a clock hanging on the wall. "*Once* maybe?" One o'clock? She wasn't too sure. "*¿Doce? No sé* exactly."

Yazzi glanced at his watch. It was almost five. The sun cast long shadows as it started its final descent. In the distance, the Mogollon Range crested like a row of worn purple teeth against a graying azure sky. The afternoon heat would disappear fast once the sun went down. If the boys left the Dairy Queen at noon, they were at least four hours ahead. Wherever they were headed, the kids had to drive thirty-five more miles to Deming, the next place with a bus station and transportation heading west on I-10. Ángel was smart enough to know that he and his brother were sitting ducks in a stolen car. Chances are they might have dumped it and were already on a bus by now.

The Navajo pulled over to think. His head felt like cotton, nothing going in, nothing coming out. He wasn't authorized. He had no warrant, no legal justification. For all he knew, he could become a suspect in a kidnapping investigation. Catching them might present a whole new set of problems. What was he doing? He started his engine, then killed it.

He continued to sit in his truck in the late afternoon heat, watching flat-bottomed clouds in the distance as they billowed into thunderheads. He inhaled slowly. Smelled like rain. Toward the north, the horizon darkened indigo blue, cold and menacing. What if they weren't on a bus but holed up somewhere? This country was no place for two kids to be spending the night, even in a car—especially in a car if there was a flash flood in one of these narrow canyons. No way. Reluctantly, he pulled out his cell phone and retrieved the last call he'd made, hoping for a signal.

* * *

Héctor sat in Carmen's living room watching the afternoon news, or rather, listening to it. First, he tuned in to the local report, then clicked over to the national news, desperate to hear something encouraging. Rachel said she would be back by five o'clock to spend the night there; she didn't want to miss another call if one came.

The old man heard the phone ring. He picked up the receiver on the third trill, hoping it was Rachel checking in.

"*Hola,*" he said, waiting for a familiar voice on the other end. When there was no reply, he asked, "Carmen, *pequeña hija*? Rachel? *¿Eres tú*?"

"*Señor* Ortega? This is Frank Yazzi—remember me? Diné, Alamo Navajo Reservation. We spoke earlier."

At the sound of the deep, throaty voice, Héctor closed his eyes. He gripped the table. A flash of light lit up his mind like an electric shock. He knew that voice. His breath caught. "*Sí, sí*, who are you, *señor*? Where are you ... what do you want?"

"I am your ... friend," Yazzi stammered, unsure exactly what to say. "I'm calling about your grandsons. I need your help to bring them home."

"Me? *¿Qué?* How can I help you? *¡Soy ciego!* I am blind, *señor*. I cannot help you. Where are you calling from?" Héctor knew he had to keep the caller on the line. That's what Flores told him because now Carmen's phone could trace the call.

"*Señor* Ortega, I'm at least three hours from you by car and I'm asking you to get someone to drive you down here. Meet me in the town of Hurley, southeast of Silver City. I know that's a long drive from where you are. But your grandsons may be out here somewhere and we've got to find them. It's urgent. I'll do my best, but I want your help."

Yazzi cleared his throat. He knew it sounded like crazy talk. He didn't care. This was his best plan. "Just promise me one thing. I don't want to get arrested, okay? This isn't my fault. I was just trying to help when I picked them up a few days ago. Now they're in a stolen car somewhere out here on their own, if they didn't board a bus already. But I'm not—authorized. ¿*Comprende?* I need you. Do we have a deal—will you get someone to drive you down here, now?"

"*Sí, sí,* I will come. I will come. *Gracias.*" Héctor reached for a pencil. "Tell me again where to meet you, please, *señor.*"

"I'll be in a tan Toyota pickup in the parking lot of the town center, right off Highway 80, in Carrasco. Look for a flare on the parking lot. You bring whoever you want. We may need help. Where I come from, there's an old saying. *Clas-tah dobahh ta'a yeni zin*—'the desert eats the innocent.' We have to move fast. I'm sorry, Mr. Ortega. I meant no harm."

"Wait, *señor, por favor,* what is your *teléfono,* the number?"

"It's 555-623-6078. Call me when you get here. I'll be waiting."

Héctor wrote the number down. He hung up the phone, stunned, overwhelmed with gratitude. Then he bowed his head and whispered a prayer of thanks to his beloved *Santa Teresa*. She had been listening after all. *Gracias, mi bendita santa, gracias, gracias. Gracias a Dios.* Buoyed with elation, he dialed 911 to get Deputy Flores on the line.

CHAPTER FORTY-THREE

On Their Own

THE THREE HOT DOGS and two pepperoni sticks did a rumba in Ángel's stomach. He wanted a cigarette more than anything, but had been out since Yazzi's woman grabbed them. He didn't dare ask the clerk at the gas station for a pack, in case she carded him. Plus, Juan had puked up his breakfast: the chili-cheese dog, the strawberry Twizzlers and most of the Pepsi. Gross. The car stank so bad. It took a whole bottle of water to clean it up. Now they only had one left. The seat reeked.

"Get me out of these clothes," Juan whined.

"I can't. We don't have any others. Don't worry, they'll dry. We've got to get out of here, Pinto," Ángel answered, pressing his sneaker to the pedal. "It's not that far to California, I bet."

When his brother refused to help, Juan threw a package of Twinkies at him and got up on his knees, screaming." Get me out of these clothes now, Ángel, now! Right now! I don't so feel good. I want to go home. I want out of here. Please. Please! I want Mama and *mi abuelito*! I want to go home. ¡*Mi abuelito*! ¡*Mi abuelito*! ¡*Quiero a mi abuelito*!"

Juan twisted and screamed and pounded his head against the back of the seat. He drooled and hiccupped and cried wet, angry tears. Poquito jumped out of the way and hid under the glove compartment on the floor where he found a half-chewed Twizzler to gnaw on. He watched Juan, bug-eyed and trembling, until things quieted down, then climbed warily back onto the boy's lap.

Juan settled, keeping himself amused by feeding the dog the last cubes of ice from the Pepsi cup. He didn't say another word. Once the ice was gone, he dumped the rest of the watery drink out the window. Then he got drowsy. His head started to nod. As the sun traveled across the sky, Juan dozed while Ángel continued to navigate a curving, two-lane road heading up and west, not weaving all *that* much. Juan finally fell asleep, his chin resting on his chest.

Ángel had no map. After an hour or so of motoring west by the sun, through the little village of Kingston and up over a low pass, they drove unnoticed through the main street of Silver City. Ángel held his breath at every stoplight, hoping no one would notice them.

Juan woke up briefly and pointed out a cop in a menacing-looking patrol car at an intersection, but the patrol car turned right. Back on the open road, Ángel breathed a sigh of relief. No one on their tail. He sensed the highway veered slightly but as long as he had the mountains to his right, he knew he was okay, because then that was north and he was heading west. He figured if they just stayed on the paved road they'd be fine.

Juan slept like a dead man. The dog snored. Then, Ángel spotted a black and white car a couple miles behind in the rearview mirror. It looked official, maybe that same cop from a while ago. Not so good.

He took the first road to his right, skidding off the pavement; a county road, just gravel and baked earth. The rusty Dodge dipped and squeaked and Ángel made a sharp left turn at a fork. Then he crossed a bridge over a ravine, turned right, and headed up the drought-parched valley rim toward the mountains again. He needed some place to hide until that vehicle passed. It had to be the cops. Their luck couldn't hold out forever.

He followed the flat road a few miles; bumpy, rock-strewn and, from the looks of it, rarely traveled. It went straight for awhile, then headed upwards, then forked again. He turned left, going west, traveling slowly for a few miles, rumbling along the bleak terrain, feeling safe, more or less. It was mostly forest around them now, the gray-blue peaks of the mountains rising to their right. Ángel didn't see a single living thing. Not a barn or a ranch house. Not a bird even. Just some barbed-wire fence and a few stunted junipers. Down below, the view was arid and empty— brush country, sand, and weirdly-shaped cacti. The dark peaks loomed closer.

Juan woke up and looked around, coughing. He seemed dazed.

"Where are we? I'm thirsty," he whined as he fidgeted, wiggled and tossed his head.

Ángel opened the bottle of water and watched his brother chug a little until he started to sputter and choke. Some came back up and dribbled onto his chest. Ángel offered him some more, but Juan pushed it away, so he took a swig himself, then gave some to Poquito in a paper cup. He screwed the top back on and stuck the bottle between the seats. Juan slid sideways and down, his head pushed up against the door, and fell back asleep.

For a little brother, Ángel thought, *Juan is doing pretty darn good. Sure is complaining less and, after that last outburst, hardly crying at all. A really good sport.*

"We'll be out of this mess in one more day," Ángel promised, "somewhere where we can get real food—get on a bus and relax. Then we can *both* sleep. When we get to Los Angeles I'll figure out what to do, you'll see. That has to be a good place; we'll find a house that won't get torn down, and we'll find new parents, too. Don't worry, Juan, everything's gonna be A-OK."

Except Ángel was beginning to wonder if he believed it. Things weren't going at all the way he'd hoped. Glancing again at his snoozing sibling, he could barely remember being seven years old. Seemed like all he ever wanted to do was grow up and be out on his own. Sure, Mom was good to him; she was good to everybody, but he and Dad were like pit bulls, always snarling, at the edge of a fight. Ever since Dad starting pushing him around and he learned to defend himself with his fists, he started carrying a small *navaja* in his jeans, just in case. He swore he'd use it the next time his father, or anybody, hit him.

He pulled over at a dip in the road and shifted into neutral without grinding the gears at all, determined to wait until the sun went down and it felt safe to drive again. Dense trees hid the car from sight. He licked his thumb and wiped the dust off the clock in the dash. It read 2:18—oh yeah right; in 1980 maybe. That thing hadn't worked in years.

Peering into the sky, it was maybe five or six in the afternoon. Clouds blotted out the setting sun. Hold on, just a few minutes more. Better that suspicious car was miles away. He turned off the motor, settled down into the seat and stared out the window at nothing, trying to stave off the fear slowly creeping under his skin.

* * *

Ángel woke up, not sure where he was. He shook his head hard, mad at himself for falling asleep. He had no idea how long it had been, but it was pitch dark—so, six-thirty or seven maybe? Juan still slept, and Poquito, too. Ángel stepped on the pedal and then remembered that the other pedal had to be pressed down too when you turn the key. Hard. As he pushed on the clutch, the old engine choked and coughed and started up. He turned the steering wheel with both hands and headed back the way he thought they came.

In the dim light of the old dashboard, Ángel could see that Juan's face looked flushed, his eyes sunken. His skin felt cold and dry. The dog had climbed up on the seat and was standing on the boy's chest, pawing the door and whining. Damn thing probably needed to pee. He did too. Well, they'd both have to wait.

As the first stars appeared between the gathering clouds, Ángel drove and drove, not certain where he was going or which direction. It didn't feel right, though. The road curved up, the going rougher. Where was the highway? Juan slept on and on, as if drugged or something. *Really weird.* Ángel hoped to see a town sooner or later. *Every road leads somewhere, doesn't it?*

He followed the road around some more curves, sensing a steady climb. Finally, the Dodge slowed, began to falter, and chugged to a halt. Ángel swore, pumped the gas pedal and turned the ignition over and over, frantically working the clutch to no avail. Blood buzzed between his ears. *Start! Start!* The car stalled and the motor wheezed and then it wouldn't turn over at all. It had simply run out of fuel. In his hurry, Ángel had remembered to feed himself, his brother, and the dog, but forgot to feed the car. *Gas! An empty tank! Man, am I a dummy or what? Crap!*

It was too late. The old hulk wouldn't move another inch. Besides, in all that time, the hoped-for pavement never did materialize. The road had narrowed, too. Ángel didn't want to admit it, but they were completely lost. The only directions he knew now for sure were up and down, and that wouldn't help. Juan continued to snore. The kid hadn't even awakened to ask for water.

Ángel let the dog out the driver side. It urinated on the front tire for what seemed forever and then jumped back into the car and onto the warm spot on the younger boy's lap. Poquito was understandably fearful since his last foray into the desert.

Ángel relieved himself too. He looked up at the sky. The stars were now covered by dense clouds, patches of gray in the night. A deep rumble of thunder sounded high above. Reaching through the window into the front seat, he shook his brother by the arm. "Hey Juan, you need to pee?" No answer. Ángel nudged him again. "Hey Juan … wake up, Pinto. Wake up!"

Why are the kid's hands so cold? he wondered. Juan's small chest rose and fell with each shallow breath so he knew he wasn't dead, but why was he unable to wake up, and why did he look so white, like some kind of ghost?

Ángel stepped back and zipped his jacket up to his chin. It was cold and blustery and smelled like rain. He shivered. More clouds hovered over the hills to the north, ominous against the inky sky, pale wisps spreading like rivulets of milk in dark water. He got back in the car and tucked the blanket they'd taken with them over his brother, then rolled up the windows so they were open just a crack. Another thunderclap shook the ground as lightning arced high over the Mogollons, lighting up the sharpest peaks, then struck again, filling the sky like wild strobe lights at a carnival. Another clap shook Ángel to the core. For the first time during their misconceived adventure, he wished he'd stayed home and never decided to run, never stolen his Mom's cash, and never jumped into that car, especially with his little brother by his side. He was tired, hungry, and scared out of his wits.

CHAPTER FORTY-FOUR

Confession

FLORES CALLED FOR BACK-UP and arranged to transfer Gerry Ortega to a cell at the Estrella station as soon as possible. Parked at the intersection of Highway 83 and Arriba Road, he wanted to get out of the public eye. Police business wasn't roadside entertainment.

"Hey, we're only a mile or so from Rosa's," he said to Rachel. "Let's hook up with Hubbard over there and get this loser back to headquarters. Then I'll take you over to your sister's."

Gerry whined shamelessly in the back seat as they drove. Judging by his slurred speech, he'd clearly been drinking. "Where you been, Rachel? he slobbered. "I been chasing you all over this damned town. You never answer my calls. You know where those boys are at? I bet you do. They playin' some kind of game or what? I think they're in trouble, man, real trouble. That means we're in trouble too. We got to find 'em."

Rachel didn't answer.

"I'm talking to you, bitch," he shouted, struggling in the cuffs. "Get me out of here. We need to make a plan."

"It looks like you've already made one, Gerry. I have no further business with you."

"Aw, come on. Our boys are gone. How could they go and do that? " Gerry hung his head and cried like a child. "How'd you let that happen? You were always so good at keeping it all together. Now what?" he sputtered.

"Don't come complaining to me," Rachel said. "Where have you been until now? All of a sudden you care? Are you kidding? Like you said to me yesterday on the phone, we're done."

Flores approached Rosa's house and pulled up behind two parked cars. Deputy Hubbard stepped out. He approached Flores' cruiser to help transfer Ortega to his vehicle. The man had passed out cold.

"Where'd you pick up this hound dog?" asked Hubbard, familiar with Gerry's habits. He hooked his hands under Gerry's bent knees.

"You might say he followed me home," grunted Flores, taking Gerry under the arms. "The jerk tried to clip me. Didn't take much to subdue him, the state he's in. Take him in and book him for assaulting an officer, driving under the influence, and disorderly conduct. Lock him up 'til we get back."

Rosa stood at her window watching the scene with interest. She opened the front door and called down. "*¿Qué pasa*?" she asked. "Everything all right?"

"*Sí. Sí*. Everything's okay."

"Let's stop in for a minute," said Flores to Rachel. "Don't want to worry her."

At the door, Flores paused, pressed a kiss to his fingers and touched a narrow silver case mounted on the doorjamb to the right.

Rachel followed, right behind him. The gesture mystified her. What was that? She stared at the silver case screwed to the doorpost. Its shape looked familiar somehow. Why had she not noticed it before? Something jarred her memory. What about the narrow case in the old wooden box? She had looked at it several times by now. It was also silver but badly tarnished and had that strange letter on the front with a small crown at the top. This one shone brightly and had a piece of turquoise set on either end. Before she could ask him about it, Flores' cell phone rang again. He pulled it out.

"Flores here."

He stopped at the threshold, listening.

"What? He called again? He said to do *what*? Where? In a stolen car? I'll be right over, *Señor Ortega*. Don't move. Just stay by the phone if he calls again. Yes, I'll take you there, *pronto*—don't worry. ¡*Gracias*!"

So excited by what she overheard, Rachel sucked in her breath and practically choked in her excitement. "What? Who was it? Oh my God! News, José?"

Flores shook his head and held a finger up, continuing to listen to Héctor who chattered on in Spanish, his voice feverish.

Blood rushed to Rachel's face and her heart bounced within her. She felt as if she was going to faint. Flores put his arm around her, just as her knees started to buckle. Rosa opened the door and took Rachel into her arms. She led her into the parlor where Father Domingo Núñez and a young bearded man were sitting at Rosa's table over a pot of tea. Rachel collapsed on the sofa, finally catching her breath. As she recovered, she fairly bubbled with excitement.

"Oh my God! I think they found them," she said. "The man who called before—he called back. He says he knows where they are. They found my boys! I have to go. I have to be with them ..."

Flores, still at the door, stayed on the line.

"*Sí, sí señor.* I'm coming right away. Listen, take a heavy jacket. It may be cold. And grab some blankets, too. Can you do that? Just take whatever is on your bed. Oh, and any food in the house? Tamales? Pack whatever's left. And water, too."

Flores stepped outside briefly and made another call. Then, returning inside to Rachel and the others, found her sitting in conversation with Israel Romero, one of the younger members of José Flores' small circle of *converso* friends.

Israel's weather-beaten face beamed at Rachel. "Everyone in town has been so worried about you. We didn't know what to do. Thank God for this news. I know José will find Ángel and Juan now."

"Let's hope so," said Rachel, getting up. "I'm going with him."

"Hold on, *señora*" said Flores. "You're not going anywhere. You may not like it, but I'm taking Héctor with me, not you. You'll stay here. We'll be meeting up with law enforcement farther south. I don't know if this isn't some kind of crazy goose chase, or the real deal, or how long we'll be gone, but we're going alone. We won't come back without those kids, though, I promise you."

"But why can't I go?"

"House rules, regulations. That's the way it is. I've contacted the State Patrol in Doña Ana, Grant, and Catron counties and requested air surveillance and ground support. The Gila Wilderness is no picnic. It's tough, even for equipped outdoorsmen. Parents are off-limits." Flores zipped up his jacket and stuffed his cell phone into a pocket.

"We'll hook up with support in Socorro and move west. I may not always have phone contact with you, but will call you if and when I can with *any* news. For now, I'll take you back over to your sister's house where you can wait, just in case that call was a prank, and the boys actually come back on their own."

"Oh please, I have to go with you, José. Please."

"No, you don't." He put his hands on her shoulders as if to anchor her to the spot. Then he guided her to the front door and led her outside. He drew her near and folded her into his arms.

"Look," he said, "it's better this way. Don't argue. You're staying here. Imagine if that call's not for real and the kids come back and you're gone? No way. Besides, Carmen's waiting for you. We'll send someone over to help you out, keep you informed."

In truth, Flores did not know what they would find. National forest land northeast of Silver City was a tough place for anyone to be on their own, thousands of acres of wild terrain. If there wasn't a happy outcome, then he didn't want her to see whatever else it was. There'd be time for that.

"Okay, I understand. Just be careful. As usual, I don't know how to thank you ..." she began.

"Shhh. You don't need to," he said. "Not now. Not ever. I'm not doing this because it's my job, or for you, even. I'm doing it because I was a kid once and I know those boys don't have a clue what they're up against. Or a chance. I'll do whatever it takes to find them. I'll bring your children home in one piece if it's the last thing I do."

"I know you will. I feel like I owe you everything," she said.

"You don't owe me anything. Ever."

Rachel took a deep breath, put her arms around him and lay her head on his chest. "You're so good to me. I couldn't go on without you," she whispered.

Flores held her tightly for a moment and then let go.

"What do I tell the others?" Rachel asked.

"Tell them you have an assignment to stay put. And that I'll be back soon."

"Okay, but one more thing," she added. "Remember, the little guy gets wound up easy, even hysterical sometimes. And Ángel carries a knife. Thinks I don't know. It doesn't take much to get him going. But you're probably aware of all that. Keep them and their grandfather out of harm, please. Héctor is almost completely blind. I can't imagine what you and that man on the phone even want with him."

He smiled. "We'll see. Not to worry. He'll be safe."

She took his hands in hers. "And one more thing before you go—quick. What's this?" She pointed to the case mounted above José's shoulder on the door frame. "This thing you touched on the way in?"

"Oh, that?" It's a way of assuring that the man upstairs protects everyone inside the house, including you and me—an old Jewish custom. My mother was quick to adapt to it. The ancient blessing rolled up inside covers everyone, coming and going. Now, don't worry about a thing, okay? I'll try to stay in touch. And relax. We won't let you down. I'll bring Ángel and Juan with me when I get back. And Poquito, too."

It was all he could do not to kiss her before they went back inside. Every fiber of his being wanted to press those lips, hard, and tell her how much he cared. *No,* he steadied himself, *not yet, not here, not now.* But he'd hold the thought. There'd be plenty of time later—more than enough.

CHAPTER FORTY-FIVE

On the Doorposts of Your Home

RACHEL BADE FLORES GOODBYE at the door. She returned to the living room and Rosa's guests.

"You must rest, *mija,*" Rosa said to Rachel. "Let him do his job. God willing, we'll all celebrate Sabbath dinner together tomorrow night. The *niños* will be back and we'll welcome in the new week with happiness and gratitude."

Rosa hoped her confident reassurance would come true. She was a mother too; she knew how hard this had to be. And she was also a woman who had fallen in love once too, and recognized all the signs of a new romance blossoming. Her son, José, clearly had this Ortega woman on his mind. Lately, she noticed he had been using the after-shave she bought him for his birthday. His eyes danced. It was very clear. But a married woman? *Ayee.* Where would it all lead? She resumed her seat and said a secret prayer that everything unfolding around her would come to good.

* * *

Israel Romero offered to drive Rachel back to her sister's. That's where Flores wanted her to wait. Rachel mused silently as she thought about the turn of events—the phone call to Héctor from the stranger filled her heart with joy. It was all she could do to stay put. Hope swelled inside her until she felt as if she were ready to burst.

Leaning back against the passenger seat of the car, Rachel closed her eyes. The picture of Flores touching the silver case on the door jamb of his mother's house came back into her mind.

"Israel," Rachel began.

"Yes, *señora* Ortega?"

"What do they call that little silver canister on the door exactly—the one that sanctifies a home?"

"It's called a *mezuzah*."

"Do you know what it says inside?"

"Yes, more or less. The words are from the Torah, from a prayer called the *Shema*. Let me think. In short, it says 'God dwells inside the home, as well as outside,'" he answered. "It's real old, a tradition from biblical times I think. The scroll inside has to be handwritten on parchment."

"What's the prayer for?"

"For safekeeping, I guess. I've memorized most of it: 'These commandments I give you today are to be upon your hearts. Impress them upon your children. Talk about them when you sit at home and when you walk along the road, when you lie down and when you get up. Tie them as a symbol upon your hands and bind them on your foreheads. Write them on the doorposts of your houses and on your gates.'"

"Oh my. Write them on the doorposts of your gates ..." she repeated. The words touched her, and his simple explanation even more. She wanted to hear them again, sing them out loud. "That's beautiful," she said, thinking how good it would be to have a home with that message on all of its doors.

"Thanks," she nodded and promised herself if she ever got her kids back, she would teach the prayer to them too. What was she saying? *If* she ever got her kids back? What was she thinking? If? She meant—*when. When! Why did the trip across town have to take so long?*

Rachel stared straight ahead, musing on the puzzle of her life. The pieces were starting to fit together at last. Just the center was missing: her boys, living pieces of her heart, gone, but hopefully, not for long. She had felt the gentle touch of a man she respected, a man who cared for her, and who cared for others more than himself. A man she could love. Most of all, she felt a new understanding of her family and its past, her place in it, and what she had inherited. A new world had begun to unfold.

They continued on to Carmen's in the dark, toward what Rachel knew might prove to be a long and sleepless night, but one she would endure. She loosened her seat belt and looked out into the dark, resisting an old urge to cross herself. Not anymore. Never again. That was the old Rachel. Instead, she thanked the God of Abraham for the encouraging news, and somehow, in the stillness, felt as if He answered her. Nothing tangible, just a feeling. Looking up, the stars shone brighter, as if spinning, giving off sparks.

"Thank you," she said, staring into the sky. "Thank you for watching over them."

As Romero drove, she felt cradled by an unseen hand, as secure as a babe at its mother's breast. She didn't know why, but somehow had the strangest sensation that the car, firmly holding the curves of the smooth, paved road, had defied gravity and instead, was simply floating on air.

* * *

When they arrived at Carmen's, Héctor and Flores were loading up the cruiser in the driveway. The old man had on a quilted nylon jacket and a blanket over one shoulder. In a bag were a large bottle of water and the rest of the tamales wrapped in foil. Flores buckled him into the vehicle and turned to Rachel, hugging her one more time.

"Try to get some sleep, will you? We'll handle it from here."

"OK. Hurry back." Rachel hugged him in return.

Before getting in the car, Flores pulled her close one more time and kissed her on the forehead, softly, with respect and just a touch of longing. "OK, *señora,* that's for you. Just a start."

She kissed him back, on the lips, unashamed to express her love. "And that's for you, my friend. Stay safe."

CHAPTER FORTY-SIX

Amsterdam 1671

A Mezuzah for the New World

AT TWENTY-FOUR, JOAQUIM BEN-DAVID Abravanel had learned his father's craft almost as well as the master himself. He'd assisted the elder silversmith, Isaac Ben-David Abravanel, for so many years in the wax work, the metal casting, and finishing of decorative or sacred silver objects that it was second nature to him now. His sharp young eyes and deft hands had an advantage over his father's dimming vision and arthritic grip. Over the last year, he had been entrusted with some of the most important commissions for Amsterdam's valued patrons.

For Joaquim, each new silver project was akin to falling in love. At first, he might conjure an idea from far away, like seeing a smile from a window on the face of a beautiful girl. But within a week, that idea would grow into a reality he could see and hold, and he'd feel the first version of it in his hands. He'd breathe his very breath into it and make it come alive. From idea to finished piece, the object made of silver filled his dreams. He nurtured it, perfected it, and savored the hours of hammering, chasing, and polishing the object into a reflective thing of beauty.

Silver is magical, he believed. It could grow warm in your palms, glow with each pass of the cloth, and almost come to life itself. And what of gold—so rare and precious—the link to infinity, the precious metal of kings and patriarchs, afire with the color of the sun?

"Indeed," he both bragged and lamented to his friends, "precious metals I have mastered—but in matters of the heart, I am not so skilled."

The time would come soon enough when he alone would add his own initials to the famous stamp that each plate or vessel bore before it left their shop. His father planned to retire one day and hand over production of the many kiddush cups, Torah pointers, menorahs, Passover plates, and other Jewish ritual objects to his beloved son. At least, that was his dream, as he explained it to his only child, of whom he was so proud.

For the many Jews who emigrated from Portugal to Holland in the seventeenth century, life was a paradise compared to what they had left behind. The Catholic Church had not yet touched Amsterdam with its persecution, a city at the heart of the Reformation, nor would it ever. Here, Catholics were reviled and Jews were welcome.

Isaac Ben-David Abravanel had arrived from Lisbon fifteen years earlier, joining hundreds before him who left their homeland to begin anew in a foreign land. The refugees were gratified by their reception in this tolerant country and determined to integrate into Dutch society without forfeiting their faith. Here they could actually live as Jews. But they were quick to adapt and embrace the language and ways of their new hosts.

Master Abravanel rented a shop on the busy *Jodenbrestraat* in the Jewish quarter, a space with two small rooms above, just enough for the aging widower and his son. He wished his wife, Devora, could have survived their escape to be with them now, but that was not to be. She would have loved Amsterdam, despite how cold and rainy it was at times, compared to sunny Lisbon.

The *Joodsie Wijk* or Jewish neighborhood was a vibrant part of life there, densely settled in the center of town. Not only could Jews worship freely in small synagogues, but they could also conduct *cheders,* schools that taught Hebrew and explored Jewish philosophy, history, and metaphysics. Some wealthy patrons were even painted by the great Dutch master, Rembrandt Van Rijn. Among the immigrants were every manner of merchant and craftsmen. All were accepted and treated with tolerance and respect—especially since there were money lenders among them who filled a need for banks and businesses. Others became involved in the stock exchange or mercantile pursuits, or worked for the Dutch West India Companies; merchants and sailors who quickly became a part of Holland's thriving hub of international commerce serving the colonies in the far southern hemisphere and even in New Netherlands, far across the sea.

* * *

"Have you heard the news?" Joaquim's friend Franco asked. "Everyone in the *Joodsie Wijk* is talking about it. The new synagogue, the *Esnoga*, is scheduled to open its doors just in time for Rosh Hashanah. There's still much work to be done, but August 2, 1675, will be a great day in our history. It's said the largest number of Jews to assemble under one roof since the time of King Herod will do so here in Amsterdam and be able to praise God without fear. *Barukh Hashem!*"

"Yes, I know, my father is making the Torah case for the ark," answered Joaquim. "And the *mezuzah* for the front gate, too. He says that even though the building was founded as a Portuguese or *Sefardische* synagogue, its design is modeled after the second temple of Jerusalem. Imagine, once finished, it will be the largest house of worship for Jews in all of Europe, no matter where they come from."

The young men passed by the compound where the synagogue was under construction, enclosed by a wall. Soon a handsome metal gate would be installed as well. The structure was built of masonry and brick, with tall arching windows of many panes, so that by day the interior might be lit with the Creator's own light. But by night, the great hall would be bathed in the glow of chandeliers hung with enough candles to illuminate the space for an enormous congregation to read by. The *heichal* in the center would allow the rabbi's voice to carry equally so that all could hear.

Joaquim labored joyfully over the *mezuzah* his father had been commissioned to create, a sacred vessel with the sacred words rolled inside. It was larger than any they had ever made before. The front and back of the case would have to be soldered together by a seam, burnished to perfection. His elegant design was a metaphor for the Universe of God himself—on the front were two pillars holding up the world, the tree of life spiraling in the center, and a three-pronged crown on the top, symbolizing the dominion of the King of Kings. Joaquim had crafted a much smaller version in wax, then cast it in silver, to show his father the concept. This they planned to show to the Rabbinical Council and the architect for approval. Both his father and the Council agreed it was the most beautiful *mezuzah* they had ever seen, and encouraged Joaquim to begin on the actual piece at once. That was just over a month ago.

To Joaquim, who had watched the public humiliations and killing of *conversos* in Portugal when he was a child, it seemed ironic. Here in a country far away from their place of birth, men who attended universities, practiced law and medicine and served in respected guilds, would finally attend religious services together in public for the very first time; men who had hidden their identities, not only from the Church, but in most cases, even from one another. God had surely devised a remarkable way of keeping His people alive.

* * *

"Have you heard?" Joaquim asked his father, slowly heating his sculpting wax over an open fire. "The Dutch West India Company traders I met at the marketplace yesterday say the future of Holland is in the

New World, in America. Their merchants will fill their coffers by trade with new cities across the sea. They say in New Amsterdam, much commerce thrives, and people of every faith can worship however they like, even Jews. And throughout this new country the trees are always full of fruit—and wild game plentiful. There's even …"

"You're dreaming again, son," interrupted Isaac. "Do not believe such tales."

"But it's true; those traders are rich and prosperous. They say the land is free for the taking."

"What would you do with land?" his father asked, perplexed. "You are a silversmith, my son, are you going to plant candlesticks?"

Joaquim did not laugh.

Isaac adjusted his spectacles and set to work smoothing the edges of the cup he was working on for the rabbi's wife. They had never been farmers, not even back in Portugal.

"I don't know," his son answered, taken aback. "But just to think of it, Father. Imagine!" Joaquim's head was full of dreams these days. But mostly he dreamed of Shulamit Malka, the daughter of Samuel de Loya, owner of the building where they rented their shop. Malka, with her fair hair and blue eyes, filled his head with many things he dared not speak of to his father.

"And there are already Jews living there too, Papa. New Amsterdam is full of them. Some came from Portugal's colonies in Brazil to escape persecution. They are building their own synagogue right in the heart of the city: *Shearith Israel.* 'A remnant of Israel,' a line borrowed from the Book of Jeremiah. I even like the name!"

He pondered that wondrous thought and gazed out the open window, dreaming again. "It's said that services are open to any who wish to attend. And the rabbi is one of us, Portuguese, from Evora, a city not far from Lisbon."

Joaquin knew that the famous synagogue in the New World, opened ten years earlier in New Amsterdam, served a strong Sephardic Jewish community. Several of their neighbors in Holland had emigrated already. At first, the Dutch governor Peter Stuyvesant did not permit

Jews to settle in his new colony, but over time, relented, and let them in, as long as they kept to themselves and only added to the overall prosperity. Joaquim also learned that his father's friend, Captain Peer Vandersteen, captain of the *Breda*, a merchant vessel of the Dutch West Indies Company, told his investors at *Shearith Israel* about the talented young silversmith who could fashion things of silver that were more than worthy of a house of God. Great interest had been expressed in bringing the young man over. But Joaquim did not tell his father that part—he didn't dare.

* * *

Tall-masted ships sailed in and out of the Dutch harbor, importing luxury goods like silk, sugar, and spices for the wealthy *burgermeisters* and their families. Dockworkers loaded thousands of guilders worth of foodstuffs, textiles, carpets, pearls, amber, and ironmongery onto outbound vessels, with special containers for their renowned tulips, in season. Many ships returning from America had furs, hundreds of bales of beaver pelts, and otter skins for hat makers and tailors all across the city. *What kind of country has so many wild animals?* Joaquin wondered.

Ha! A wild one, of course. Sooner or later, I will be on one of those ships and see for myself. Paid passage is mine, if I would only bring my tools and silver ingots to open a workshop. That's what they said. I could start my own life and become a rich man in New Amsterdam. Just how, or when to tell father, is the problem. He has his old heart set on my continuing in his footsteps.

"What brings you to the wharf?" a charming voice interrupted his thoughts. He turned to see the young woman he had long adored, standing before him in the flesh. For several months, the two had been sharing a quiet flirtation, meeting "by accident" here or there, watching one another from afar and waving hello. She had been shopping in the marketplace that morning and held a basket in her arms. Beaming at the good fortune of finding him alone, Malka smiled and waited for his reply.

As modesty required, she wore the typical long skirt and vest of Dutch schoolgirls over a simple blouse with a woven gray cap that barely covered the ash blonde curls peeking out around her face. The ensemble served a proper Jewish girl as well. Her blue eyes danced with happiness.

Joaquim faltered. His face flushed and his tongue seemed to have disappeared down his throat.

"I ... I was just counting ships," he said. "So many, bound for ports around the world ... ah, here, let me carry that for you."

He reached for the basket and brushed her hand, a first touch he would always remember. How many months had he been scheming for a way to merely touch her? And now his fingers burned with the heat of it. Her skin was even softer than he imagined.

"And why would it matter?" she asked, "How many ships there are? And why should you care, Joaquim Abravanel?"

"Because I shall be on one of them someday."

There. He said it, told her. Too late to take it back.

"But please, don't mention it to anyone, I beg you. My father would have none of it."

"Of course not, Joaquim. I would never say a word. You know ... I too dream of sailing away," she said wistfully. "I want to go to the colonies, in the New World."

"You too, to New Amsterdam?" Joaquim couldn't believe his ears. "You—you have thought of this?"

"Yes, but I dare not speak of it. How can a young girl travel alone? My parents have other plans for me I am afraid, though I want none of them."

Joaquim's dark eyes blazed with excitement. "Would you risk traveling with me? I mean, trust me to take care of you? To make sure you're safe? What if I told you I can get passage for us both? Would you find a way to come with me?"

"You can't be serious, Joaquim! Do you mean it? Because yes, I would go with you. Gladly, I would! I dare to say it, but I would follow you blindly. Just tell me when," she answered, taking his hand in hers. "I am ready when you are."

That night Joaquim couldn't sleep. His mind raced with ideas. He couldn't imagine his good fortune. She was ready to join him! But how? The possibility of a new life loomed with a future of unknown adventures, to be shared with the one woman he wanted to make his wife. He recalled the tales a fur trader had told him about the rest of the continent with clean rivers and high mountains and abundant game, of a people who lived off the land and hunted wild beasts with horns. He spoke of gold and the glory of exploration.

Joaquim tossed and turned. He held his pillow in his arms. *Malka, oh Malka!* He would make her his own. If he could not get their parents' blessing now, then they would travel some way together, perhaps feigning to be cousins, and then marry in New Amsterdam later on. He turned to one side. The small silver *mezuzah* lay on the table by his bed, gleaming in the light of the moon slanting through the window.

The wondrous *mezuzah* had brought him so much good fortune already. Never had he felt so inspired as when making it. His father told him that the small model was his to keep. Perhaps to use for his own purposes someday, wherever that would be. Once he arrived and got settled, he would pay back the cost of passage by working hard for the new synagogue. That much he owed them. He would give them all they asked for and more. But that would be only the beginning.

In time, he would take his bride and travel to the lands conquered by the Spanish he had heard so much about. The explorers went in search of the legendary Seven Cities of Gold. Had they found them? If not, and he couldn't settle there, he would seek a place that would fill his heart with beauty, a kind of paradise. He imagined a place where the sun and the stars were equally bright, where a man was perfectly free. Wherever it was, it would be a place where love was all that mattered, and gold and silver glittered in the earth, asking to be found. He would wait to tell his father after services on *Rosh Hashanah* that he was headed for the New World. Whether Father approved of his plans or not, the time had finally come.

CHAPTER FORTY-SEVEN

A Family's Truth

CARMEN CAME HOME FROM work to find her sister fairly alight with happiness.

"Thank God," said Rachel." The search parties are on the way. At least now they know where to look." Carmen hugged Rachel with tears in her eyes. She set about making coffee for what they both assumed would be an all-night vigil.

Israel Romero brought his laptop with him and found a website that broadcast radio traffic from the Grant County sheriff's office. The site was dedicated to Search and Rescue transmissions and screened, but at least they could listen to dispatches and information from the Silver City area police until they received more specific news directly from Flores.

Rachel decided they'd take turns listening and getting some much needed sleep. Unable to relax, she paced the empty living room, thinking over what had happened that day. Finally, she went into the kitchen where Carmen was making sandwiches and took her sister by the hand. "Listen. We need to talk."

"Whoa? What's the big deal? What about? The house again?"

Rachel led her to the back porch, ignoring the evening chill. "No. Not really. It's about everything else. You, me, Mom, Dad—our life, their past, our past, who we are. Plus the old box that was found in the house." She paused. "Let's just start with our family. "

"Wait a minute. What in the world are you talking about? You want to know exactly what about our family right now?"

"Who we are, *mi hermana*. About who our grandparents really were, and theirs before them—about our old house, and a Bible that goes back over five hundred years tracing our history. And why no relatives showed up at my wedding when I married Gerry. Not that I knew any of them very well. But still. Why?"

"Well, that's one question I can answer, so slow down. Let's start there—the wedding. I can't be sure, but I think it's because you married outside the community. Gerry wasn't one of us. No one trusted him."

"The community? What community? The Church? That's the only one I ever knew of."

"I don't know. Something that set us apart. It was just the difference between us and everyone else. A difference I still don't really understand, Rachel, nor do I care to. But why are you asking all this now?"

"Because you seem to know more than I do. And because after what's happened lately, I feel like the entire world has changed, turned upside down. Whatever I was standing on just isn't there anymore. Do you get that?"

"Maybe. Maybe not."

"I feel lost, Carmen, just like Ángel and little Juan. Really lost. It's not just the house and Gerry. According to Father Núñez, the feeling is a symptom of not knowing who we are. It appears we're something other than what I always thought we were, with a past that's different than I remember. So why don't you tell me what you know—right now. Exactly what did you mean by the word community?"

Carmen sat down on the two-seater porch swing and zipped up her sweater in the cool night air. "Well, I sure didn't see this coming. I'm not sure I know what to say. I have to think about it for a second. Whatever it was, it's not like it's that big of a deal anyway. I meant the community of others who were like us, like Mom and Dad." She pushed her feet back and let go, letting the old swing come gently forward.

"Then you knew? That we're different? Descendants of *conversos*? Catholic on the outside, Jewish on the inside? You knew Mom and Papa lived a secret life as Jews?"

"A secret life? I wouldn't go that far, but yes, I did, in a way. I never really understood what they were doing or why. Honestly, I didn't. You used the word 'Jews.' I never thought we were *Judeos*. I'm not so sure Mom and Papa knew that much either. Papa didn't seem to care much about it. Mama just kept some old rituals that seemed kind of pointless to me. And I really didn't care to know more. After they died, well— there was nothing more to do. I couldn't see why I should change anything in my world. I took what worked for me and went my own way. That's it."

Rachel pulled up an old lawn chair and sat down. "Oh come on, that's it? You never even thought about it again?"

"Not really. Look, Rachel, my own situation was rocky back then. I had my own problems. When Mom and Dad died, I moved back here to pull myself together and help you out. I should have stopped you from marrying Gerry, but you seemed so happy and in love, so ... that guy was a loser from the start. But I had to get a job and support myself; the rest was up to you. I figured maybe he was better than he appeared. You sure thought so. I got things worked out, rented this place, and went on about my business. Life goes on. We can't hold on to the past, especially one that's so vague and meaningless."

Rachel stood up fuming and faced her sister directly, hands buried in the pockets of her jeans. "Meaningless? *Are you kidding?* The past is what makes us who we are. At least that's the way I see it. Did you know that our great-grandmother five times over was raised in a convent here in Estrella, but lived the rest of her life as a hidden Jew? Imagine that, our own ancestor. Afraid of her own self. It's all in the church records. You can't make this stuff up. I mean, come on. It's our heritage!"

"I don't know much about heritage, Rachel. All I know about is survival, and I'm not all that great at that. Right here, right now. Where do you want me to go with all this anyway? I'm almost forty. Religion is something I've taken for granted my whole life. That is, we're Catholics, always have been. Maybe not such good Catholics all the time, but not bad ones either. That's about it. What do you want from me?"

"I want you to help me, like you always have, Carmen. Only now I want you to help me find out exactly who I am!"

Carmen, speechless at the request, looked at her sister with a puzzled expression. "Whoa, take it easy. That's a tall order. Well, guess what, Rachel? You're the only one who can do that."

Rachel glared, stunned by her reply. *Damn. She's right, as usual.* Rachel stepped down off the patio and stared up into the night sky. A few faint stars gleamed high above. For some reason, finding her boys and finding herself were inexplicably tied together. To move forward, to find her sons, she needed to know exactly who she was and what she wanted to be. And she knew from here on out, their future was in her hands, and her future in theirs. They needed to have a sense of pride about who they were and where they came from, as did she.

Carmen stood next to her, not knowing what else to say. Rachel helped her out. "Don't take this wrong Carmen, because I don't mean to hurt you, but honestly—I don't ever want to be like you. You don't even have the courage to ask what it means to be Carmen Martínez Ortiz. What about the sense of obligation that comes with family, with the debt we owe to those who went before us, who gave their lives for us? We wouldn't even be here if it wasn't for them. I'm sorry I even bothered you!"

Rachel turned, entered the house, and slammed the patio door behind her. She headed for Héctor's room to be alone, leaving Carmen, baffled, standing outside. Rachel shut the bedroom door and lay down on the bed, disappointed more than anything. She kicked off her shoes, looked at her watch, and decided no one would miss her if she took a quick nap. She'd never felt so exhausted. She turned off the night lamp and hugged her cotton knit jacket close around her. Within minutes, she managed to shake off the turmoil of her confused emotions and the weight of her fatigue, and drift into another world, sound asleep.

CHAPTER FORTY-EIGHT

Time and Memory

RACHEL DOZED FOR MORE than an hour, lying on Héctor's bed. All along the windowsill, a row of carved wooden *santos* looked on, their silent blessings easing her heart. In that nether world of dreams where she now rested, her history—in fact, time itself, flowed back and forth without boundaries. There, in that place where past and future merge, she could let go of the illusion that the present moment was the only one that mattered. The ancient box had already taught her how very far from the truth that assumption was.

Somewhere near Silver City, search dogs, trackers, helicopters and men on horses combed the hills of southwestern New Mexico, hoping to find two young boys alive. Here, inside a small house north of the Rio Grande, one desperate woman wrestled with unforeseen choices, coming to terms with a revised version of herself and her family's hidden past.

On the dresser, the aged Bible sat, secure as a sentinel, its secrets locked amidst the list of names written within, its pages heavy with history—Rachel's story, as well as her mother's and her mother's before her, all laden with tales of commitment, survival, and loss, its many previous owners begging not to be forgotten.

Rachel could never know any of them personally, nor all that they endured, but the book itself would hold their signatures and their spirits for eternity; its contents having touched their souls. The continued survival of the Bible and the ritual objects found inside the box would now be her responsibility—hers alone. She was their steward, their keeper and their host. Her sleep grew restless as her ancestors appeared at the foot of the bed, one by one, sharing some of their tales.

* * *

"Mother, please, wait! Slow down. I can't keep up with you!" Miriam called as she scurried down the broken trail behind Catalina. Her breath came in sharp bursts.

"*Cuidado, mija.* Be careful, my precious. Give me your hand."

On their perilous journey northward over so many weeks and months, far away from *San Miguel el Grande,* Miriam Sequerra followed her mother closely, the two silver candlesticks sewn into the hem of her skirt bumping against her booted calves. She had calluses on her shins beneath her high boots, her pale skin bruised to the ankles.

The family had walked under cover of night for days, then weeks, then months; enduring heat, then cold, ignoring all. Except for game caught along the trail and the mercy of strangers, they had nearly run out of food, but at least they were still alive. The thieves who finally stole their horse and mule spared the frightened mother, daughter, and infant, but asked no questions.

Catalina was grateful that Ephraim had not been there when their camp was discovered. Surely he would have been killed had he tried to defend them, or hold on to the animals. He had gone on to scout for the best way through the mountainous trail ahead.

Helpless and terrified, Ephraim watched from above as the two men threatened his wife and children with swords, then made off with their tethered mounts. No matter the horse and mule. His family was safe. According to the map, they were but a day's journey from the outskirts of Santa Fe. He had the name of one who would protect them there, a *converso* like himself, and a blacksmith as well. He'd know where to find new horses. They would continue on foot and find him.

In time, he would settle his family in the mountainous area far to the north at the edge of the empire and plant his vineyards anew, the earliest beginning of the prized vines one day to be found in Corrales, rich concord grapes raised on the famed Black Mesa of New Mexico. In time, these would eventually be exported across the New World.

Young Maria would grow to womanhood, become a skilled weaver and seamstress, and at seventeen, marry one of their own kind, a *señor* Béjar García from the town of Mora, a crypto, or hidden, Jew like themselves. Together they would bring forth six children: five sons, and a beautiful daughter, their precious Lilliana, or Lilly, all raised carefully in what they remembered of the secret tradition, yet under the direct gaze of the Church. At the age of twenty-two, Lilly would accidentally be discovered by a suitor; a road-weary traveler who stopped to ask for water and a night's rest, a Spanish-and Portuguese-speaking fur trader by the name of Joaquim Abravanel.

Seated around the family table, young Lilly was charmed when she heard his stories of the Dutch colony with the great harbor on the sea from whence he'd come. She hung on to every word of his descriptions of Amsterdam, and Lisbon too, great cities in Europe where his family had first started their journey long, long before, so as to be far from personal threat and danger. But all that, he said, was in another time, another world far from here—at least he hoped. At thirty-seven, he was ready to settle down and start a family. The year was 1692 and his lust for wandering had come to an end.

Lilly had never met a man so worldly, or who could speak more than one language. She could barely breathe during the family dinner, his presence affected her so.

Seated at her parents' table, Joaquin eyed the handsome silver candlesticks upon the mantel. "A fine example of casting," he said, examining the pair by hand. "I used to do work like this myself. Not for myself alone, but in the name of *El Dio*. It is how I came to this land."

Maria and her husband looked at each other, then directly into his eyes. None of them spoke a word. They didn't have to. "For God," he had said, in the singular form, so deliberately. Not for Jesus. Not for the Virgin. And from that moment on, they knew.

"I came to America with dreams of a future," he told their comely daughter. "I lost my betrothed, however, shortly after our arrival. A typhus outbreak on the ship took my beloved Malka. I never imagined she wouldn't survive. After a year in New Amsterdam working as a silversmith, I went into the wilderness to heal my broken heart and become a trapper. But I was naïve. My sorrow followed me there."

Lilly held her breath, waiting for him to continue.

"I was willing to learn the skills needed from those who hired me, but discovered that we came too late, wild game for hundreds of miles had been decimated by those who came before us. But the land still called. I headed farther and farther west. I will never return to New Amsterdam. It's here I want to stay, where the great river meets the mountains. At a gathering of trappers I heard of opportunities in Santa Fe where I can work with my hands, of plans to rebuild the church there, earlier destroyed by an Indian revolt. A silversmith always has a job. Therefore, I am on my way."

Joaquim departed. He found his way to the northernmost trade center of *Nueva España* and was soon hired by a metalworker who allowed him to use his forge. In time, he became the metal smith for the new church, responsible for grills and hinges, as well as for chasing vessels, cups and bowls for the sacristy. He was glad to be a part of the building of the Cathedral of Saint Francis of Assisi, soon to be begun on the main plaza. But as his success grew, he vowed to return to the vintner Sequerra one day and ask for his granddaughter Lilly's hand in marriage.

It did not take long. Within two years, the fated couple wed in the Christian tradition, secretly celebrating their Jewish roots. They soon had a daughter, Rafaela, who, within two decades married into the wealthy Morales family farther north in the village of Rio Grande, successful ranchers originally from Spain near the Taos valley. In time they bore a son, Enrique Carlos Morales, who would grow to be the infamous rancher and father of a beautiful daughter, Rebeca, cloistered and hidden, ill-fated to live two very different lives.

By the late seventeen hundreds, Morales' wife died while giving birth, leaving her infant girl to be cared for by others. They called the girl after her mother, Rebeca Elena. By the age of three, she was placed in the convent of *Las Hermanas del Sagrado Corazón* for education and safekeeping. She would grow up, marry, and learn to keep her ancestor's faith, if God willed it so. Somehow, the tiniest flame of her secret Jewish past had survived within her unknowing heart, to be brought to life through love and matrimony once again.

* * *

Following the loss of her unborn child, Rebeca Elena Morales Martinez dedicated herself to the God of Abraham. She prayed in earnest that she and Moisés be blessed with more children, and set about to work the land with her husband, tilling the earth and increasing their fine herd. They returned to their bed each night, determined to raise a family true to their heritage and build a great ranch worthy of its horses. Soon Mexico won its fight for independence and the country changed and grew.

By the end of Rebeca's life, at eighty-two, she had borne four sons and two daughters and died leaving twenty-seven grandchildren and great-grandchildren. Her youngest grandson, Louis Samuel Martinez, one day to become the grandfather of Rachel Martinez Ortega, would take over the old adobe house in Estrella and start a new family in what was now the state of New Mexico, carrying on the pride of the Martínez name.

Louis Martinez's Jewish roots, barely remembered or understood, were very distant indeed. But he knew what his grandparents had told him. They were once Jews. He and his wife had two daughters, sisters five years apart. They raised them with the barest identification with the tradition, but gave them whatever remnants they could, certain customs and rituals, whatever had been handed down. Neither husband nor wife ever imagined they wouldn't return that night when they drove down to Truchas to visit distant members of their family.

* * *

One by one, Rachel's ancestors assembled before her, passing by the foot of her bed in a ghostly procession, whispering their names, showering her with their love. Behind them, as if through a frosted glass window, pressed the faces of her two children desperately trying to reach her.

"Do not forget us this night, or ever," beseeched the voices of the deceased, their collective breath and earnest pleas a caress of wind over her body. The rush of air startled her. A cold draft swept in from the open window.

"Ángel! Juan!" she shouted, waking suddenly. "Please, don't leave me!"

The dream left her shivering. First, strangers at her bedside, and then the faces of her sons, all fading to nothing. It couldn't be. Where were they now, and where was Flores? Why hadn't he called and this horrific nightmare finally come to an end?

CHAPTER FORTY-NINE

Storm over the Mogollons

THE TEMPERATURE HAD DROPPED some twenty degrees by the time the thunderstorm struck. Ángel dozed off and on in the back seat where he had placed his little brother, who was still sleeping as if dead to the world. Checking on Juan, he made sure the blanket covered him. The stranded car offered little protection against the cold, but at least it stopped the wind.

Ángel's teeth chattered and his hands ached, but little could be done. He wrapped his arms around his chest and curled into a ball next to Juan, trying to stay warm any way he could. Soon, the roll of thunder and crackle of lightning shook both boys where they lay. Poquito cowered and whimpered with each new peal and clap. The heavy rain fell in sheets so dense Ángel wondered if the road wouldn't wash away beneath them in the downpour.

He couldn't sleep. He knew his brother hadn't taken another bite since throwing up his breakfast earlier that day, and whatever had gone down sure didn't stay long. He hadn't drunk much either, except for those few sips of water, which didn't make sense because the afternoon was so hot. Ángel knew he had to be thirsty. On top of that, Juan slept most of the day and hardly responded to anything. When he did, his answers came out confused, just babble.

Ángel had never seen Juan this sick. He himself was hungry and thirsty too, but the real discomfort was deeper than that: guilt and shame for having brought his brother along on his stupid quest for freedom. *Some freedom.*

The heavy rain lasted over an hour. Brief showers pelted the car the rest of the night, leaving them parked in a sea of mud. By the time dawn lit up the sky, Ángel felt paralyzed by the unknown. His breath came in short gulps, a kind of panic. Afraid and exhausted, all he knew was that Juan was hardly moving, felt ice cold, and his breath was shallow and weak.

He had to go for help. After all, Uncle Tomás told him he had to act. He couldn't wait for someone to come down this muddy track in the middle of nowhere. The road was probably impassable anyway. He decided to crack the windows, lock the car doors, and leave Juan covered with the blanket. Then he would head out on foot and find a bigger road.

He scrawled GONE FOR HELP in the dust on the dashboard, in case Juan woke up. He thought twice about taking Poquito, but knew if Juan awoke, he'd be frightened and lonely without his dog, especially since his older brother wouldn't be there. So he locked the dog in too.

"Sorry, Poco, gotta go find help for Juan. If you have to pee, just go on the floor of the car."

Determined to find someone, and soon, he headed out, following the road back the way they came. He never realized he'd driven the car so far up into the mountains the night before. The Dodge had stalled on a flat section of a logging road cut through the deep woods. Tall pine trees grew up straight along either side, blotting out the peaks beyond. He'd made an awful mistake. There was only one way to fix it—and only he could make it right before something really, really bad happened.

CHAPTER FIFTY

From Out of the Past

THE FOLLOWING MORNING, FATHER Núñez arrived at Carmen's at two minutes to eight with warm *buñuelos* and *biscochitos* for breakfast. It was Friday, a week since learning of Rachel's plight. Two of his parishioners, Joe and Gloria Delgado, followed right behind him, bearing a six-pack of Coke, tortilla chips, and Gloria's special ground beef casserole for the day's vigil. Gloria, a school social worker, often worked with law enforcement to help families through a crisis. She had been briefed on the situation and greeted Rachel with a warm hug.

Rachel looked at Gloria warily. She'd been buying tomatoes and peppers from her husband's farm outside of Estrella for years. *Is it possible?* she wondered. *Them, too?*

"Good morning," said Father Núñez, pouring coffee from a carafe on the stove, then helping himself to the *buñuelos*. "What's the news?"

"Nothing, and it's so frustrating," said Rachel. "I would have thought we'd get some word by now, but I guess no news is good news, right?

I'm sure Flores will call when they find something." She attempted a smile and squeezed Father Núñez's hand.

"I need to ask you a favor, Padre," said Rachel. "Please don't think I'm crazy, but I've been thinking about our conversation the other day. About my 'family.' Could we make a quick trip to the cemetery this morning? Just for a few minutes? I want to visit my parents' graves. It's something I have to do. Would you go with me?"

"Now?"

"Yes, now. I know it sounds nuts, but I need to. I just have to. I'll have my cell with me if José calls. We won't be gone long."

Núñez nodded. "Of course we can, my dear. I'd be glad to. Just let me finish my coffee and we'll be on our way."

As Núñez sipped the hot brew, Rachel poured another cup for herself, and turned to him with a troubled expression on her face. "Please don't misunderstand, Father. I don't mean to pry. But I have to ask you something. Something personal. You've been more than just a clergyman for me these past few days; you've been a real friend. You've spent countless hours; more like family. In fact, you've been with us every step of the way. Tell me, if you don't mind—why?"

Rachel didn't care how blunt her question sounded. "I mean, you're a Catholic priest, but you seem to care an awful lot about these *conversos*. Especially me. Why? Father Núñez, are you a *converso* too?"

The priest looked across the kitchen table, avoiding her eyes, and remained silent. He downed the rest of his coffee. "Rachel, could we discuss this in private?"

As they closed the front door behind them and headed for the car, Núñez stopped.

"Look, I really don't know how to answer you, Rachel." He continued to the car and turned when he got there, leaning against it, facing her. He folded his arms and cleared his throat.

She had never seen Father Núñez so hesitant before.

"But the answer, plainly spoken and without equivocation, is ... yes. Indeed, I believe I too am a *converso,* or crypto-Jew as some call us—at least, the son of *conversos,* born of Jewish ancestry."

"Are you a true Catholic then?"

"Are you asking me about my religion? What I believe in? That's another matter. My faith remains a personal issue. My parents, who were devout Catholics, allowed me to go into the clergy, actually against their will, as a very young man. They wanted me to stay and work in the family business, but serving God was all I ever wanted, to carry forth the Word. I've since learned where we actually came from, and some of my own family's history, here in the Southwest. It has called me back to New Mexico and a search that's ongoing. The return has been a source of conflict ever since."

"I can only imagine," said Rachel. "I understand. And thank you for your honesty."

"You know," he continued, "back in the Middle Ages, many crypto-Jewish families required at least one son in each generation to enter a Catholic seminary and be ordained. That, at least, provided a link between the family's secret world and the Church, allowing for advance warning of any hostile actions. Priests also had legitimate reasons for keeping secrets, thanks to the confessional seal. When a crypto-Jew went to confession, he would always go to his own family priest. Secrets were passed on that way and Hebrew texts could be obtained for their underground services. It was the perfect cover."

Rachel leaned against the car beside him. "Fascinating."

"History repeats itself I think. As I grow older, there is much I can't resolve, so—I leave it up to God. I have a parish and a congregation and I truly love my work. But when I found out about my heritage, I had to come to terms with the most important questions in my life. Does one merely inherit belief? Or do we self-determine? Do we carry on what was, or do we choose our own way? Is our spiritual life one that evolves over time? Trust me, the answers don't come easy."

"But it appears you've made a choice."

"Ah. Appearances are deceptive. A choice I struggle with daily. I am no longer certain of many so-called religious doctrines, but if what one truly believes brings fulfillment, perhaps that's good enough, whether it's true or not. Don't you agree? After all, Jesus was a Jew. So I continue to lead and minister as best as I can. To be candid, let us just say—I have my moments."

Núñez opened the car door for Rachel and she slid in. He strode around to the other side, got in the driver's seat, and turned to her.

"I have never told this to anyone. But every night I get on my knees to reconcile my soul to the father of Isaac and Abraham, and to Jesus, too. I continue to ask and question. That's more than enough. But there's no need for you to be concerned about me. My quest is ultimately my own."

"Then how can you urge me with such conviction to embrace my ancestors' faith?" she asked.

"I am not urging you to embrace anything, Rachel, only to consider. You must come to your own conclusions."

Núñez started the engine and headed down Road 59. The drive to the cemetery was a blur. Rachel couldn't see past her own hazy vision of the present and the priest's confession to her, even as the bright New Mexico sunlight filled the morning sky.

The town of Estrella shrank behind them to a scattering of barns as they approached the cemetery from the north end, just past the lumber yard. Núñez parked his car outside the low stone-walled enclosure across from Hermanos's peach orchard. Late fall remnants of dried fruit on the ground filled the air with a musty sweetness.

He opened the gate and Rachel followed him through. Before them scattered a profusion of colorful plastic floral bouquets, religious statuary, ornamental iron benches and folded lawn chairs, along with small, well-kept altars next to headstones of wood, granite and sandstone. Rachel carefully wended her way between the graves, squinting in the sun's glare. Like a child, she followed the priest through weedy aisles, their feet making soft crunching sounds on the dry grass. Together, they picked their way past statues of Jesus, various saints and the Madonna.

Time and weather had worn many of the inscriptions off the markers, especially the wooden ones. Some were barely readable, but still legible headstones could be found from as far back as the early eighteen hundreds. Rachel was surprised at the many Old Testament first names people had back then: Isaac Hernández, Ezekiel Adobada, Abraham Tafoya, Rebeca Hererra, all of them passed on before 1880. The name Martínez surfaced in every decade.

Here and there, the priest stopped and asked her to look more closely, showing her a Martínez or Morales marker with a small carved candelabra or six-pointed star inscribed on the back, invisible if only viewed from the front. One had a pair of lit candles carved in stone, yet another a crown, like the one on her ancient *mezuzah*, alluding to the King of Kings. She ran her fingers over their rough lines, feeling their inarguable truth.

She had to look very closely at some inscriptions; on others the signs were more obvious. Incised six-petaled roses and other flowers seemed to hold secret meaning, a coded language, beyond words. The pistils of certain carved flowers resembled the Hebrew letters seen in her Bible. Some stones bore a series of symbols so obscure that perhaps only the stone carvers themselves knew what they stood for. But wherever she turned, she was convinced beyond any doubt that many of the dead interred here were once her people—her family's people. *Conversos.* Hidden Jews. She could never turn her back on any of them again.

As she turned down the next row, she found herself standing at the foot of her parents' gravesite, two brownish grass-covered beds, slightly sunken, with two gray granite headstones, undecorated and austere. Only their names, plus birth and death dates.

Rachel closed her eyes, and silently begged her mother and father to forgive her for so many years of neglect. Welcome tears slipped from beneath her lids. Father Núñez stepped back and stood in respectful silence.

The date of Rachel's parents' death could be seen carved in sharp relief; June 16, 1991. It was not only a day that left Rachel an orphan, but also one that plunged her into ignorance. She knew now just what she'd been robbed of. The time had come to take it back. She returned to the car without saying a word, but squeezed the padre's hand, filled with the deepest gratitude.

CHAPTER FIFTY-ONE

Countdown

TEN MINUTES AFTER THEY got back to the house, at exactly 9:35 a.m., things began to move. Rachel's cell phone buzzed in her pocket. She practically jumped in excitement. Flores, at last! She put him on speaker phone.

"It was a long night, folks, but we're close. Hell of a drive. We hooked up with this Yazzi guy, a Diné from Magdalena, and waited in Silver City overnight. He seems okay, straightforward type. Says he picked up Ángel and Juan a few days ago to help 'em out; then they ran. Not sure he's telling the whole truth, but I'm convinced he wants to help find the boys. For some reason I trust him."

"What have you learned so far? Rachel asked. "Does he know where they are?"

"They're in a stolen vehicle. A 1991 gray Dodge sedan. Air patrol has spotted the car. Somehow they ended up in McKenna Park, by the west fork of the Gila. The river's pretty low right now but that rain last night didn't help. It's almost impossible to bring a chopper down anywhere near there but we'll get as close as we can and go in by foot. We're headed that way now. Let's see, it's about 9:40. If we pick 'em up, and every one's all right, your boys ought to be back home in time for lunch."

"Thank God," said Rachel. "Thank you. Thanks so much." She turned to Núñez, embraced the padre and this time, wept unbridled tears of joy.

* * *

Almost an hour passed before they heard from Flores again. Rachel grabbed the phone on the first ring.

"Rachel, it's ..." Flores' voice crackled through a bad connection. For a minute they lost touch, then he was back. "... Rachel?"

"Yes, I'm here, José," she answered. "Talk to me. I can hear you. Tell me something good."

"We found the car. Juan was inside, freezing cold, but wrapped in a blanket and still breathing. That little dog of his was lying on top of him. He's okay, but unconscious—dehydration's my guess. They took him to the chopper, hooked him up on fluids right away. He's on his way to the hospital in Las Cruces."

"Oh! My poor baby. But thank goodness, he's safe. I need to get down there right away! Tell them I'm coming, okay? Just give me a few hours. But where's Ángel?" she asked, clenching her hands so hard her nails left marks in her palms.

"Um ... not here. Looks like he went to find help. Left a note on the dash. Rachel, why don't you just stay put for now? No need to drive all the way down here yet. Juanito's safe and he'll be well taken care of. Maybe send your sister instead. Seriously, Ángel could show up any minute at your door, and then you can both drive down. I need you to stay where you are."

"But ..."

"I mean it. If he's not on the road already, and still in the forest here, we'll find him, but there's no telling. We have four men on the ground right now, but more support should be mobilizing soon: a mounted patrol and additional trackers with dogs. A posse arrived with horses this morning. With thirty thousand acres of forest land all around here, we need to get the ground search going ASAP. They're mapping a grid of the area as we speak. Please. Not to worry."

"You can't mean it, José," Rachel said, "Come on. Is it possible he's out there alone in the Gila Wilderness? He doesn't know how to survive. He never even liked camping." She buried her head in her hands.

"Oh my God. I was afraid something like this would happen." She walked away from the table and leaned her forehead against the wall, closing her eyes. "Ángel, where in the world are you?" she whispered. "*Where?*"

"Hey, Rachel, you still there?" The voice crackled over the phone again.

"Flores," she said, putting the device to her ear, her voice barely audible. "Please, find him."

"We'll do our best. Just be strong. Stand by. I'll be in touch."

"Call me. Call me soon."

Rachel opened the front door. She went outside. All eyes in the room watched as she walked a few steps and then slowly fell to her knees on the cold ground. "Dear Lord, don't let me down now. Thank you for giving me back my little Juan. But Ángel needs you too, just as much as I need him."

Father Núñez walked outside and knelt beside her. He put his arm around Rachel's shoulder and bowed his head.

* * *

Yazzi had been on edge ever since the cop and the old man met him down in Hurley, just after midnight. Cops made him nervous. That deputy grilled him pretty hard. They waited out the night's rain in the parking lot of a 7-Eleven in Silver City, then at daybreak, continued west to rendezvous with other searchers in the Gila, waiting for a report from the air surveillance after sunrise. They were lucky. Tomás Begay's old Dodge four-door was spotted shortly after seven-thirty by the chopper. After getting the call, they headed north into the hills.

Now, sitting in his pickup, the Diné meditated, eyes closed. Héctor sat next to him in silence, listening to the increasing gathering of men and vehicles assembling with the search team. He could smell the horses as they headed out. As the white man's assemblage grew, Frank Yazzi opened his eyes and blinked: he did not like what he saw. *Too many men. Too many machines. Distractions. This is not the way.*

He shook his head, grunted at Héctor, and climbed out of the truck. Walking a few feet up the hill and into the trees, he sat down on his heels, both hands touching the ground with his fingertips. He closed his eyes.

"Um—excuse me, but what are you doing, Mr. Yazzi?" asked Flores, approaching the Navajo. He carried Juan's dog under one arm.

"Listening to the mountain."

"Oh, sorry. Don't let me interrupt."

Flores went over to Yazzi's truck, still carrying Poquito. Héctor sat perfectly still in the front seat of the cab, his blank, clouded eyes staring straight ahead.

"You okay, *señor?*" Flores asked Héctor. Flores felt unsettled by Yazzi's performance and wasn't sure he wasn't interrupting another one of a similar nature. "Uh ... 'scuse me, but would you mind watching the dog here, *mi amigo*? I have other things to look after."

The old man turned his unseeing eyes to the voice at the window and nodded, accepting the Chihuahua as Flores passed it through the window onto his knees. Poquito wagged his tail and yapped, recognizing a familiar human, then settled in. The small dog in his lap felt like a good omen, as if they were already on the right track. Héctor stroked the dog's head and smiled.

"*Hola, Poquito poco, ¿Sabes ónde está Ángel*?"

Yazzi opened the driver side door and got in. Turning to Héctor, he touched him on the arm.

"*Yá'át'ééh*, old man—heya. What do you think?"

"And what about you? What do *you* think?"

Almost in unison, the two men spoke the same word. "South."

The Indian smiled at his blind passenger and knew he had made the right choice in asking old Héctor Ortega to come. *Haashch'ééłti'í* spoke to this grandfather. And after all, since when did an old man need sight to see his grandsons?

Flores, who was watching and overheard the exchange, shook his head and cocked it to one side.

"South? How can you both know that? What makes you so sure, Mr. Yazzi?"

"Couldn't speak for *Señor* Ortega," answered the Navajo. "But the mountain told me. That's the way we're going to go. Look, Deputy Flores, you manage the crew here and whatever trackers you got. We're going to follow this road back down and then go after him on foot. Kids usually go downhill. We will too."

"You need a compass?"

"Got one," Yazzi said, pointing to his head.

"Uh huh. Well, take this anyway." Flores handed him a small case. "And here's a radio—let us know what you find. It's tuned to the right channel. Just press here to talk. You sure you don't want help? We've got plenty of men now."

"No, sir. I'm a well-known tracker in my tribe."

"OK. Do what you can."

Flores watched the Diné's truck rumble away down the muddy road that Ángel had come in on. It went over a hump and disappeared. Given the short amount of daylight, they had four hours, maybe five, to find him. Unless they got lucky, there was a good chance the kid would spend the night on the mountain and have to find shelter wherever he could. Forecasters predicted rain, again.

He wished the searchers would hurry up with the rest of those sniffer dogs and get to work. Imagine being on Rachel's end, having nothing to do but wait and hope. It couldn't be easy. At least they'd found Juan and his little dog. Now—just one more boy.

CHAPTER FIFTY-TWO

Shabbat Shalom

SIX DAYS HAD PASSED since the world had begun to unravel; since Rachel's house was demolished and the wreckers found the box; five days since the boys had run away and Rachel began peering into her past. To Rachel, it seemed like a lifetime. For her, an entire world had been lost, yet a brand new one was under construction. It could only be complete with her children by her side—both of them.

Friday dragged on without much news. Carmen drove down to Las Cruces to be with Juan until Rachel could join them, based on Flores' orders. Like he said, Rachel needed to stay in one place, for security's sake.

Rosa called Rachel shortly after three to hear how things were going. She invited anyone who wanted to come over to her house for dinner. After all, they still had to eat, and the worry could be eased by being together. The Sabbath came early in October, since sundown occurred around five-thirty. Although some light might still grace the western sky, candle-lighting would begin shortly thereafter.

Rachel said she didn't feel very social, or much like eating, but she appreciated the invitation. She'd still heard no further word from Flores. Oh well, at least there was no additional cause for alarm.

Carmen arrived at the hospital in Los Cruces and settled in by Juanito's side. She called Rachel to say he was stable and improving with hydration, though somewhat groggy. She gave him a big hug and a stuffed dog to hold, and told him Mama was coming soon. Real soon. She promised to call again if there was any change.

Rachel joined Israel Romero as they headed over to Rosa's for dinner, cell phone in hand. Father Núñez drove over on his own. Rosa welcomed them cordially, her table set with white linen and her best dishes laid out for the Sabbath meal. Leading the way into the house, she enveloped Rachel in her arms, pulling her close.

"*Ven, mi cariño,*" she said. She pulled a clean handkerchief out of an apron pocket and dabbed her eyes. "This too shall pass. You'll see. They'll be home safe. Here, sit down. How are you feeling?"

"I don't know. I'm so happy Juan is safe now, but Ángel is out there somewhere on his own, or maybe on his way to find help. I'm really worried. I need to get back to Carmen's soon, okay? He might show up there. I don't know what to do except pray."

"*Bueno*. That's good. Ángel will be fine. You'll see. You will get through this night and many more, together, I am sure of it. Here …" she said, fishing a silver amulet on a chain from around her neck and beneath the collar of her blouse. It was a six-sided star made of sterling silver.

Rachel's eyes widened. "It's beautiful."

Rosa lifted it off over her head and handed it to her, folding the chain and star gently into her open palm. "Here. Use this to help. It's called a *Magen David*—King David's shield. My son gave it to me when I told him I wanted to live this way, like our forefathers. It helps me pray. Perhaps it will help you."

"Oh, Rosa, I … I don't know what to say."

"*Toma,* take it. It's your shield too, you know."

"Mine?"

"It is time, my dear, to own what is yours by birthright. Use my amulet to call God's name. He listens, of course, without such things, but you never know. It might help. Put it on if you wish. I would love to see it on you."

"*Gracias,* Rosa. But, first, you have to tell me—are you like José? Do you believe what he believes?"

"Yes, and no, my dearest. I hide no longer. I don't broadcast who I am to everyone, as you know, but like my son, I live a Jewish life now. I began this journey to honor my mother, and her mother before her. Now I do it for myself. I am full of pride for our people. Who else could last all these thousands of years, never to be extinguished, even after all we have been through?"

"That's a wonderful way to see it."

"It's the only way. And every week, whoever cares to, comes here to share a Sabbath meal at my house to be together. It's time you joined us."

She beckoned those present to gather round. "The prayer over the Sabbath candles this night will be recited by Rachel Ortega," announced Rosa, as the Romeros and Delgados assembled. "We are using your silver candlesticks this night, Rachel. I polished them for you."

"They look beautiful," she beamed. "But recite the prayer?" Rachel asked, surprised at being included. "I don't know how."

"Then you will learn. It's not the speaking, but the feeling that's important. Don't be afraid. I'm still learning it too." Rosa smiled and took her prayer book from the table, the page with the Sabbath service marked by a worn red ribbon. The men, including Father Nuñez, covered their heads with skull caps. Rosa handed Rachel a white lace scarf.

The older woman lifted a struck match to the first taper. She instructed Rachel to close her eyes and move her hands in a circular motion over the flames. "Repeat after me," she said. "*Barukh atah A-donai, E-loheinu melekh ha'olam, asher kideshanu be'mitzvotav ve'tzivanu lehadlik ner shel Shabbat.* Blessed art thou, O Lord Our God, King of the

Universe, who has sanctified us by thy commandments and commanded us to kindle the Sabbath lights."

When Rosa asked Rachel to light the second candle, Rachel took the match, then noticed her own reflection in the silver candlestick's shining base. How she wished these remnants of another time could speak to her and tell her of their long journey to this night, to this room, to this very moment in time.

Rachel repeated the words from the simple prayer used in part to usher in the seventh day of the week at Jewish Sabbath tables all over the world. "*Barukh atah A-donai. . .*"They sounded simply magical.

Father Núñez said a prayer over the wine, each person took a sip from their glass, and then they all took turns washing their hands over a basin on the side table, using a two-handled cup. Together they recited the *Hamotzi,* or blessing over the bread. Israel Delgado took a chunk from one of the freshly baked *bolillos* and passed the remainder to his left. It continued around until all were served.

For most who were seated at the table that night, the following day, ideally, would be a day of rest. Except for Rachel—there could be no rest until Ángel was found. But perhaps this ancient ritual would somehow lighten the wait.

Rachel's eyes brightened as she took this first step toward embracing the faith of her ancestors. It felt good. Yet, night was falling and she'd still received no call. Worry clawed at her every move. But here in Rosa's dining room, life went on as if nothing had changed, and the gathering seemed protected by something sacred and eternal. Surely, no harm could come to her boy.

Rachel shared in the prayers over the bread and wine, accepted some food on her plate, and then retreated into herself. Anxious, she could hardly eat. But at least she was with friends who were kind and supportive. As the meal came to an end, singing replaced the prayers that had come before. Each person at the table took the hand of the person next to them. Together they formed a circle of love and hope, their spirits flowing as one. In the light of the two glowing candles, Rachel knew that this was where she belonged. With smiling eyes, she fingered her silver amulet, her shining, hidden star. It rested just above her heart.

CHAPTER FIFTY-THREE

Discovery

ÁNGEL FOLLOWED THE ROAD with a giddy elation that took him down the first quarter mile at a trot. He panted, slamming one foot in front of the other against the muddy earth, pumping his fists. The road descended gradually, with frequent switchbacks on the steep grade of the mountainside. All around him, the dark green trees dripped with dew, and the rocks along the side of the road glistened like black tar. He looked behind him just once, a chill raising goosebumps as he did. Even in his panic over Juan, that feeling of being chased by cops was still with him.

The dense forest closed in on either side as the road wound its way down, back and forth, back and forth. He could see the switchbacks now in his mind's eye, like at the moto-cross track, etching the manmade hills he knew so well. These were just bigger, filled with pines—except for the occasional clear-cut, where there were just stumps. All he knew for sure was he had to get to a highway fast, or find somebody somewhere with a phone.

Oh Juan, my stupid little brother. Why did you have to get sick? Don't die Pinto, please don't die. The words kept running through his head, over and over. *Why didn't you wake up? Why didn't you make any sense?* He couldn't forget Juan's sunken eyes and raspy breath. *Please hang on. I'm really sorry. Really, I am.*

Maybe if he just took a shortcut down the mountain he would run into the road again, only a good ways farther along. Sure he would; it only made sense. All he had to do was cut to the left, go straight down, and the road should be right there, curving around below. Easy. He broke into a lope and headed down the hill, scrambling between pines and scrub oak, ducking under low-hanging branches. He pushed one pine branch and winced as it snapped back and stung him on the face. Pausing long enough to rub the welt with the back of his hand, he wiped the blood on his jeans, then slipped and scurried down the thick, wet covering of pine needles as the mountainside grew steeper. Before long, he spotted a small creek below. Its steep banks were fringed with sawgrass and a thick green crest of low-growing willows.

Water! Ángel suddenly became aware of how thirsty he was, his throat so dry he could barely swallow. The stream didn't appear to be too far below the bank. Maybe he could just cup some with his hand if he held on to a rock and reached. He sat down and slithered on his jeans toward the bank on damp grass, never seeing the root in front that caught his sneaker, twisted his foot, and pitched him over the edge, snapping his ankle with a sickening crack.

"*Aaahhhh!*" Ángel screamed, then slammed face forward onto a flat rock in the creek jutting out just above the icy current. He jerked, rolled once, then collapsed, his torn cheek and bruised forehead pressed against the wet stone, its surface already turning a bright crimson. The water washed gently over the edges of the rock, a steady splash that lapped at his broken ankle and the injured side of his face. The forest, Juan, and the mountain had suddenly ceased to exist. Unconscious, Ángel lay still, his bare foot twisted sideways, his broken ankle already beginning to swell.

* * *

Frank Yazzi drove down the narrow road for several miles, looking for any sign of a boy: a footprint, a discarded item of clothing or remnant of food. Nothing in the late afternoon light told him he was on the right track, other than a feeling in his gut. The truck rumbled over a flimsy bridge, rattling the planks. A ways farther and Yazzi could see a deer path leading off into the pines. An owl flapped up from the fir trees beyond the stream. Hours had passed. They didn't have much time before it grew too dark to see anything.

"*Señor,* stop here, *por favor.*" Héctor said, breaking a long silence.

"Here?"

"*Sí, sí, aquí.*"

Yazzi pulled over and parked. Poquito squirmed and stood up on his hind legs in Héctor's lap, whining, his nose against the window.

"My grandson is that way," said Héctor, pointing towards the deer path. "I can feel him. He needs our help. *Caminemos en esa dirección a Ángel.*"

"Over there, huh? ...?"

"*Sí*, that way."

"I'll go look around, see if there's any sign. Maybe Ángel followed that trail. I'm going to ask you to stay here, old man, in the truck. I'll be back soon if I don't find anything. Just wait."

Héctor nodded and clasped his bony hands around the dog's chest. Poquito whined as the Navajo reached into the space behind the seat, pulled out a flashlight, and stepped down out of the cab.

Yazzi started down the trail searching for signs: a footprint, blades of flattened grass, a broken twig or fallen branch, the smallest stones dislodged. But he saw nothing, except a double set of tracks where two deer had come through. He continued moving down toward the murmur of the creek heard clearly to his right. The trail faded and disappeared into the thick dark green of the pines.

Héctor sat alone in the truck with the window down, listening to the wind passing through the trees; the faint sound of a distant stream faded in and out with the shifting direction of the breeze. But mostly, he listened to the silence of it all. The silence spoke to him. This forest felt like a place of salvation, benevolent and calm. He closed his eyes, remembering his dream of the boys' faces appearing on his altarpiece. In subsequent nights of fitful sleep, that dream had been replaced by visions of the boys walking by a creek in the mountains, or along the banks of the Río Grande, and once, even floating in canoes on Heron Lake. His dreams had placed them in a dozen locales. But water—streams, rivers, and creeks—had figured in them all, over and over.

He could barely hear the sound of that water rushing somewhere nearby, but it was there. He licked his lips. Boys are thirsty. Thirsty and hungry; not only for friendship and guidance, boys need to drink, a lot more than dried-up old men do, and he was very thirsty himself. Ángel must be by the water. He would find his grandson if he was anywhere in this wilderness at all—blind or not. *Santa Teresa* would help him.

Héctor bent his head, offered a prayer to his blessed saint, then crossed his chest and opened the door. He would find that creek no matter what. He might not be able to see, but he was not going to sit like a lump while his grandson needed him. Using his cane, he got out of the truck. Poquito leapt to the ground and darted fitfully around his feet.

Héctor knew that Yazzi would not be pleased, but felt something pull him, something he couldn't resist. He'd find his way to the water by sound alone if he went slowly, and probed in front with his cane as he always did, inching through the trees. It couldn't be that far. Poquito would know the way. The sound of the coursing stream called to him from the woods.

"*Ven, Poquito,*" he called to the dog. "*Vamos a encontrar a Ángel.*"

Poquito danced ahead, sometimes running, sniffing the ground, then circling back again. The old man stumbled and groped down the mountainside toward the sound of the river. He pushed ahead to find his way between the trees and forced his way through their branches, ignoring the scratches they left on his face and arms. At one point, he tripped and fell, landing on his knees in the damp and stony earth. He pulled himself up by a stump, cursing in Spanish, and started downhill again. The welcoming sound of the water increased. Finally, Héctor felt damp grass against his ankles and knees and heard the stream babbling loudly below. He stabbed the ground with his cane to find where the bank ended and the creek began.

Poquito began to bark excitedly, running up and down the water's edge, back and forth, then clawing wildly at Héctor's leg. Héctor stopped to listen, his heart beating fast. The dog stopped at the lip of the bank and barked furiously.

"Ángel," the old man called, cupping his hands. "*Ángelito*!"

Frank Yazzi, standing on the slope of the hill not more than one hundred yards above the river couldn't believe what he saw—the old man, calling out Ángel's name at the water's edge. Impossible. But there he was.

"*Heya!*" called Yazzi. "Don't move! *Por favor, señor. Cuidado*! You'll fall! Yazzi scrambled down the hill toward Héctor. "You're right by the edge and an eddy in the water, *señor.* A whirlpool, just there. What the hell are you doing out here? I told you to stay in the truck, you crazy old ..."

Then he saw the tennis shoe, wedged under a root near the water's edge. But Poquito already knew. He was clawing at it with both front paws. Looking downstream, Yazzi saw the still form of the boy, farther down, beyond the bank lying on a rock, the foaming water swirling around its tip. Ángel's white T-shirt glowed in the beam of the flashlight. *Ahéhee'!*

"There he is!" said Yazzi. "Right below you! Looks like he's hurt though. He's not moving. I need to get down, into the stream." He turned to Héctor. "Please stay right here this time. But *hey-ya*—good job, *amigo.* You found him."

Yazzi went along the bank to a cleft, then clambered down the rocks into the eddy. He lowered himself into the turbid water and waded into the depths where Ángel lay, still as death. He called the boy's name softly, then again louder, putting his hand on his shoulder and shaking him. Ángel moved his right hand, moaned, then opened his eyes. He looked up to see the Indian peering down at him.

"Ángel, Ángel Ortega, are you okay?"

No answer. Nothing but a dull, blank stare.

"*Ashkii*, answer me. It's me, Frank—Frank Yazzi."

Ángel groaned and blinked his eyes, looking down at his twisted foot in amazement and then at the stranger, but still said nothing.

Yazzi called up to Héctor. "Call him, *señor*, call your grandson. He doesn't seem to recognize me."

"*Hola, Ángelito*," called Héctor from the bank above. "It's me, Grandpa, *tu abuelo*. We've come to take you home."

Ángel struggled to get up, leaning back on his elbows. "Is that ... is that you, Grandpa? Is it really you? You were in my dream. I saw you! How did you find me? C-c-come get me, please? We have to get Juan—he's, he's sick! He's in the car..." Ángel's voice dissolved into sobs, his teeth chattering. Yazzi took off his jacket and wrapped it around the wet boy.

An ugly bruise discolored the right side of his face, and a clot of blood was forming on an open cut.

"J-just tell me, mister—did you find Juan? Is he okay?"

Yazzi answered. "Yeah, he's okay, kid, we got him. He's safe. Take it easy. How ya' doing, son? How's your head?" He shone his flashlight on the huge bump on Ángel's forehead and felt around it gently. "Think you could hang on around my neck while I lug us both up this bank? We'll get you to a hospital and fixed right up."

"I uh ... I think so." Ángel shivered furiously and swallowed "...My h-hands are so cold they hardly work. But, yeah ... I think I can."

"Try not to hit that foot on anything, now. Looks broke pretty bad, kid."

"I know, but it's so f-f-froze it don't hurt that much."

Once he got up the bank, Yazzi laid Ángel down on the grass and told Héctor to hold the flashlight. Quickly, the Diné made a rough splint for the broken ankle with a tree branch, binding it tight with his bandana. Yazzi helped Ángel up onto his back, and the three began a slow ascent up the mountain towards the truck, led by Poquito whose keen nose had them back on the trail in no time.

When they finally got back to the vehicle, Yazzi pulled down the jump seat in the back and locked it in place. He laid Ángel upon it and buckled the seatbelt tight, holding him close. Then he pulled his emergency kit from under the front seat, unfolded a heat-conserving space blanket, and tucked it around the boy like a cocoon.

Héctor, sitting in front, turned and reached over the seat with his left arm and took Ángel's hand in his. He would warm it with his own. He wiped away tears of joy with the other. Thank God, the child was alive.

Yazzi grabbed the two-way radio he'd been given to call Deputy Flores. He pushed the button. *Yes, sometimes the white man's toys are good.*

CHAPTER FIFTY-FOUR

The Deal

RACHEL SAT ALONE AT Rosa's table with Israel Romero's laptop in front of her. The dishes had been cleared but a carafe of coffee remained in the center. Rosa knew Rachel needed to be alone after dinner, and herded the others into the front room.

Romero had opened the PC to the site with ongoing state patrol reports. Rachel sat on edge, listening for every new dispatch that might have an update from the search. Some of the information coming over the Grant County sheriff's band had nothing to do with Ángel, but still, she jumped at every sound from the speaker.

It seemed like hours since she'd last talked to Flores. Carmen however, had called from Las Cruces right after dinner. "*Hola.* It's me. Things are looking very good down here. Someone is up and feeling much better. Ate some Jell-O, drank some apple juice; even named the toy dog Poquito. Surprised? He sure misses his mama. Here, say hello."

"*Pinto*, it's Mama. Yes, it's me. I'm so sorry I can't be there just yet, but I love you, *mijo*," she said, barely holding on. "Do everything the doctor says. Auntie Carmen will take care of you 'til I get there."

"When am I going home?" asked Juan.' "I want to go home. Where's Poquito?"

"Soon, sweetheart. You're coming home soon. Mama's coming and we'll all come back together. Poquito is just fine. Get better and sleep tight, OK? See you tomorrow!"

After an hour or so, she pushed her chair away from the table and got up, heading over to the dining room window. Her eyes focused on the big cottonwood by the front drive, dimly illuminated by the porch light. Fall had stolen all its leaves and the skeletal trunk awaited the first chills of winter. Before long it would be laced with snow. Rachel shivered and took a deep breath. Only one thing was left for her to do; she knew it in her heart.

If Ángel was found—*when* he was found—she would give the word *home* a new meaning. She would return to the faith of her ancestors and reframe their lives, giving her children a safe place to come home to every day, a place where every day would be a blessing, a celebration of life. It wasn't too late for her boys to grow up with a strong sense of who they were, and a connection to their past. It was important they understood that they were a part of something much, much larger than themselves. Together, they would become a part of Flores' circle and the larger *converso* community beyond that. Rachel would ask José to help her—to show them the way to a better life. He was always so good with her difficult teenage son.

She knew Ángel desperately yearned for a father figure, someone he could count on for more than an arm wrestle, an argument, or a tease. Until that day when Angel could understand Gerry and have some kind of better relationship, were it ever to happen, he needed a real dad. Someone who cared for him, guided him. And she, God willing, would find out what it meant to love a man who cared about who she was, too.

Sitting alone before the pair of flickering candles on the sideboard, sipping a glass of sacramental wine, she felt like the moment had finally come to reconcile everything that hadn't worked before. She never understood that being shut out from her family's history had taken her so far from the Creator, as well as herself. But she knew He was listening now. She could feel it, a connection way beyond anything she'd ever felt before.

She could sense her mother with her in the room as well; the way the candles flickered and danced. She inhaled the lingering scent of Rosa's dinner. Her mother used to make *posole* like that when she was a little girl, the rich hominy soup that was now a favorite in her own kitchen. Rachel sensed her ancestor Rebeca as well, another woman who had accepted a new path once she learned exactly where she came from.

She ran her fingertips softly around the silver rope accent at the base of one of her candlesticks, now used to light yet another Sabbath meal among friends. Who would have ever believed that Juan and Ángel had shown her the way; that their leaving would lead them all home?

When children go missing, Rachel mused, it's like a knife that cuts your very soul to pieces. But perhaps that's how it has to be. God shows us a sign, and if we're not listening, not paying attention, he tries again in more persistent ways. He loves us too much to let us live broken and unfulfilled.

Rachel heaved a heavy sigh and closed her eyes. Acceptance was a strange balm. It soothed her soul with an unexpected peace. She finished the wine, then bent her head in prayer.

Almighty, You have given me one boy. Please don't leave the other behind. Let this night be my redemption. If I could trade my own life for Ángel's, I would, gladly. Take me now, or allow me to give my life to You in service, in the path of my ancestors, in exchange for the return of my first born.

It was all she had to give; an essential part of who she was. She looked out into the night sky. A full October moon hung low on the horizon. She was grateful for its light. She pondered further what she had just done—offered her life for Ángel's—that, and her sworn devotion, in trade for her son's future. It felt right. She remembered the story of the Exodus, when the Jewish slaves were freed and wandered in the desert. There they found manna. She had always loved that Bible tale as a girl:

lost people surviving on food sent by God. He protected them, gave Moses the Ten Commandments, led them to freedom, and parted the Red Sea. What tales—those ancient scriptures. Indeed. But in return, they had to live according to His laws.

Those were the kind of Bible stories she loved most. Did she believe that they were true? It didn't matter. But if they were, all of that had to have been very complicated stuff compared to this. This time, God had only to find one small boy in the wilderness. Just one boy. Such a thing should be easy. *Oh please, Father, let him survive and grow to be a man.*

Rachel closed her eyes, hoping that Flores would call that very instant; that Ángel had surfaced, that the hunt had come to an end. The minutes ticked by mercilessly. She got up to walk around, pacing the room. Maybe she should ask Rosa to start a fire in the fireplace; a cold night lay ahead. She glanced at her cell phone, lying on the table. The digital display read 7:43 p.m. Why didn't he call?

She pulled on her heavy sweater with the hood, searched for an Advil in her purse, swallowed two with a sip of water, then sat down and buried her head in her hands once more. Fatigue tore at every bone. She looked up, waited, listened. Nothing. Nothing but silence and the low murmur of voices in the other room. She sighed the empty sigh of one who waits and hopes and waits again. She remembered the Sabbath prayer and began to recite it softly again. *Barukh atah A-donai.* That's when her cell phone lit up and started to ring.

CHAPTER FIFTY-FIVE

Trucks Can Fly

FLORES WATCHED THE DARK ridge where the road cut through the trees. The moon shone down, outlining the mountain's profile against the sky. He saw the Toyota's headlights ripple through the pines as it came around the mountain.

"There they are," said the deputy. "Unbelievable. We assemble the best volunteers from three counties, roll out with dogs, horses, terrain maps, four wheelers, night-vision goggles, flares, flashlights, and a chopper. Then a Diné Indian and a blind man head for the hills on a hunch and find the boy in just under six hours. Go figure. Makes no sense."

The helicopter whirred noisily behind him, on the ground waiting to airlift Ángel to the hospital. All eyes were on the headlights of Yazzi's truck as it slowly lumbered down the final grade, including the unexpected moment when the vehicle started to slip. First it went into a slide, then wobbled wildly out of control on the muddy gravel of the logging road, bouncing from one side to the other.

"*!Ay cabrón!*" shouted Flores, peering through his binoculars, "What the hell is he doing?"

A dozen concerned trackers with field glasses focused on the bright headlights dancing through the trees as the truck picked up speed down the steep descent.

Frank Yazzi grabbed the steering wheel with both hands. It twisted in his grip like a bucking horse. They were in serious trouble. The gearbox had blown. In the back, Ángel screamed over and over in pain as they bounced down the deep ruts in the road. Héctor yelled something in Spanish, trying to hold on to the dog. Yazzi smelled burning brake pads and cursed himself for using the brakes too much when they started. What had been his goddamned hurry?

He yanked on the emergency brake. It held momentarily, then gave. They started veering toward the mountainside. Not much time. His head smashed against the ceiling with the worst bump yet. Ángel howled. Héctor screeched. Poquito slipped all over the cab, claws extended, scratching at whatever he could reach, trying to hold on.

Yazzi had to calculate the risk of crashing into the mountainside against careening off the road into thin air. Maybe the thick-growing pine trees down the slope to their right were their best bet before they all became a trajectory with no hope of recovery and slammed headfirst into a granite wall, or worse, tumbled forward, straight off the cliff.

He somehow kept the madly bounding truck on its tires as it accelerated with every foot of descent. But when he heard something under the truck snap with a loud crunching sound, he knew he had to make his last move—before they lost an axle and flipped, or veered smack into oblivion.

"Okay everybody, I've got no choice. Transmission's gone. I'm taking her airborne!"

Heading straight for the blanket of pines, down and to the far right, Yazzi hoped it was the best choice, though he knew the impact of hitting the trees below could kill them almost as easily as the rocks. But it looked like a young and healthy stand; heavy pine needle branches, broad like fans, slender poles. Maybe, just maybe—she'd cushion and roll.

"Hang on, Héctor!" the Navajo screamed, his hands clenched around the shuddering steering wheel, pulling it far to the right. "Get down, *señor.* Way down. Cover your head and your neck with your hands. Hold that dog tight between your legs. Ángel, brace yourself. Two more seconds, we're gonna fly!"

* * *

From the mountain's base camp, José Flores gasped as he watched the headlights swing to the right, fly off the road, then soar, blink out, and disappear among the pines. He could hear the tree branches snapping and cracking with a hideous crunch, creating an avalanche of timber and green. Then the truck rolled, tumbled over once more, and smashed through the lower stand of trees near the clearing of the camp, skidding on its side some one hundred yards from where the rescue vehicles stood. The battered vehicle miraculously slid to a stop upright; scraped and dented, its tires blown and rims crushed, steam rising from under the crumpled hood. At least the doors on either side still held.

"Mayday!" shouted Flores, grabbing a flashlight out of the car. "Mayday! Mayday! Hey, Franklin! Garcia! Get moving! Let's get 'em out of there before the tank explodes." Six men dashed toward the wreck.

From somewhere inside the steaming hulk came the tinny bark of a dog. Poquito's small pointed nose poked above the shattered driver's window, then two terrified eyes appeared and a pair of tiny paws followed. The dog jumped over the edge and down, limping away, only to collapse on the ground, whining softly.

Frank Yazzi, stunned but conscious, bleeding from the nose and mouth, shook his head and looked around him in the dark. Even the dash lights were out. He felt around the cab, moved his arms and legs. Body parts still worked. Except for a throbbing broken nose and a bleeding gash on the left side of his lip, he seemed to have come through unscathed. He shook his head. "Ángel, Héctor—you okay?"

No answer. Yazzi unsnapped his seat belt and reached back over the seat, searching with his hand to see if the boy was still strapped in.

"Ángel!"

The boy groaned. "Ugh. Still here. I'm okay. But my foot hurts. Owww. Wha … what happened?"

Yazzi turned his attention to Héctor, still strapped in beside him, but doubled over, slumped against the dash. "*Señor, Señor—Señor* Ortega!" Héctor didn't answer.

Someone was coming. Flashlights shining—closer, waving, voices shouting. In the beam of light bouncing in the cab, Yazzi could see Héctor's head hanging limply, blood oozing from his ear and mouth. He had a serious gash on the side of his head. He didn't move.

Two Grant County deputies, John Franklin and Tip García ran straight to the mangled truck. Flores, a step ahead of them, dashed straight for the driver's side where he found Yazzi dazed and bloody in the glare. Franklin pried open the door, then Flores helped Yazzi out and onto his feet. The Indian staggered briefly, but was able to stand. Flores went after Ángel next who seemed surprisingly alert—and talking normally. Helicopter medics arrived. They undid the jump seat straps and lifted Ángel onto a gurney, then carried him down to the chopper, over a quarter mile away in a clearing.

Héctor still lay unconscious and limp. The medics returned to the truck and lifted him carefully from the wreckage, onto a second stretcher and took him down the hill to the helicopter as well. García spotted the whimpering dog, picked him up, and quieted him in his arms. The animal seemed to be in shock.

Flores paced beside the chopper as each victim loaded up. "It was nothing less than a miracle they weren't all killed," he said, shaking his head. "Rachel's never going to believe this. Never. Never! I'm not even sure that I do."

Héctor's head wound was bandaged and a neck brace strapped on while he lay motionless on the stretcher. Suddenly, the old man moaned and arched his torso, bending one knobby knee. His right hand jerked. His head twisted to one side.

"Please, don't move sir," said the paramedic. "You want to lie real still now. Don't try to talk. Just stay calm please."

The copter emergency crew secured Héctor on one side, across from Ángel, who was already tucked in against the chopper wall. Yazzi sat on the floor between them. Flores looked in from the doorway.

"*T'ahee.* That was the dumbest thing I ever done, riding the brakes all the way down," Yazzi said. "We almost lost everybody. I did the only thing I could think of—took her up and over. Sorry *Señor* Ortega is hurt. So sorry, *baa shíní'.*"

"Don't you be saying sorry to anyone," Flores said, signing the paperwork needed to get the victims on their way. "Any landing you walk away from is a good one—I swear, that's the first truck I ever saw fly. Remember, you found Ángel, and you're all alive. You did damn good."

Ángel reached over and touched Frank Yazzi's shoulder. "Thank you, Mr. Yazzi," he said with a weak smile. "You saved me. You're my friend, forever."

"*¿Ángel, eres tú?*"

Héctor had come to with a start and asked in a frail voice, "Ángel, is that you?" He tried to turn his head in the direction of the child, but couldn't because of the neck brace. "*¿Qué me ha ocurrido? ¿ Ónde estamos?* Where are we?" He gathered some strength and asked again "*¿Ónde*?"

"You're safe. *Señor* Ortega. And thank God, you're awake. You're on your way home, sir," Flores said. "You're going to be just fine. Had a little roll down the mountain, but everybody's here, everybody made it, even Poquito. So lay real still now, okay? This chopper will take you to the hospital *pronto.*"

"*¿Ónde estás Ángel?*" Héctor asked louder, turning his head as much as he could. He blinked. Then he blinked again. He gasped. Tears began to spill from Héctor's rheumy brown eyes.

"Ángel," he said, his voice rising, with a frantic edge. "Ángel, is that *you,* my grandson?"

He reached his hand out toward the boy's stretcher—thrashing, grabbing at the air. The medic held his arm and tried to restrain him.

"Take it easy, sir. *¡Cálmese!* You have to lie real still now, like I said, please."

"Ángel, Ángel, *¡Es un milagro! ¡Ay Santa María! ¡Ay!, ¡Ay!*"

The old man turned his head, in spite of the brace, this time toward the medic. *"Deme su mano, señor.* Give me your hand," Héctor demanded. "Give it to me!"

The medic extended his arm. Héctor took the man's hand firmly in his own.

"*Jesucristo ¡Gracias a Dios!* Thank the Lord! I can see your hand, ¡*Señor*! *Su mano* … your hand!" Then Héctor turned toward the boy, in spite of the pain, "*Ángel—niño, mi Ángelito, ¡Puedo verte!* Look at me! I can see you at last! I can see your face—I can see! I can see!"

CHAPTER FIFTY-SIX

Night Eyes

JOSÉ FLORES WATCHED THE helicopter rise into the night sky and fly high above the ridge line, carrying its passengers away to civilization and the hospital where Juan waited in Las Cruces. Below him, the volunteer rescue workers began to pack up and move out, one by one, their taillights disappearing into the night.

Instead of more rain as the weather forecaster had predicted, the clouds cleared above the highest peaks of the Mogollons and a bright harvest moon shone overhead. A blurry halo of light glowed behind it, as if sanctifying the sky. Stars blazed with clarity impossible to imagine at lower altitudes. Their multitude peppered the endless realm, magic pathways of light through the void. Flores remembered his grandfather telling him once that stars were "the eyes of the night seeking hope in the dark for the Queen of Heaven." Surely she had smiled down on them this night, that Queen, and maybe the King of Kings too. Something bigger than all of them, that's for sure.

Flores zipped up his leather jacket and shook off a chill. The thick woods all around had given way to a luminous clearing where even the shattered frame of the truck and the mangled and twisted trees took on a comforting kind of grace. The site seemed hallowed in Flores' eyes, a place where a great miracle had just occurred. *No,* he thought, *not one. Maybe two. Maybe several.* It was time to call Rachel. Good news at last.

Flores walked uphill toward a rocky platform amid the pines. He inhaled the night air as if drinking in life itself. Sitting down on a log, he started to dial the most important call of his life. His heart beat harder with each number he punched into the cell phone. Waiting. Waiting.

Her phone began to ring. Incredible. Another miracle, right there.

His heart thudded in his chest. Rachel. Rachel Ortega. How had he ever lived without her?

"*¿Hola*?" she answered. "José, *mijo,* is that you?"

"*Sí,* Rachel, it's me. Everything's all right. We found him. Yes, yes—really ... yes, I know, I know—it's true! He's safe. He's on his way to the hospital, sweetheart—a little banged up, but okay. Yes, Grandpa, too. Your Ángel has a broken ankle, but the medic said it doesn't look too bad and should heal up fine. You'll have to thank that Diné, Frank Yazzi. He's an amazing guy—and a helluva driver. Rachel? Hey—Rachel?"

The connection faded for ten unbearable seconds, then came back on.

"You there? Good. We couldn't have found Ángel in time without Héctor, either. This whole thing is impossible to describe. Oh yeah, and Poquito, too. He's in the trailer with his new best friend, García. Broke his little tail though. Hon, this is one for the books. In fact—what happened here tonight should be written down in that Holy Book of yours, that Bible you found, so you and your kids and their kids' kids from here to eternity will remember this story."

"I love you," said Rachel. "Did you hear that? Can you hear me?"

"What? Yeah. Listen, I hear you. Me too! I'm loading up and hitting the road. I'll meet you at the hospital whenever you get there, OK? And when you do, I'll tell you all about it. Main thing, the boys are safe. Hon, I can't wait to see you, hold you. Be with you. Meanwhile, let everybody know the search is over. For you, Rachel, and for me. It's time to celebrate, *mi cariño.* For all of us, it's finally time to move on."

EPILOGUE

Córdoba, Spain, 1528

In the Beginning

HER FINAL AUDIENCE WITH the tribunal lasted over an hour. Doña María Consuelo Velásquez, thirty-nine, born and raised in Seville, mother of two boys, and the widow of Carlos Esteban Velásquez, could not convince even one accuser of her innocence. To these men, fire was mercy. She stood with her hands in shackles, heavy chains below her wrists, her bare feet against the cold stone floor and wept, ashamed she could not hold out much longer against such vicious cruelty.

"*Atención*, *Señora* Velásquez. We, the Inquisitorial Tribunal of Cardinal Nicodemo Castilón de Sevilla, in Córdoba, Spain, on this day of our Lord, February 23, 1528, shall hereby pronounce, in the name of Queen Isabella and King Ferdinand, and by the right of the Council of the Inquisition, the divine *Suprema*, your final sentence. It is based on accusations brought against you by members of your extended family, certain "*familiares*" about whom we shall not speak. We leave that to you. Surely, you know who they are. You are encouraged to name them."

Doña María stood bewildered. "*Lo siento.* I know not of whom you speak. I don't understand why I am here."

The three inquisitors looked at one another and then back at their prisoner—like three raptors on a fence studying their prey. "Specifically, it is stated, you are a false Christian—a *Judaizer*—and have fouled the body of the Church of Rome with your Jewish heresies. You have lied about your behavior, your intentions, and your very being—disgraced those who had confidence in what you pretended to be, and seduced true believers from their righteous path."

The sunken-eyed accuser in the center paused for a moment, gazing motionless at the woman, his expression blank. He cleared his throat, adjusted the *pluviale* around his neck and settled deeper into his padded chair. Her case bored him. It was not unlike many he had already come to judge at the *Casa de Penitencia.*

"Shall we be more specific? Reports confirm you have been seen eating meat on a day of abstinence, and donning fresh clothes on a Saturday. Although you buy pork in the market place, you feed it to dogs. You have been accused, tried, and now shall be sentenced to punishment, perhaps even to burn at the stake in the name of Our Lord, unless you recant your previous statements to this court, thereby admitting your heresy, and acknowledging that the charges against you are accurate and true. Have you anything to say in your defense?"

The accused stood speechless, not sure what to say. She felt dwarfed by the inquisitors' chamber, a long barren space with high windows, a stone floor, the judge's bench, chairs for the two clerks and notaries, and nothing else but a door at one end. This led to the *cárceles secretas,* a room of unimaginable horrors. She gazed straight ahead as if transfixed, her eyes boring into theirs. The *sanbenito* or linen shroud that she and others like herself were forced to wear had been removed and she stood naked before them. She dared not think about her bare breasts, exposed by these evil men for who knows what reason?

If this was the Church, she wanted no further part. They were like no Spaniards she had ever known, as if from some strange, faraway place where all respect for good people had been utterly lost. What would such men, supposedly servants of God, think if their own mothers were stripped bare in this way, shamed forever? Who could know what such iron-eyed monsters feel?

Her bosom burned in their gaze. The hard floor made the bottoms of her swollen feet ache as she shifted her weight. She blinked and defiantly continued to stare, looking into the tribunal's expressionless faces, searching for any shred of humanity.

"Once more, *Doña* Velásquez. *¡Hable!* Time is running out. Do not tax our patience. Is it not enough your husband has already been burned to ashes for conducting obscene heretical rituals, casting filth on the Church of Rome, shaming you and your children? How dare you continue to protest your innocence when we know you have relapsed from your conversion, fasting on certain days, even seen lighting two oil lamps on those nights?"

"But sir, I ..."

"Further, we found hidden in your home, a Bible, written in Hebrew. That is proof enough. The outcome of this trial, whatever the result, shall therefore be entered in your Holy Book. Others in your family who have accepted Jesus as the true Messiah and truly practice our faith as prescribed will then know what has taken place here and take heed from it. Let them realize the fate of those who stray. You cannot hide from the Holy Office, *Señora*. God sees all, and we are His eyes. And we see you, María Consuelo Velásquez, as unrepentant—an apostate, and a sinner of the worst kind."

"Please. *Se lo ruego.* I beg you. I beg Your Excellence for mercy," she answered. "I have attended every mass, taken communion, and baptized my children according to the sacred laws of the Holy Mother Church. If I was ever seen doing any of the things you speak of, it was merely coincidental, but a meaningless habit of mine, nothing more—nothing at all to do with the traditions of our ancestors, which I no longer follow. I beg of you, *Licenciado.* I never meant to sin; I did nothing wrong. My customs never hurt a soul. They were only habits learned long ago. Mother of God, have pity on a poor Christian woman."

Doña María hung her head, not daring to endure their stares. Her gaze shifted to the scribe seated at the far end of the table, hastily penning each word uttered by either side. She marveled at his speed and dexterity, the plumed quill racing across the page. What skill. How did he do it? Entertaining the thought was almost ludicrous, considering the circumstances. Her survival was at stake.

The inquisitors settled deeper into their chairs. "*Doña* Velásquez, you vex this panel with your stubbornness. You will confess your sins, admit your false Christianity, and admit that you secretly followed the old dispensation of Moses. If you cannot comply, we must consider the eventuality—consumption by fire, where you will be relaxed until your soul enters heaven, or more likely, hell. But for now, perhaps we can help you remember. Six turns of the wheel will crack your bones until the truth and names of your accomplices sing out!"

She knew torture was sure to follow. She dared not think about the pain. "If I cannot convince you to have mercy on me Your Eminence, then do that which is in your heart to do. Tear me, break me, even burn me if you must. Force me to say what you want to hear, for you are seeking something I cannot give."

The three judges looked at one another in silent exasperation. The eldest, the *fiscal,* motioned to the hooded guard to proceed. Her reticence would be met by more aggressive "questioning." The tall man shackled her wrists behind her back, then led her to the iron door of the dreaded cell, followed by a pair of notaries. Desolate, she cast her eyes to the floor, trembling. She stood bare and alone in a chamber with a huge wooden rack—the *potro,* a trial with no escape.

"Do not hold back, dear lady. We are ready at any time to hear your truth." In minutes, the warden positioned her upright between the wide wooden arms, securing her wrists and ankles, each bound several feet from each other. The machine was designed to pull her body apart one turn of the wheel at a time. The operator placed his hand upon the crank and initiated the first rotation. *Doña* Maria gasped as the first shock tore through her back and numbed her brain. She shrieked as she heard her left shoulder crack. Another turn and immeasurable pain ripped through her joints like fire, her very spine stretched to breaking. Tears spilled from her eyes. Her agonized screams echoed off the stone walls, to no avail. By the third turn she was sure she would faint, her vision blurred, her mouth filled with froth and foam. "*Dio ayúdame!* God, please help me!"

The trio watched, impassive, through the open door. A volt of vultures could not have hovered with less emotion.

"Once more," said the Chief Tribunal, "and this shall be our last offer. We are merciful, but lenient within limits. Should you oblige and confess fully to these charges, then your two sons, Fernando and Umberto, shall live, though they are as guilty as you, albeit through no fault of their own. It is known they are circumcised, in that barbaric practice of your kind. Too old to be adopted by good Christians, tell us what you know now, and we will give them penance, to be assumed in service to the King's army as it settles the empire in the New World. They shall toil and help build a church in *Nueva España*, in service to the name of our true Lord. They shall not be put to death for your sins, or investigated by this Tribunal, but give their lives to the Holy See. Now—are you ready, or shall we consider this investigation merely suspended?"

Doña Velásquez's eyes grew wide. Her shoulders ached and her wrists burned in their shackles. Her head hung limp, but tears of joy welled up. Her sons would live? Her lower lip trembled as she mumbled softly, "*Gracias.*"

She raised her head, painful as it was. "If that be true, Your Most Merciful, that they be spared, if it might be for them—then please, my Lordship, I beg you take this admission from me now. Write this down, Notary of the Secret: I am guilty of all charges!" At this, she broke down weeping, desperate tears dripping onto her naked breast.

"Finalmente."

Three pairs of eyes met in approval. "We are listening, *Doña* Velásquez," said the second judge, raising his right hand that the hooded henchman might cease. "You have come to your senses. But first you will tell us who else you have seduced into these practices."

"No one, I swear to you. But as for me, it's true. I am a Judaizer and have sinned. From this moment on, I will accept your holy doctrine and renounce any practice of the religion of my ancestors, for my life has no meaning if my sons are murdered too. No rack could rend my heart as much as their death because of my faith, our inheritance. All that the great God of Abraham ever asked is that we keep his commandments—which I attempted to do with my very heart and soul. At least I am not guilty there. But no one else knew of my observance, I assure you, least of all, my husband and my children. The sin is mine alone. And I have no idea who could have accused me thus. I merely wanted to raise my children to be law-abiding, God-fearing Jewish citizens of Córdoba. Let them live and I have succeeded. I shall abandon the faith of my fathers and take your merciful Lord in spirit and name forever. I trade my life for theirs. Break me or burn me, but let my sons go free."

"Excellent," said the Grand Inquisitor, with a crooked, satisfied smile. His breast puffed with pride. "You shall therefore only be coerced further, but not burned. We hope your memory grows more sharp. The names of others may yet come to you. Call on Our Lord Jesus to sustain you if the pain becomes too great. It's for your own good, for your very soul. The body is nothing. If you survive this test of faith, then you are worthy of reacceptance into the Church, and purification. If not, then we were just and true, ever righteous in our task to purge Cordoba of all heretics so that we may spare the pious from further harm. Repent *Doña* Velásquez, for after we are done with you, imagine—you may yet be saved."

The judge raised his hand that the torturers might begin again.

"*¡Esperen!*" said María, preparing herself for the worst. "Wait!"

Were she to die at their hands regardless, would she want it to be this way, as a traitor to her people, and her beloved mother and father before her? To her husband who went to his death ever faithful to his God? Dare she proclaim her unquenchable love for the children of Zion and her heritage instead, knowing that the words she just uttered in cowardice might be the last ever heard from her lips—other than her tormented screams?

For a moment, silence filed the room. With one more confession, she could still redeem herself and live. If not, and the Holy One willed it thus, she might then die with honor. She parted her lips to speak but could not find the words.

The scribe, looking up for the very first time, met her terrified eyes. He raised his pen and waited.

AUTHOR'S NOTE

A STRONG SENSE OF identity takes years to develop. Yet even when we think we know who we are, the present may hide a hidden truth. Our sense of self may change over time. Imagine waking up one morning and discovering all your core beliefs masked by a different story entirely. Such is the experience of the many Spanish Catholic *conversos* who have begun to ask who they are, who their ancestors were, and how they got here.

During my research for this book over the last decade I met many on the path. Some had actually returned to Judaism. Of these I asked, "What was the 'aha' moment, the reason for the leap of faith?" The answers were myriad, but almost exclusively based on emotion, not logic—on a sense of arrival and acceptance. For some, it took a crisis to accelerate change or begin the dialogue. For many, it's still an ongoing conversation.

For those who wish to know more about the subject of crypto-Judaism, or suspect that Sephardic Jewish ancestry figures in their own family's background, here a few select sources.

Author, historian and one of several founders of the Society for Crypto-Judaic Studies, Dr. Stanley Hordes addresses the story of the Spanish Jews in the New World in his seminal work, *To the End of the*

Earth: A History of the Crypto-Jews of New Mexico, published by Columbia University Press. Another important resource is Dr. Seth D. Kunin's *Juggling Identities: Identity and Authenticity among the Crypto-Jews* (New York: Columbia University Press, 2009).

The late author and photographer Cary Herz created a photographic essay titled, *New Mexico's Crypto-Jews: Image and Memory* (New Mexico University Press) featuring personal interviews with many who are descendants. Renowned university professor and author Dr. David Gitlitz wrote the encompassing work, *Secrecy and Deceit: The Religion of the Crypto-Jews,* also by the University of New Mexico Press, and Dr. Jane S. Gerber's academic investigation, *The Jews of Spain: A History of the Sephardic Experience,* covers the wealth of a culture and measure of the disaster that befell an entire civilization when ousted from Spain practically overnight in the 15th century. (Free Press, Simon & Schuster.) To each of these scholars, I owe a debt.

Historically, we live in an unusual time; a time when anyone may choose who he or she wants to be, and what they choose to believe, at least in the Western world. Many organizations exist to educate and explore the subject of this story. Some are academic, others are genealogical, some are cultural, and others still intend to reach out and bring the newly-awakened home to Judaism. That particular goal was never my purpose. Rather, I hope to inspire in each and every one of us the right to question who we are, who we dream of being, and how we relate to the Creator.

Corinne Joy Brown
2016

CORINNE JOY BROWN IS a multi-published author, professional writer and editor who lives in Colorado. In addition to a passion for Western history and culture, she's devoted her first two novels to the question of identity: *MacGregor's Lantern*, a story about Scots in the frontier West, and *Sanctuary Ranch*, a saga of love and transformation. The history of crypto or hidden Jews in the American Southwest, descendants of those who fled the Spanish Inquisition more than five hundred years ago, became the ultimate stage for questions about selfhood and belief. Current editor of *HaLapid*, the journal of the Society for Crypto-Judaic Studies, Corinne is a past president of the Denver Woman's Press Club, a Fellow at the University of Colorado at Colorado Springs, and was a presenter at the inauguration of the Anusim Center for Return in El Paso, Texas.

To contact the author go to **corinnejoybrown.com**

ABOUT THE COVER ARTIST, Sushe Felix, whose painting of a New Mexico night captured my imagination. In her own words: "My work involves a combination of my ongoing interest in the American Regionalist and Modernist Art Movements from the 1930s and 40s and my desire to find new and different ways in which to depict the natural rhythms and movement found in nature. As a native of Colorado, I feel my work is all about the brilliant color, dramatic forms and shapes, and the intense lights and darks of the American Southwest. I wish to instill a sense of joy, along with a feeling of mystery and playfulness, and hope it brings the same to those who view it."

CPSIA information can be obtained
at www.ICGtesting.com
Printed in the USA
FSOW01n1046141216
28577FS